MAJOR CRIMES

A NICOLE LONG LEGAL THRILLER

AIME AUSTIN

AIME AUSTIN
www.AimeAustin.com

LOS ANGELES, CALIFORNIA

ALSO BY AIME AUSTIN

The Nicole Long Series
Outcry Witness

Major Crimes

The Casey Cort Series
Judged

Ransomed

Caged

Disgraced

Unarmed

Kidnapped

Reunited

Contained

Poisoned

Abused

MAJOR CRIMES

A NICOLE LONG LEGAL THRILLER

AIME AUSTIN

Major Crimes

This edition published by
Moore Digital Media Inc.
1125 N Fairfax Avenue
Unit 46071
West Hollywood, CA 90046
www.aimeaustin.com

Copyright © 2022 by Aime Austin
ISBN 13: 978-1-64414-091-8
eISBN 13: 978-1-64414-090-1

Cover Designer: Wicked Good Book Covers
Cover images © Depositphotos, Shutterstock

Major Crimes/Aime Austin. 1st ed.

Vengeance is in my heart, death in my hand.

— WILLIAM SHAKESPEARE

1

Sarah Rose Pope
July 20, 2007

"This is the last time, Sarah," Tyisha Cooley said.

If I had a dollar for every time someone had said that to me, I'd be a millionaire with zero reasons to be standing in this Cleveland Heights living room, hand out, hoping for a bed to sleep in and a pot to piss in.

"I know." I nodded in mute appeasement. She was right. I did need a plan. The guy I'd been staying with had found a younger girl. One who was willing to pay his rent and sleep with him.

Yesterday, she'd rolled up in a pickup with her stuff. That's when I'd known she was real and he wasn't just holding some fake relationship over my head to get me to cook or clean or do something I didn't want to do in bed.

I hadn't even fought it—this time. Just put my stuff in my pack, called Tyisha, and had begged for a place to stay. She hadn't sounded happy, but she'd said yes, which was all I needed.

"No, I'm serious. This is the absolutely last time you can come to my house high. You need to get into rehab. For real. I'm not joking this time."

"I'll go. I promise." I tried to move, to skirt past her. Put my stuff in her guest room and wait for her to go to sleep so I could get out and score.

I'd get back.

We'd both get a good night's sleep and she'd probably be over her impulse by morning. Then…then, I'd be fine. I could chill here for a few days until I figured out my next move.

"Good." Tyisha looked a little too triumphant for my tastes. "I found a bed for you," she announced.

"Wait? What?" Panic flooded my veins. She'd never gone through with this threat. Not really. Not even after the Pat Bailey debacle. "I'm not—"

"You're not what? Ready?" she challenged. The tiger eye ring Bailey had bought caught the light. Inwardly, I sighed because I knew I'd fucked up her life one time too many. Maybe she was right. Maybe it was finally time.

"Don't I get time to get my affairs in order?"

"What affairs? You can leave your car here. I'll even put it in the garage for you. If you had somewhere to stay, I could take care of that too. But if you're indeed here with that huge backpack, then I'd guess that you're not carrying a lease."

"That eviction was unfair," I improvised. It wasn't a lie exactly. Just wasn't the reason I was here today. Hadn't happened to me.

Undeterred, I continued with my lie, "I was subletting. How was I supposed to know that my friend was dealing? No one told me. Landlord said he wasn't interested in the government coming to forfeit his property. Said that place was his retirement plan or some such. I told him I wasn't dealing, and could stay. But he threw me out...like the baby and the bathwater."

"Probably a safe bet. It's hard to prove a negative. Lots of people get caught up in that forfeiture net, especially people of color. Daddy knows some people who've done some advocacy work around that for profit policing."

"Of course he does."

"What's up with the attitude, Sarah? Momma and Daddy have done nothing but be nice to you, help you where they can."

"Your dad sounds like he's the face of the Innocence Project or the Southern Poverty Law Center or even the ACLU. Lots of limousine liberals who say all the right words, but have no idea what it's like down in the trenches."

Despite all the ungratefulness in my tone, I liked Mr. Cooley. I loved both her parents. Sometimes, though, I wanted some real world stuff to happen to them. I almost said that out loud, but held myself back. A lot of his reading and volunteer work had come on the heels of his son and Tyisha's brother's death. That was a topic best left alone. They didn't exactly blame me for his murder, not explicitly anyway.

"Advocacy has to start somewhere." Tyisha's voice was cool. "But that's not the issue here. Daddy's not the addict Sarah. You are. You're the one who needs help. You have to promise me that this time you'll get it."

"Fine. Tomorrow. Whatever." This time when I made a move toward the bedrooms, she didn't exactly stop me, but didn't quite step aside either. My mind clicked slowly. "Um, there's no one back there right? No surprises?"

Whatever held Tyisha's face together fell. Every one of her fifty-two years showed. Her sigh of resignation was heavy.

"You know I'm too old for that."

"But you're not. Not really." My attempt at upbeat fell flat. I pushed on anyway. In my own way, I wanted the best for her. "Your parents have the best marriage. Haven't you ever desired something like that for yourself?"

"Pat Bailey was that chance, and…"

And that I'd ruined it went unspoken, but not unsaid.

"You deserve someone who loves you. Everyone does."

"I ran into Pat a couple of weeks ago. Did I tell you?"

Tyisha knew very well that she hadn't mentioned it to me, otherwise I wouldn't have said a thing. I shook my head, though the reason for the ring was clearer.

"I was at the Shaker Heights library picking up Eat, Pray, Love."

"I loved that book. See…anyone can reinvent themselves. Start over."

"I was standing in the check out," Tyisha continued as if I hadn't spoken. "Pat came in with a kid about fifteen."

"Wow."

"They were picking up a guide to the PSATs. He was talking to the kid about colleges." Tyisha fanned herself with her hand. "It wasn't déjà vu. That's not the word for it. It was more like watching a movie, getting a peek into the life I could have had."

"I'm sorry. Really sorry about that. You could have married him."

"He wouldn't accept you as part of the package, Sarah."

"But—"

"You're family. Have been since I was a kid. After losing Wayne, I couldn't lose you too. Not for some promise of a picture perfect suburban life."

Some part of me had never moved past my teen crush on Tyisha. I pushed it down ninety-nine percent of the time. Deliberately not thinking about it. But in this moment, I wished I could comfort her. Give her what she'd been missing all those years since she'd walked out on what Pat Bailey had offered.

I gave in to a single impulse and moved forward to tuck a hank of curly hair back under the scarf she was using to keep it away from her face. We stood there for a minute or two, me with a hand on her face. Her with a hand on my shoulder. Though I was mute, I hoped she could sense all the love and remorse I was feeling.

Without a word, Tyisha finally stepped aside. I dropped my hand and went into her guest room. It wasn't really set up for guests anymore. The daybed was still there, and that's where I dropped my bag. There wasn't much available floor space. That was dominated by clear plastic storage containers which looked like they had a lifetime's worth of crafting stuff stored inside.

I wanted to tell her she was not going to be the black Martha Stewart, but I didn't. She wouldn't appreciate the joke, I didn't think. Our humor hadn't really synced up in years. Instead, I pulled my little phone from my pocket. My ex hadn't thought to turn off my extra line. Eventually, he would. In the meantime, I'd use as many plan minutes as I could.

I put in a call to the one person who'd never abandoned me and more importantly, didn't ask too many questions, Ja Roach. Asked him to bring something by. He was one person where I still had credit. He'd always let me pay him later. Sometimes, he forgot altogether and said I didn't owe him at all.

When I came back to the front of the house, Tyisha was fiddling with the television remote. She muted HGTV when she realized I was back. I didn't say a thing about the crafts or the channel and neither did she.

Neither of us could go back to being eighteen or twenty with a whole world of opportunities in front of us. Some had been snatched from me. I'd squandered others.

"Do you have a beer?" I asked. It would take a while before Ja Roach could get over here from the westside. In the meantime I was ready to mellow out. "Maybe we can start to audition for living together as little old ladies. Maybe even get a couple of cats."

My childhood friend gave me a side eye that hadn't changed since we were eleven. She went to the kitchen anyway and came back with two brown longneck bottles.

"No Heineken?" I wondered what had made her ditch her longtime favorite.

"It's an IPA from a black owned microbrewery." She held up the bottle in a mock toast. "Trying to support where I can."

"I'm surprised you let me drink." She'd always tried to control my consumption during my past stays with her. Especially after that unfortunate couch situation years back. Though it was hard, I held my tongue. I'd apologized too much for that and everything else. Didn't want to jog her memory and get her so mad she kicked me out.

"One last hurrah and all that." She held up her bottle. Took a long swig. I parroted her.

"What are you up to tonight? Got a guy I don't know about? You didn't actually answer the question, you know. I've always thought you deserved someone special." Once I'd gotten the questions out, I knew I'd spoken too quickly, made it awkward between us. The beer wasn't working fast enough.

"Did you invite someone over?" Her arched brows did not accompany another swig from her bottle. I very much wished she were three deep.

"Why would you think that?" If I could have pushed back farther into the chair's cushions, I would have, but the chair springs were already pushing up against me.

"You're not overly interested in my nearly nonexistent dating life except when me not being home serves you."

"That's not true—"

"Who'd you invite over?"

"Um…"

"I've known you for more than forty freaking years. Can we skip the hemming and hawing and lying and get to the truth of it already."

"Just Ja Roach. A friend of mine. You may have met him before."

"Another junkie?"

"He's not like that," I cut in. "He's got a place and a job and everything." Two things I couldn't put to my own name.

"And a heroin habit."

"He manages it."

"Why is he coming over?"

"I...uh..." There wasn't a single excuse I could muster.

"Oh, God." Tyisha did drain her bottle then. "You were planning to shoot up here? Again? After that last time, you promised no more."

"Well, if this is my last hurrah." It was weak. I hoped it would work because I was fresh out of other options. "I really will get clean this time, Tyisha. I never see many people out here much older than me. I don't want to die. Not now. Not yet. I may never find anyone like your Pat Bailey or even someone as good as Wayne, but I'm thinking that my life doesn't have to be over. That there's an apartment and a job and a woman who could love me like your mom and dad love each other."

"Why were you living with a guy anyway? I thought... You've always said—"

"Because they're easier. They never want to get to know me or even try. As long as I make them coffee and spread my legs, I can stay warm and dry most days." It was a truth I'd never shared.

"Fine." I tried not to cringe from the obvious pity in her eyes. "I really want nothing to do with this." Tyisha pulled a phone from her pocket.

"Oh my God. Did you get one of those new iPhones? I heard they're great."

"It does the job. You know, if someone had told my kid self I could have all my music and a computer and phone in my pocket, I wouldn't have believed them."

"Too bad you can't read a book on it. That would be killer."

If there's a single thing Tyisha and I had in common all these years it was books. They were my solace. Got me through nights in my car. Sleeping on cold pavement. Rolling over after letting a guy treat me like a dumpster for his lust. Sometimes, I think books were the same for her. After Pat Bailey, she'd turned from serious five hundred page tomes displayed in the windows of Appletree Books, and nonfiction lent by her father to paperback romance. Stories where women found love despite any odds against them.

"Kind of a small screen for it. But I agree that carrying all my books like I carry my music would be cool." Tyisha flicked her thumb, then turned the phone in my direction a calendar on display. "We're scheduled for one in the afternoon. This place came well recommended." I wanted to ask who in hell did she know who needed a bed, but kept that to myself.

"Where are we...am I going?" I was already thinking of how many days I'd have to suck up to drug counselors before I could check myself out, where'd I'd camp once I left. Then remembered my promise to her and myself.

Maybe I could stick it out this time and come out the other end a better person.

Tyisha pointed the phone at me one more time.

"It's in Hocking Hills. Three hour drive. We'll need to leave here at nine thirty at the latest, okay? I'm going to watch TV in my room. Behave."

2

Ja Roach was knocking on the front screen before Tyisha had closed her bedroom door. He'd always had good timing.

"Long time no see, girl," he said as we walked in. Wrapped me in a big hug. "How are you?"

"Going to rehab tomorrow."

"For real?" He'd never been for or against it one way or another. It's one of the things I liked about him. He was a lecture free zone. "Good for you. Who's taking you"

"You remember Tyisha? This is her house. I just found out it's my last night of freedom, apparently. You bring the stuff?"

"Police are out everywhere. Got the word from a friend that they're doing OVI check points this weekend.

Must not have made their quota of tickets from the fourth of July. Got the guy's phone number, though. He delivers. All I gotta do is say the word. Is she here, your friend? She gonna have a problem?"

"As long as he doesn't stay. She's in her room. If we turn up the TV here in the living room, she won't be able to hear us." I found a DVD of 300 and slid it in the player's plastic tray. In a moment loud, angry shouts drowned out any other sounds in the room.

"She gonna be mad?" Roach's eyes darted around like a cop was going to jump from behind the slim space between couch and wall.

"I agreed to take this bed down at some place called Journeys, so she's giving me amnesty for the night."

Ja Roach's nod was stiff, tight. I couldn't figure if he was angry that I was going to be clean while he wasn't or jealous that my people cared for me more than his did for him.

"Let me call the dealer before it gets too late. Let him brave the police."

Roach flipped open his phone and punched in a number. He cupped his hand near the bottom, but I still made out that he was getting two dime bags with a little something extra. My mouth practically watered in anticipation. Whatever he was ordering up, it was going to be good. I'd tried to kick the stuff once, but had quit after sweating and hallucinating through two days on some religious stranger's couch.

I should have asked Tyisha if this rehab place had some kind of drug that would take away the side effects. Someone had said treatment centers sometimes offered that. I blocked those thoughts out of my brain. If I dwelled on them too long, I wouldn't have the guts to stay the night. The weather wasn't hot, so I could disappear for a few days until Tyisha lost the bed.

Instead, I got Ja Roach situated on the couch that had replaced the one I'd ruined. Got him a beer and a tray with two wedges of French silk pie. Mary Cooley used to make them for us as a special summer treat. This one looked store bought, but I wasn't going to look a gift horse in the mouth. Before I knew it, I'd eaten my slice and Ja Roach's.

"You not hungry?" I asked when there were only crumbs on the tray. "You usually love a dessert."

"Nah. Ate too much before I got here." His leg jiggled uncharacteristically. "You know how my sister can be."

I did. I remembered that first meal at his apartment. If he didn't have a guy, and they came and went, then his sister cooked for him. There wasn't anything that woman couldn't make.

Just then the screen door rattled.

"I'll get that," Roach jumped up before I could push the food debris off my lap. In less than a minute, he was back.

"You want anything else?" I asked. I wasn't trying to push my hospitality on him, but once I got my shot, I wouldn't be up to opening cabinets and loading snacks into a bowl, much less anything else really.

"Nah, let's get into this. I gotta be good by Monday. Work. I'll do you, first, okay. I can do myself."

"I never got good at it." That was another thing men were willing to do for me. I'd never gotten used to needles. But I hadn't mentioned that part to Tyisha.

Ja Roach got up and retrieved his lunch box kit from where he'd left it by the TV stand. All these years and he stood by the seventies metal throwback.

He prepped, got everything ready. It had been a cool day, so my blouse had long sleeves. I pushed one up to my shoulder. He tied rubber around my skin, pulled tight. He filled the needle. Tapped at my arm. Once. Twice.

"Looking bad here."

"Other arm?"

"You know that's shot." My veins had been only one of the many casualties of my lifestyle.

"Look, I'm going to be honest here. You're going to need to do this in your groin. I would never normally suggest it because maybe smoking or snorting would have worked, but I've already mixed it. I don't have any money to go back to him. But I don't feel comfortable doing that to you. Can you do it?"

I tried not to panic. Relief was so close, just on foil outside of my body when it needed to be inside. "You know I've always been squeamish with needles. I—"

Ja Roach tapped the syringe impatiently already jonesing for his own high. "Will your friend do it?"

"Tyisha...God no."

"She's not big on partying. I get it." He made a sweeping gesture with his hands. "There's no one else here. You have to ask her."

"You sure you can't do it? Please..." I didn't care that I was begging. Times like this I had no shame. I wish I could have offered to blow him, but he was gayer than I was. Just the thought of a woman near him like that made him twitchy.

"My momma didn't raise me like that. I'm just not familiar with a lady's area and I don't want to get a crash course today. Okay?"

"Fine." I rose up and walked to Tyisha's bedroom, heavy footed and not caring. I knocked hard on her door. I heard the TV stop and go mute.

"Yeah? You need something, Sarah?" she called through the door, obviously not moving from where she probably was on her bed.

"Can you come out here a second?"

Tyisha shuffled out, tying a robe around her thin pajamas. I wanted to point out that Ja Roach didn't care to see anything but decided against it.

"What? You still going in the morning, right? You're not bothering me to tell me that you and your friend are off to go somewhere and not coming back." Her impatience was wearing her love for me thin.

"No, I one hundred percent promise I'll go with you tomorrow. But I need a huge favor from you tonight."

"I'm already in my pajamas. Took off my bra, so I'm—"

"I don't need you to go anywhere."

"Give it up, then. I don't have time to dig for gold here."

"I need you to give me a shot."

It wasn't hate in her eyes, but it wasn't love either. She closed them for a long moment. Opened her lids, stared me dead in the eye.

"What. The. Fuck." She rolled her neck. "You've got to be kidding."

"Look, Tyisha, I already promised to go tomorrow. I don't so much want to do this as I kind of need to do this.

I just can't start detox here…tonight." Getting kicked out and landing here had taken all my willpower. I'd already gone too long without a fix. For a brief moment, I let go of my control, let her see what it took for me to be here, to ask for this one thing.

"Fine." She squared her shoulders, doing the thing women do when they have to get through an unpleasant task no one else will take on. "Only this one time. To-morrow is a lock. What do I need to do?"

"Ja Roach will show you."

"Why don't you do it yourself?"

"I'm afraid of needles."

"Ironic." She gave a half-hearted laugh. I joined her.

"Yeah. Not gonna lie."

"I'm only going to do this because I love you. You've been my person for nearly four decades. I want the best for you. We both know that this isn't it, but Sarah, this is really your last chance. We're past fifty now. If we don't have our health, we've got nothing else. We going to need that for the last thirty or so."

"Thank you." I meant those two words more than I ever had. "It'll be different this time, I promise. I need to find my person, my other person. I was so afraid of who I was for years, but I'm more afraid of being alone." I don't know what had come over me, but I was done with all the pretending to be something I wasn't.

"I hear you."

"Why did you never find anyone, Tyisha?" I asked again. It was as if figuring her out would make it easier to figure me out. "You're so normal."

"You know what? It's bigger than Pat Bailey. He wasn't the only one who loved me, who I could have shared my life with." She shook away the ghosts of memories clouding her eyes. "Maybe we'll have that conversation another time. When you're out, okay?" She patted my shoulder, then kept her arm loosely around me as we walked back to the living room.

"Ja, can you please show her what to do?"

Ja Roach showed her how to tie a tourniquet. How to find my veins. How to poke the needle in. Then he walked to the other side of the room to take care of himself.

Tyisha had always been a fast learner. Once she set her mind to something, she did it. She pushed her lips against each other and squinted in concentration. The rubber pinched around my legs, catching on hair I hadn't shaved in years. She thumped at my vein and the needle. Did a swab from the foil packet, tossed it all down. Then her eyes met mine.

I saw love and compassion there. I wanted to reflect that, but I was only thinking about the sweet oblivion that was coming. She poked the needle through my skin, then pushed the plunger. I helped her pull up my pants. Then I waited, but something was off.

"I don't feel so good," I heard myself say. I got cold really quick. I leaned over and let everything in my stomach out knowing I'd ruined her house again. Then I got very sleepy. Bad damn batch. I was too old for this.

As I nodded off, I promised myself: *This is the last time.*

3

"I'm Nicole Long." I extended my hand for shaking. Bennie Gross took it reluctantly. After that I sat down across from her at the brown wood conference table. I could tell Gross was nervous, so I moved as slowly as I would have around a skittish cat, slowly taking the file, then a pad and pen from my bag. Finally situated, I said, "I'll be handling the prosecution of your perpetrator in your case."

"So, if he's the perpetrator, does that make me a victim?" Gross asked.

"No." My pause was for dramatic effect. "It makes you a survivor," I said.

"That's not a label I ever wanted," she said, her voice just this side of a whimper.

I had to take a deep breath. Push away my own memories of being in her shoes with someone a lot less sympathetic on the other side of that table so many years past.

"No one does." I patted the back of her hand.

"So how bad is this going to be?"

"First, I'm sorry your victim advocate couldn't be here today. She's on maternity leave. She'll be back next Monday, but I wanted to accommodate your schedule, so this meeting will just be me and you today, okay?"

Gross nodded her understanding.

"On Monday, we're going to have our last pretrial hearing. That means, the defendant will be in court while the lawyers argue over what evidence will be allowed at trial."

"What are you arguing over?"

"Many years ago, our state, and nearly all state legislators, passed something called rape shield laws. The revised code requires a separate hearing on whether the defendant can introduce any evidence of your prior sexual activity."

"I thought it wasn't permitted. That's what the...advocate—I forget her name—said when I first met her."

"It isn't permitted. That doesn't mean the defendant won't try to get it in."

"Oh, God. What does he want to dredge up from my past?"

I tried to swallow my sigh. In nearly every case, defendants tried to bring in a victim's sexual history. In nearly every case, the judge excluded it for all the reasons the rape shield laws had been enacted. Because women were still judged by different sexual standards from men. And because a jury could still be swayed by the idea of a promiscuous woman. America was nevertheless puritanical in many ways.

"First, I want to assure you that the chances of any judge permitting any of this is tiny."

"But not zero."

"Nothing is certain in a courtroom."

"Okay…"

"I'm sorry to tell you that, but every case and every trial is unique. The defendant wants to bring in the fact that you were assaulted as a minor. He's arguing that your earlier rape by your stepbrother made you…into a person who solicited sex from men to make yourself feel better."

"Jesus. I'm the one who told him about my stepbrother. I know that case was sealed. There'd be no way for him to find out, otherwise. I'm so stupid." For a long moment, Gross' hands went up to her face, covering her eyes. She pressed hard as if pushing the tears back inside, then lowered her hands. "I trusted him. I thought I could share my secrets. And all he did was use them against me."

"I'm not sure if it will help you, but this is something predators do. Win your confidence. Use it against you. Target previous victims. He dug for your vulnerabilities, found one, and used it to his advantage."

"What an asshole. I can't believe I trusted him."

"He's in the wrong here."

"Thank God you didn't say 'it's not your fault.' You have no idea how much I hate that stupid phrase."

I looked at my witness, could sense that she was on the fence. She hadn't admitted it yet, but I could read in her eyes, in her body language that Bennie Gross was thinking of bailing. No way was I going to let my first case back in the office go like that.

"Can I share something personal?" When Gross nodded, I continued. "I was once the victim of sexual assault. Back before there were rape shield laws. The perpetrator, the police, and my parents convinced me not to prosecute. The hardest part of all that? It's that my rapist is out there to this day. These rapists…these men—they never stop until something stops them. Do you remember in high school physics the concept that only an immovable object will stop an unstoppable force?"

Gross nodded.

"You and me and the judge and the jury that will convict your rapist. Collectively, we're the immovable object."

"Tell me what I have to do," Bennie Gross said.

After that, it was just a matter of going over what she may be asked in chambers by the judge. When she left our early morning meeting, I knew that she was solid. That my return to work would be capped by a successful rape prosecution. There was no better way to come back than with a winner.

When I finally got to my office, the extra desk was gone. I hadn't exactly been assigned a bright and shiny new workspace with a plate glass window facing Lake Erie. At least I wouldn't have to share, though.

One desk.

One office chair.

And two guest chairs was more than I'd expected…or maybe even deserved.

I set the Bennie Gross file, my purse, and empty briefcase on the single flat wood surface and set about getting reacquainted with my desk. The top middle drawer had some crappy ballpoint pens, their leaky tips covered in mystery crumbs. I wondered who'd helped themselves to my good ones.

Everything else appeared to be in place. I pressed all the necessary buttons to bring my computer and monitor to life, then realized my bags were in the way of actually using my keyboard to type in my password. I'd always kept my personal stuff in the bottom right hand drawer. I gently tugged at the handle. It was exactly as I'd left it—locked.

I fiddled for the keys I'd dropped in my purse the moment I'd come into the building. Fished them out. The tiniest key on the ring fitted in the equally small lock. The turn to the right was smooth as if the mechanism had been oiled. As I pulled the drawer open, my extra pair of black pumps came into sight. I tugged a little harder at the metal handle. The high pitched tinkle of glass was music to my ears. Two tiny bottles of Maker's Mark were exactly where I'd left them. The bottle labeled Madagascar Vanilla was still there as well—empty.

Reaching in back, I grabbed both bourbon bottles with a single hand. The little red wax seals hadn't been disturbed by movers, cleaners, or sticky-fingered office mates.

I poked my thumbnail at an irregular drip trying to decide if I needed to transfer the contents to the brown glass flavoring bottle or the toilet in the restroom down the hall.

Undecided about that, I let the wax draw my attention again. When Daddy and I had gone to the bourbon distillery in Kentucky, every visitor was allowed to dip their souvenir bottle in hot wax. It had been one of the coolest things my dad and I had done that was just the two of us. The bottle from that day was long gone. The memory of the drink from that souvenir that had led to the assault I'd been candid with Bennie Gross about, left a bitter taste in my mouth. But these little ones made me smile.

I used my perfectly French-tipped thumbnail as a knife and cut through the wax. Peeling the red seal back filled me with more satisfaction than something like that had a right to. I twisted off the cap. Downed the bottle in less than three seconds. The empty one and the full one clinked like musical notes as I shoved them to the back of the drawer. Nostalgia trumped sobriety any time.

"Early bird catches the worm, huh?"

I nearly jumped out of my skin as I reflexively slammed the drawer shut hiding the offending items.

"You startled me," I said in greeting to the woman who'd entered my office unannounced.

"Can't recall seeing you here before nine-thirty ever," my boss said.

Lorraine Pope was the prosecuting attorney for Cuyahoga County, Ohio. Every pleading, every letter, every document that left this office had her name at the top and the bottom. In this county, there was little doubt as to who was in charge of filling jails and prisons.

I stood as tall and straight as an Army private during boot camp. A salute and click of my heels wouldn't have been out of place.

"Ready to make a fresh start," I announced. I left off the "because this chance may be my last." That was understood between us.

"Did you see the door?" She gestured to the wide open door that was taking full advantage of its hinge and the rubber doorstop behind it.

"Yes, ma'am. Thank you." My tone was full on southern polite.

Three brass plates adorned the faux wood. My name was actually affixed to the metal slides along with the plaque for Major Crimes. Below that was the title Deputy Director. The three metal bars made me feel like I'd been promoted to staff sergeant.

"I kept up my side of the bargain," Pope said as if a job were a favor.

"You must have gotten a good report from Journeys, otherwise I wouldn't be here." I'd had to waive any and all confidentiality during rehab as a condition of keeping my job.

I have no doubt my substance abuse counselors were serving as low key spies, regularly feeding information to Pope or someone in her office. The knowledge of such a file's existence, with my personal information, in this building was all the behavior modification I'd need to keep on the straight and narrow.

"How many days sober are you?"

"Forty-five," I answered. Or zero minutes. But one little bottle didn't count. One and a half months of days was math I could do in my head without a thought. Adding one tortuous day after another had been hell.

"Are you ready for your first case assignments?" Pope inartfully switched topics. She'd always saved her grace and charm for the higher-ups.

I'd been so worried about her seeing the alcohol in my drawer or demanding a search that it was only at this moment I noticed the razor thin oak tag file folder in her hand. The kind the office sometimes had for "off the books" cases. My debt repayment was starting immediately.

No grace period for me.

4

"C'mon, Sorry, don't be such a scaredy cat."

I hated when my big sister called me that. Not just the "Sorry," part, which I really super-duper hated, but scaredy cat. I wasn't scared. When my cat Oreo got scared, her back went up and all her black-and-white fur looked like she'd put her tail in a socket. I was nothing like that. I swiped at the back of my neck to make sure my hair was indeed flat. It was.

Rainey didn't understand that I was just following the rules. When I did what Momma and Daddy said, I didn't get into trouble. Rainey never did what they said, and she was always in trouble.

My sister's eyes were shooting lasers at me. She looked like the kids in the Village of the Damned from her stick-straight blond hair to her creepily glowing eyes.

See now that was trouble. Momma had been real mad when she'd caught me watching that late night movie after my bedtime. Momma had said it would cause my too young, ten-year-old self nightmares. She'd been exactly right.

Okay, maybe I was scared. I didn't want to tell my sister, though, because Rainey would make fun of me for days. Once my sister got a hold of something, she never let it go.

"But Daddy told us to stay home." I knew I was whining, but I didn't care.

"'But Daddy told us to stay home,'" Rainey mimicked in the sing-song voice she knew I hated.

"Why do you want to go over there anyway?" I asked. "Did you see the news? Walter Cronkite said it's a race riot."

"I want to see it in person," Rainy answered as if going to Hough were the same as looking at outer space meteorites at the natural history museum. She continued, breathing the last words like she was whispering in church, "To see if it's for real."

"Of course, it's for real," I huffed. "Daddy hasn't been home at all. Momma said that no one in the police department can leave their post or something like that."

"Your momma says a lot of words." Rainey's voice was clipped. "Get your tennis shoes on."

I tried to back away from my sister, get to my room so I could shut the door. Sometimes Rainey didn't bother me if she couldn't see me.

"I don't—"

Rainey's hand gripped my arm so hard, I was afraid she was going to leave bruises. I was tired of trying to explain the black-and-blue marks that would appear. I'd even stopped letting Momma come in when I was taking a bath. I missed that. Momma sitting on the toilet seat while I lay in the foamy bubbles. She would wash my hair and rub my scalp, then we would chitchat until the water got cold.

"Your mother's asleep."

Reluctantly, I shoved first one foot, then the other into the red, white, and blue sneakers I'd begged Momma and Daddy to buy me for the summer.

Five minutes later I was in the front seat of Momma's car. Rainey had somehow gotten the keys. After the first time Rainey had "borrowed" the car, Momma had started keeping her metal key ring in the drawer next to her and Daddy's bed. Momma was a light sleeper, though, and the curiosity as to how she'd gotten the keys without waking Momma was eating away at me.

I thought about asking Rainey on how she did it, but the way she squinted at me made me think twice. I kept my big mouth shut.

"I used to live in Cleveland, you know." The gears of Momma's car ground a little as Rainey jammed the stick shift into reverse. She turned the car around from facing the garage toward the street.

Cleveland wasn't New York or Detroit, but the city was still miles from our driveway in Rocky River.

I wanted to ask my sister if living in the city had been scary. Did she worry about being murdered in her bed at night by a guy coming through her window? Daddy said it wasn't a safe world when you went east of the Cuya-hoga River. That he was doing everything in his power to keep our family and people like us protected.

"Yeah, but you had Daddy. Everyone knew he was a cop, right? All of our neighbors say to Momma all the time how glad they are that we moved on the block."

"He wasn't ever home at night," Rainey spat out. I hated that tone of voice she used, as if I was too stupid to understand anything. I wasn't sixteen like her, but I was ten and that felt old enough to know how stuff worked in the world. She couldn't yell at me if I didn't say anything, though, so I shut up.

"Your dad is home almost every single night." That one came out with a hiss, not a yell. I hoped that meant she wasn't mad at me anymore for having a better life than hers.

It wasn't long before we were on the expressway and Rainey wasn't grinding gears because she'd stopped moving the stick after she'd switched to the highest one. She must have been driving Momma's new Mustang at least ninety miles an hour in the left lane. I didn't exactly know, though, because I'd closed my eyes when I saw the needle go past the number eighty.

I only opened my eyes again when the car came to a stop. Everything was quiet while Rainey waited for the light to change on the wide and empty Cleveland street. A big stone church stood silent on the corner. I craned my neck to look for street signs. We were on Euclid Avenue and East Thirtieth street. When the light turned, Rainey ground it into first and we drove what could only be further east.

Fear gripped my throat. I could only breathe again when my eyes finally got used to the dark. It was nothing more than brick buildings and tall steepled churches. I think I saw a theater, but it was closed up tight.

Then the air changed. It wasn't like a thunderstorm was coming in, but the air felt electric anyway. The streets were not dark anymore. Even though I was afraid, I rolled down the window and stuck my head out. Even though streetlights were all broken jagged glass, it was as bright as daylight.

Then I understood why.

First, it was thick smoke coming from somewhere just past where I could see. I pushed my glasses up my nose, but it wasn't much better. Rainey was moving a lot slower now. Suddenly my arm got hot and my head snapped to the open window again.

Something was on fire. It wasn't a building because whatever it was half blocked the road. It was a garbage can, maybe. I tilted my head to the right and held my glasses up with my index finger. No, it was a car. Some kind of small car. The smell was awful, the smoke thick and oily.

A group of angry-looking Negro men ran by. Then a group of men came behind them. They had guns and uniforms, but weren't police.

"Who's that?"

I pointed my finger out of the window toward men in camouflage.

"National Guard."

"What do they do?"

"What you see them doing. Keeping order."

The car was crawling now. The fires were bigger. The shouts louder. Negroes were running everywhere. Some were throwing rocks and bottles with rags sticking out. Others had stuff in their hands like they'd been shopping without a cart or bag.

I nearly jumped out of my seat at the sound of shattering glass. Momma was going to kill Rainey if something happened to this car. It had been a birthday present from Daddy.

Ponies were stitched into the seat leather. Some days I swear Momma loved it, more than she loved any of us and the dog. The dog had been Daddy's present to me the year before, but the Shih Tzu loved her best. At the sound of something else breaking, I forgot all about Lady.

"We should turn back, Rainey. You can see what's happening. People are throwing things. I think I heard a gun go off. We could end up dead. Then Daddy would be really mad."

"If we're dead, we won't care how Daddy feels," she said. She was one hundred percent right. My heart started beating really fast. Sometimes I lay awake in bed at night squeezing Oreo too hard while I tried to imagine the nothingness of death. Even though Momma promised me I'd go to heaven, Rainey said she was lying. Rainey said I'd be in the ground feeling like I was suffocating and being eaten by worms. Then after that—nothing—forever.

"I don't want to die," I gasped.

"No one is going to die." Rainey was turning the car this way and that. "Look, I think I see Daddy now." She pointed through the windshield.

"Really?" I pushed my glasses up again. Tried to find him through the hazy smoke.

"Yeah. Look, you're right. This was stupid. Let's get him to drive us home or find someone to get us out of here safely."

"That's a really swell idea," I said. It was the first good one she'd had all night.

In a second we were reversing too fast. The car thumped and someone screamed.

"Did we hit somebody?"

Rainey didn't answer, though a smile played around the side of her mouth. Something twisted in my belly. Instead of saying anything to me, or checking to see what might have happened, my sister put the Mustang back into gear and turned down an alley. It was blocked by a burned car and other stuff.

"Get out!" Rainey had turned to me. She was screaming the command in my face.

"What?" My body suddenly went very, very cold.

"Daddy's right there around the corner. Just past those garbage cans. You see that sign on the ground, the one that says, '79ers?'"

In front of us, there was a giant half burned piece of wood lying on the pavement.

I nodded.

"He's there. Right there just past. I'm going to go around to the other side of this alley. Pick you both up there. Got it?"

I nodded again. My heart slowed down a little. She had a plan.

Right then I saw a burly cop poking his head and shoulders down the alleyway. It was Daddy. Swell. I just needed to get to him. Then we'd get home. Rainey would be punished. I would be safe.

My sweaty fingers pulled at the lock until I could get it to open, then I lifted the door handle until the heavy door of Momma's new car opened. I stepped out and slammed it. Before I could say anything to Rainey confirming our getaway plan, the car was peeling out of the alley in reverse.

Though I couldn't figure out why I was doing it, I found myself booking it toward her instead of Daddy. She was smiling at me. That smile filled my belly with balls of lead and my chest with fear and dread. Rainey rolled down the driver's window. Her face going from pretty to ugly in an instant.

"This time, you're going to be sorry you were born, Sorry."

It's what she meant every time she called me by that nickname. I was as good as dead this time.

5

I already met with a sexual assault victim this morning."
I straightened up and stood at attention when I answered
my boss, Lori Pope. "So, yes, I'm more than ready to get
back to work." The bourbon had gone straight to my
head. Kept me looking unruffled as I fished through my
top drawer as if looking for a pen. I pulled one of the
leaky ones out along with an equally janky legal pad. My
Oscar worthy performance made the subsequent mint
find look like a surprise. After I popped the small square
candy into my mouth, I continued. "The counselors suggest keeping busy in the beginning." Though I was sure
Lori Pope already knew that.

"Good. Here you go." She walked toward the desk,
thrust the single file across it and toward my chest. "Two
murders."

I accepted the oaktag all the while waiting for her to say something about my last disaster of a murder case, where I'd indicted the wrong defendant. Or clue me in on the second murder. Pope did neither.

When she remained quiet, I flipped the folder open because none of the usual heft was there: murder photos, detective investigative notes, autopsy report. There was only a single sheet police report.

"Where's the re—"

She cut me off.

"That's it."

When Pope didn't budge, I took a step back and a moment to scan the single Xeroxed sheet. It was from the Cleveland Heights police department, one of the forty-nine municipalities in Cuyahoga County that our office had jurisdiction over.

The incident report detailed the logistics of a body found in an abandoned house. When I first started working in the prosecutor's office a decade ago, this kind of incident would have sparked an investigation. Nowadays much of Ohio was in the grips of both foreclosure and heroin crises, and this kind of death was becoming an everyday occurrence. These were cases where no one person was to blame.

No crime.

No prosecution.

No punishment necessary.

I didn't dare look up or meet Pope's eyes. No doubt I was supposed to figure out on my own why this particular file was important; why the normal rules didn't apply. So I skimmed again. No time for perusal with my boss practically breathing down my neck. My heart beat out of my chest when I finally cottoned on. The lede had been buried under the victim's name: Grace McNeill.

"I thought we talked about this in a staff meeting before I...left." Talk was a more polite word than the debate that had nearly ended in fisticuffs. "You said we weren't going after these nonviolent offenders." I read carefully this third time around, my manicured nail grazing the tiny handwritten words. "It says here McNeill died of an overdose."

An overdose was a tragedy. It was a tiny snapshot that encapsulated all the issues in rustbelt Ohio. What it wasn't, was a murder.

"I know what it says, Nicole. But the fact remains that she was murdered."

I don't know if the jolt I felt was fear or excitement. Either way, I tried not to let my boss see that I was affected by her statement.

"How do you...by whom?" I stuttered out.

"Whom? Funny how you talk sometimes. Are you asking who killed her?"

I nodded, then stated the obvious.

"A crime needs a perpetrator."

It was the lesson I'd learned the first day of my Criminal Law class in my first year of law school. A lot of what I absorbed in those three years wasn't practical knowledge. My school had been heavily immersed in theory back in the 1990s. But the fundamentals of criminal law were the same now as they were then. Some person had to be identifiable so they could be charged with and held responsible for a crime; otherwise it was at best an unfortunate incident and at worst, a tragedy.

"Then I think you'll need to find one Libby Saldana," Pope said.

"Libby Saldana?" I rolled the name around in my mouth because I had a feeling I'd be saying it more than a few times.

"She's the one who gave this McNeill girl the hot shot. The one who recklessly killed her. The one who needs to pay for this crime."

"Sounds like you know her."

Pope's chin tipped down in what could have been a nod. "We may have crossed paths a time or two. I wouldn't say she has a reputation for honesty. All about the self-preservation, this one. Whoever takes this case better watch her back because Saldana has been around the block a time or two."

"And for the other?" If it was vendetta week, I needed to know all the players in the game.

But Pope wasn't going to give an inch. She was the kind of politician that always came up smelling like roses even when everyone else around her was covered in shit. If anything ever rubbed off on her, she said it was chocolate. What's worse, everyone believed her. If push came to shove, I wanted enough facts for plausible deniability.

"One case at a time," was my boss' parting shot.

I guess I was going to stay in the dark. I wanted to ask more, to press harder. I didn't chase her out the door because I already knew the penalty for bucking the stystem—reliving my worst nightmare.

I'd been warned about the repercussions of crossing my boss just a few weeks ago when I'd been treated to an unexpected visitor just two weeks into my stay at Journeys. Since I had no friends, I hadn't bothered to ask who the visitor was. Sure it was a mistake, I'd planned to disabuse, whomever was here, of the notion that I was their friend or relative. Mistaken identity cleared, I'd planned to go back to my monastic cell and grind my way through the rest of the treatment.

I have to say that I was surprised to see my boss sitting quite primly in the visitor's area empty save for the two of us and one burly orderly.

"Checking up on me?" I asked Pope in greeting.

"I need to make sure I hadn't made a mistake," she retorted. "Stuck my neck out for you. While I may have a kind place in my heart for addicts—I've told you about my sister—not everyone else does. You really need to get it together. This is your last chance."

"I am grateful," I said with a slight bow to my head. That was mostly true.

"Glad to hear it."

We sat in silence for a moment. She had some other reason for visiting. It wasn't like we were friends. I waited.

"I got a call from an old acquaintance of yours yesterday."

Something about her tone made my heart beat just a tiny bit faster. That had been happening off and on over the last few days, but I knew my racing heart wasn't caused by the effects of withdrawal.

"Of mine?" I couldn't help asking after she remained silent.

"Your old boss, Seth Collins."

My chair tipped back, and before I could regain my balance, the back of it hit the floor. An orderly ran toward me, picking me up like I was a fragile bit of china.

I'd overheard the director calling those of us whose insurance companies paid full price—special cargo.

"You bleeding or anything?" the orderly asked.

"No, I'm fine," I insisted. "Just embarrassed."

"Well, miss, let me help you up so you can finish your visit with your friend here." Though I wanted to, disclaiming friendship probably wasn't the right way to go. So I let him put me back in the chair and be pushed forward toward the low accent table between us.

"You were saying?" I asked as if I hadn't just showed my hand.

"Yes, New Day pastor. He's quite famous now. I met him back in ninety-five. He happened to be in town during some protests of the Simpson verdict. We had a common cause."

"What's that?"

"Justice."

I didn't point out the irony of that. That man, Seth Collins, would never be brought to justice, never see his day in court for what he did to me, much like the famed football player.

When I didn't respond, Pope continued, "I did thank him for referring you all those years ago. I hope you thanked him properly for that. You were only one of a handful of hires in a year when the county had frozen our numbers. I was only able to get you guys in based on attrition. Expansion was out of the question. Glad I hired like crazy after that because we're back in a slump. Don't know when I'll be able to add more attorneys to our ranks."

"It was a favor to my father," I lied. "I'm sure we're all even."

"He's offered to visit. To help counsel you spiritually. Would you like that? It's only a phone call away."

I knew then that Pope had somehow learned about my biggest secret, my biggest shame. I couldn't begin to figure how it happened, but I'd have bet all the money I got from Collins and New Day in a confidential settlement that this was going to be my personal sword of Damocles.

"This place, Journeys, is good. No need for anything more. It's a full service program."

"Glad it's working out. If all goes according to plan, you'll be head of Major Crimes when you get back. The offer of having Seth Collins help, still stands. Let's just keep that as an open offer, shall we? Great seeing you. Gotta get back to the big bad city. The place would go to hell in a handbasket without me."

Blackmail firmly in place, she had taken her leave.

That memory lay heavily on my shoulders like a wool cloak wet from Cleveland rain. Someone was going to get hurt, me or Libby Saldana. I swallowed my morals and ethics with the second bottle of bourbon then scribbled a few spirals to get the ink in the Bic flowing smoothly.

I got to work doing what I did best—put people in prison. Saldana was going to have to give up her freedom in exchange for mine.

6

Justin McPhee
February 22, 2008

I kicked out my tasseled loafer and braced it against the leg of my desk. My head snapped as my chair stopped spinning in an instant. I'd been going round and round and round for the last five minutes. Now the room spun as my eyes darted about. Gradually, slowly, my world came to a complete standstill.

That's how it felt without Casey Cort in my life, like I'd gotten off a carousel seconds ago. Casey and her fiancé Ron Pinheiro and everyone else was still moving forward and I was doing nothing but watching the blur of life and laughter and love from my solitary perch.

In exactly two months, Casey was having a baby. A boy or girl I was quickly starting to believe had half of my DNA even if she'd decided to marry the other prospect. I could be there, right now, at her apartment, holding her hand. Taking her to birth classes or breathing classes or whatever classes pregnant women went to. Playing happy family. Instead, I was here, my life shoehorned into three hundred square feet of buttoned up office space.

A pit of emptiness opened in my stomach. I didn't even know what hospital Casey was giving birth in. Cleveland Clinic was top flight, famous for flying in the King of Jordan, the emir of Kuwait, and president of the United Arab Emirates, not to mention professional athletes. University Hospital wasn't a bad runner up either. Cleveland had more than enough doctors for her to have a safe birth. I had not one reason to worry. Anxiety gnawed at me anyway.

I shook my head trying not to dwell on the decision I'd made. It had been a sound one. Casey wanted love and marriage and kids and a white picket fence around a bright green lawn in front of an eastside brick Tudor. I was not that kind of guy. I would *never* be that kind of guy. I *could* never be that kind of guy.

Fortunately my phone's intercom buzzed cutting my one man pity party short.

"Your client is here."

"Thanks Ernie," I said before pushing the off button.

I'm not sure what Casey had done with her half of our big money judgment, but with mine, I was giving back to the community.

Legal Aid was sending me working poor clients who needed a lawyer but were too well off to qualify for free services. The first few cases had made me feel good, better than I had in most of my years practicing. Helping the cancer stricken children of Brighthill had only been the beginning. I wanted to keep that feeling going.

I stepped outside my door. A woman was coming down the hall toward me. She emanated cold. As she got closer, I could see tiny crystalline snowflakes were turning to beads of water on her coat.

"Justin McPhee," I said to her.

"I think you're the lawyer I'm supposed to see."

"Why don't you step into my office."

The woman was a little worse for wear. In her frazzled state, she undid the three buttons of her black wool double breasted coat revealing less than clean hospital scrubs. Then she was fishing through a blue paisley quilted bag as if the holy grail were hidden in there. Patiently, I waited. I'd learned that I had to give clients a moment to gather their bearings. For many, coming to an attorney was intimidating. They wouldn't be here if something big like their children or freedom weren't on the line.

In less than a minute, the woman had pulled a crumpled paper from the blue bag. Smoothed it on my desk. All the while standing and pacing on a small patch of industrial carpet. Her steps and turns were so tight that for the first time ever I worried a client could wear a hole through to the concrete subfloor.

"You're Justin McPhee, I guess," spilled from her. "This woman from over at Legal Aid on West Sixth Street put your name on this paper. Said you could help me because they couldn't."

"You know who I am." I worked to make my voice calm, my speech slow in hopes that she'd mirror me. "Can I ask your name?"

"Libby. Libby Saldana." She was speaking so rapidly it was as if I were billing her by the millisecond, when in reality it was a free consultation.

"Well, Ms. Saldana, please have a seat."

"I don't have any money." She paced in an even tighter square. "This is a nice office you have here." Saldana spun on a flowered clog. Pointed a gloved finger at me. "I can't keep you in leather couches or yachts."

"Fortunately, I already own this couch. I don't much like the water." My attempt at levity fell flat. I extended my hand in invitation again. "Have a seat in one of the chairs, please."

Saldana didn't seem like the kind of person who used chairs when otherwise wearing a path in the carpet would do. Ignoring me, she continued to pace. I didn't make a third offer. To gain some semblance of authority, I went to stand behind my desk. Words kept spilling from her despite my movement.

"I'm in a lot of trouble, I think. I can't go to jail. I have a little girl. I mean she's at my mom's house, but I'm almost ready to get her back."

I nodded in understanding. Like many of the clients I'd served when I'd worked for practically nothing in Juvy, Saldana had what they called a 'kaleidoscope' of the usual client problems. Kid in foster or relative care under the watchful eye of children's services. If I had to speculate, I'd add boyfriend with felonious tendencies, and some kind of substance abuse. Instead of guessing, I jumped right to her biggest issue—potential incarceration.

"Jail?" I asked. I meant prison. But that was a word that scared the shit out of people. I needed information.

Saldana could not be in such a panic that she wouldn't be able to help herself.

"Yeah. Some deputies came by with this."

Saldana dug through her bag again. More papers emerged. She thrust them at me. I really wanted to sit down because I could think easier that way. It didn't feel right in the face of her frenetic energy, though.

I gently pulled the documents from her hand. The bold black type at the top spelled out 'indictment' in bold and capital letters. Which meant a felony. Which had a much higher probability of jail, er, prison. Suddenly her nervous anxiety made a lot more sense.

"Sit, please."

I needed her to stop moving so my mind could think instead of being occupied by the dizzying pattern of her swaying bag.

Finally she let herself plop into one of my chairs. So I did as well. It took a lot for me to look away from her bobbing leg and cuticle exploration and focus on the documents in front of me.

After I smoothed out the sheets, I took a look at what Lori Pope had in store for this woman. To say it wasn't a walk in the park would be an understatement. It was, actually, a bramble filled path that could lead to a very long prison sentence.

"Have you read this?" I worked to meet her gaze.

"Yeah, a few times. I think there must be some mistake though—"

I interrupted her before she went down that well-trodden path. There were thousands of people in the care and custody of the Ohio Department of Rehabilitation and

Correction who'd started with the false belief that there'd been some kind of cosmic error.

The county prosecutor's office didn't make mistakes. And when they did, they acted as if they didn't. Which in the end was the same result; a defendant trying to dodge a prison sentence. I used my thumb to flick at the papers. The rattle of processed tree pulp was the only sound in the room.

"It says here," I started, "upon information and belief—"

"What's that?" Saldana's interruption was a question.

"Just legal jargon. Anyway, you're charged with," I read the sheet on the top, "involuntary manslaughter." I flipped from one page to the next all the while trying to keep my eyebrows level. She was not the typical homicide defendant. "Corrupting another with drugs," Flipped. "Possession of heroin." Turned to the last. "And tampering with evidence."

"Tampering?"

That wasn't the headline, but we'd get back to that, I guessed. My index finger ran along some black and white text.

"It says here that you deleted some text messages."

Saldana lifted a single shoulder in a shrug, then dropped. The unspoken message was clear. She was guilty of at least that much.

"Possession of heroin?"

"I'm guilty of that one, too."

"Let's go back. What happened that led up to these charges."

"Do they have a case? Are you going to be my lawyer?"

"I can't make a decision about that until I hear the story."

"What would make you not take my case?"

Saldana had me there. Not being desperate meant that I could pick and choose what cases I was working on. When I'd agreed to be on the Legal Aid referral list, my first inclination was that I could help people who really needed it, not choose cases to line my pockets or burnish my reputation.

The rich could pay for legal services. Much of the middle class as well. There was a gap, though, between those people who could pay and those people the government deemed poor enough not to have to. Not to mention that the attorneys at Legal Aid or the public defender's office were always overburdened. Often they couldn't even adequately help those that qualified for their services.

"If I don't think I can help you, I won't waste your time," I equivocated.

"Can you...help?"

"It's not that simple. Can I call you Libby?"

That shrug again. I'd misinterpreted it as apathy the first time. Now I realized it was a nervous tick. Saldana was anxious she'd leave my office without a lawyer...without any bulwark between here and a cell block.

"Sure, call me whatever." Her shoulder only twitched a little this time.

"I need to hear about what happened to make the prosecutor's office indict you."

Her head shake was incongruous.

"They indict everyone," she said.

Saldana didn't want to talk about what had happened. Unfortunately, her street-smart instinct to remain mum was at odds with her need for a lawyer.

"That may be true, but you're the one who's going to be on trial." I pointed to the papers in my hand. "This here is your name on the indictment. Whatever happens to anyone else is their business. But this here means the county prosecutor's office wants to put you in state lockup a good long time. I'm going to guess that you don't want to go."

"A long time? No. That makes no sense. Everyone knows that they're not prosecuting nonviolent—"

"Nonviolent drug offenders," I finished. "The prosecutor's office *has* made diversion available to more defendants."

"Can I get that...diversion? I need to be here for my baby." Head shake. "I'm not innocent. No one is. But I'm not guilty either."

The prisons were full of people in that gray area where the scales had tipped a little bit toward conviction. I didn't tell her that either.

From my experience, all this would probably go away. She'd been overcharged. It was from page one of the prosecutorial playbook. Indict for everything. Plea the defendant for far less. That way a conviction for *something* was nearly guaranteed and Pope's stats looked great come election time. Saldana didn't need to know she'd probably skate on these charges, this time around. I needed her fear to keep her focused.

I scooted my chair closer to my desk and in turn closer to her.

"So, what happened?" I asked again.

"I didn't mean it. I really didn't. But I can do needles. I'm a certified phlebotomist." Libby waved her hands at her scrubs in mute explanation. "She couldn't poke herself. Grace needed to get straight. Really needed it."

Phlebotomist. That was a new one.

"What did you do Libby?"

"I gave Grace..." she swallowed, hard. "Gracie McNeill. I gave her a shot. Her last one..."

"That favor is going to cost you..." I did quick math in my head. Roughed out her longest possible sentence. "Twenty years."

"What are you saying? That I could be in prison until I'm fifty years old. My little girl would be almost thirty. She would have graduated from elementary and middle school and high school. She'd be married. Have kids. All without me. No, no, no. That can't be right. Nobody gets charged with this. We all help each other out."

The shrug-twitch again.

"Sometimes it doesn't work out," Saldana continued. "That's the nature of it. It's not like heroin comes in pretty packages on a drug store shelf all weighed and tested. Some of us have demons. This is the only way to chase them away. Most of the time it's good. We get straight. Sometimes it's cut with something bad.

"That's what happened." Suddenly her voice was full of emotion. "There was something else in there. Something that made her sick. Grace just had a seizure and od'd right there. I tried to save her. I tried CPR. I called the police. The paramedics, they couldn't do a single thing. The cops, they took me to the hospital. Turned me over to the doctors there. I got into treatment right then. Some social worker found me a bed. I've been...sober ever since. Got a new job. Getting my girl back. I'm done with the life. Can you tell them that? The judge? The prosecutor? Let them know that I'm sorry. It'll never happen again. I'm a solid citizen now?"

It was that last plea that got to me. She'd made it past the bad part, all on her own. Saldana deserved a fresh start. I could probably do that for her. I wanted to do that for her because a fresh start was something everyone deserved. I should know.

"I'll take your case." I used my most soothing voice. "I'll represent you."

"Good. When can we talk to the judge? Can you call there now?"

"There's a process Libby. It's not going to be that easy. I'm going to do everything in my power to convey your message to the other side, to the court. To a jury if necessary."

"A jury. You mean like a trial? I don't want to do that, having people judging me. I'll do community service or whatever they need me to do. But I can't go to jail."

I wanted to promise her that she'd never go, but I'd made that mistake once before with a client who was still behind bars. Instead, I gave her my warmest and most reassuring smile before speaking the harsh truth.

"Unfortunately, neither you nor I get to decide that."

7

"Daddy!" I yelled toward the stocky, shadowy figure that we'd watched step around the corner.

There was no response. I ran down the alley. I couldn't see Daddy in the mess of people. There were just too many bodies. Men, women, and even some children were running back and forth. I couldn't tell where anyone was going. Were they trying to get home? Or were they trying to escape their neighborhood before the entire place went up in flames?

Glass exploded to my left. A few seconds after, I felt a sting in my shoulder, like a swarm of bees had come at me. I didn't yank my top down to check what had happened. Daddy could figure that out later. He'd always been more patient than Momma with tweezers and a magnifying glass whenever I'd gotten a splinter or tick stuck in my skin. That almost always happened when we went hiking. Rainey said I was plain bad luck.

Hope filled my chest. My sister wouldn't have just left me here. I must have imagined her backing out of the alley. I whipped my head around toward the way we'd come in. Momma's car wasn't there.

No Rainey.

No escape.

I needed to find Daddy.

I ran to the street. Looked right. Looked left. There was a cop, gun raised. I knew that uniform. My daddy had one just like it. I tugged at the belt. He jumped like a cat and spun on his heel toward me. The shiny black gun was pointed straight at my head. My hands flew straight toward the sky.

"Don't shoot! My dad's a cop!" That's exactly what Daddy had taught me to say. "My dad's a cop" was supposed to be my get out of jail free card, like in Monopoly—only this wasn't a game.

"Who are you? What in the hell are you doing down here? It's dangerous for a girl like you."

I didn't have any kind of answer to that question, so I asked one instead.

"Officer…" The cop didn't have a name tag or any badge that I could see. Daddy had always told me to look for the name tag. Memorize the badge number. That way he could thank whoever helped me. I never planned on needing help. "Have you seen my daddy? Is he here?"

The officer looked right and left, then pulled me back into the alley where it was quieter than the street.

"What's your name?"

"Sarah Pope."

"Who's your father?"

"Frank Pope."

"What district?"

Someone screamed and I couldn't think.

"Sarah—"

Officer no last name looked like he was going to leave me here alone if I didn't get with it.

"Sorry. First. West One Thirtieth."

"Don't know him. I'm on Fulton in the Second."

"I'm not lying," I whined. Rainey would have pinched me for that. I didn't care how I sounded right now. As long as I got help. "I think I saw him. I need him to take me home."

"Alright. Alright. Girl like you does not need to be out here for any damned reason." He pointed to something behind me. "See those trash cans? Hunker down over there. I'll make sure someone comes to collect you. I gotta get back out there. Looters are going to steal everything that's not nailed down. Gotta try to save something for the honest hard-working business owners here."

"Okay. If you see my dad, tell him I'm here."

He nodded, then lifted his gun and ran toward what looked like another car in flames. Why were people setting things on fire if this was their own neighborhood?

The sound of fire crackers or maybe even gunshots bounced off the brick behind me. Daddy always put his gun in a locked box when he got home. He said that weapons were deadly. Hands over my ears, I hunkered down. These people had to go sleep eventually. They couldn't keep this up all night.

Three sets of shoes ran by me. A bottle fell. Some kind of oil splashed on my brand-new sneakers. Momma was going to kill me. If these people didn't.

I was starting to think Daddy had never been here. That Rainey had done this on purpose. Rainey had left me out here to die. She'd never said it outright, but I knew that my half-sister didn't want me on this earth. Even if no one else would ever believe it if I told them.

No matter how many times she'd said I was stupid, I didn't really think I was. My teachers liked me well enough. I didn't get called up to the board to answer math questions or diagram sentences, but I wasn't in the back with the boys who couldn't read, either.

I don't know how many hours passed before it finally got quiet—no shouts, no shots. The sky wasn't dark, but it wasn't daytime, either. I wondered if it was the fires that was keeping the dark away or whether it was already getting light. I tried to move one of my legs, but it was asleep. I crawled out on my hands and knees from behind the cans. I couldn't feel my foot. It was as if I was dragging a sandbag behind me. The tingling everywhere else was like pins and needles of torture.

The clang of one of the metal trash can lids on asphalt shocked me to standing—wobblily. Fortunately, a discarded door hid my imbalance from view.

"Somebody's back there," I heard a man's voice say.

"Should we check?" that one was from a girl.

"Could be hurt. Can't wait for no police or ambulance to help. We gotta help ourselves," he said.

"Hello!" the girl called out.

To me.

I was pretty sure they were talking about me. That they were looking for me. For the first time in hours, I actually wanted to be found.

I was hungry. I had to pee. They didn't *sound* like killers. I could hear everyone's voices in my head telling me this was a bad idea. Rainey's voice was the loudest. But she's the one who had left me here, so that one I ignored.

"Here," I tried to shout. My voice was hoarse. It burned my throat to speak.

"Did you hear something?" the man asked the girl.

"I'm here!" I shouted again. This time it was a little bit louder.

Two people emerged from behind some piles of trash. It was a man and what was probably his daughter. For a moment I was so jealous that she had her dad when mine was nowhere to be found that I wanted to cry. Pushing back the tears, I just looked between the two of them curiously.

"I'm Tyisha," the girl said. She was Negro like her dad. I'm not sure if I'd ever seen any Negros up close before last night.

"Nelson Cooley. What's your name?"

"Sarah," I croaked out.

"What are you doing *here*? Do you live around here? Are you hurt? Are you okay?"

"My sister wanted to see what was happening," I explained. "She...we got separated when I went looking for our dad."

"Your dad?"

"He's a...police officer."

"Where is he?"

"I don't know." My nose started tickling, then the tears came. I tried my best to hold them back, but it wasn't any use.

"Oh, Sarah, don't worry." Tyisha patted me awkwardly. "Are you okay? I mean are you hurt at all anywhere?"

"Yeah." At Tyisha's raised eyebrows, I tried to answer better. "No, not really. I'm fine, not hurt, maybe a cut. Mostly just tired and a little dirty."

"We'll take you back to our house," Mr. Cooley decided. "You can clean up and eat a little something. Then we'll call your mom or dad. Is that okay?"

As I nodded hard, I could feel my chin bang against my chest. "Yes. Thank you so much."

When the three of us emerged from the alley, I could see that dawn was breaking. Smoke was rising from random places, but it was otherwise pretty quiet. Only a few people were wandering about looking scared or bewildered or lost, as if they couldn't believe what was happening in their own backyard. I couldn't imagine what it would be like if this kind of thing actually did happen in Rocky River.

"You okay to walk?"

"Yes. Yes, sir. Yes, Mr. Cooley. Sorry for my manners. I was just surprised that anyone found me."

"If you're okay, then let's keep it moving. I'm not sure how safe it is out here."

I followed them seven blocks to a skinny Victorian house on Eighty-fourth street. It was a lot of different colors: forest green with cream windows and dark red on the eaves. My mother would never have gone for anything like it. I thought it was pretty cool looking, though.

"Your house is nice," I said in awe. I'm not sure what I expected, but this wasn't it. Daddy and Rainey said the people here lived like animals. I thought that meant people were living in caves or burnt-out buildings or something else other than a regular house.

"Tyisha, try to be quiet," Mr. Cooley said as we walked up the front walkway. "I think your momma is probably still asleep."

"Okay." His daughter nodded. I nodded too, though he wasn't talking to me. Good manners should have made me turn around and try to find my father, my way home, but my bladder was too full for that.

I forgot all about having to pee really bad because the moment Mr. Cooley pulled open the screen door, the interior wood door flew open and a woman barreled out.

"Where did you go?" she asked. Her voice was full of worry, probably like my own momma's would be the moment she realized I wasn't in my bed, or in the house, or in Rocky River for that matter.

"I wanted to take Tyisha out. Escort her. It's a unique moment in history and she needed to witness it in person."

Maybe Rainy wasn't trying to kill me. Mr. Cooley sounded a little like my sister had. Maybe a riot was something people *should* see in person. Probably one of those "history repeats itself because no one listens lessons," the teacher had talked about during civics class.

"No eleven-year-old needs to witness a riot, Nelson John Cooley."

She'd used his full name. I knew that meant trouble.

"Hi, I'm Sarah," I interjected. Fights made me nervous. "I'm almost eleven years old, too." I would have stuck out my hand for a shake, but I didn't want her to see my black palm all covered in God-knows-what from the dirty ground.

"Excuse my manners." The woman stepped back a bit. Blinked at me in confusion. "I'm Mary Cooley. Are you a friend of Tyisha?"

She didn't stick out her hand, either. Instead, she wiped it on her apron. Maybe hers was dirty too, like mine.

"We found her huddled in an alley," Mr. Cooley explained. "I think her family had the same idea to come down and see the riots, but she got separated."

Suddenly my urge to pee nearly overwhelmed me.

"I'm sorry to be rude, but can I use your restroom?" My legs were crossed real tight.

"Oh gosh. I'm so sorry." Mrs. Cooley stepped back from the threshold. "Run upstairs. It's the first room on the left."

Pushing past them, I ran through the door and took the wood stairs two at a time. I flipped up the toilet lid and released all I'd been holding in all night. The relief was immediate, and I could breathe deeply for the first time in hours. I looked right and left until I found the metal toilet paper holder. It wasn't anything like mine at home. The roll just sat on a bar. I pulled too hard and the roll came flying off. I lunged for it and missed. The paper unrolled on the floor.

Once I'd wiped myself and the seat and flushed, I rescued the roll and tried to put it back as neatly as I could on the spool. After that, I stood and looked around the small room. I grabbed and pulled at the light chain and the room suddenly got a lot brighter.

Everything was spotless. A clawfoot tub hunkered under a big window covered with a frilly mint green curtain. The sink was small, but a bunch of lotion bottles were crowded on one side. I spied some soap and washed my hands. There was one of those fancy guest towels hanging next to the sink. My mom said to never use them in our house. But it had to be okay here because I was the guest this time.

I pulled at my top until I could see my shoulder. It was pink and red and blood had dried around what I thought was glass, but it was hard to see at any angle.

"What time is it?" I asked when I came back downstairs. Following the murmur of voices, I wandered into the kitchen where Tyisha and her dad were sitting at a small wood kitchen table.

"Early." The mom pointed at the clock over the stove. It was quarter after six. "I'm making some breakfast. Why don't you eat first. Then we'll call your family? Is that okay?"

Before I could pull up my shirt, Mrs. Cooley pressed a finger against my shoulder. Breath hissed in my mouth before I could stop it.

"Glass…a window exploded."

"Don't move."

I stayed put at the bottom of the steps until Mrs. Cooley came back with a washcloth and long, skinny tweezers. She wiped gently. It wasn't water, but something that smelled like flowers. In another second, she'd pulled out the glass.

"It's gone. I hardly felt that."

"Let me get a bandage." In a flash she was back with the familiar metal Band-Aid tin, only this one had "Stars 'n Strips" on the front above colored Band-Aids with stars on them.

"Those are cool."

"They don't have them in our color, so we got these. Which do you want?"

I had to think a long moment about what she meant about color, then it hit me. They didn't come in brown. "Oh...I'll take blue. It's my favorite color."

Carefully, she pulled off the wax strips and pressed the bandage to my skin.

"So eat, then call?" Mrs. Cooley asked again, abbreviated.

"Yeah. That's a good idea." I had no idea what Rainey had told Momma or Daddy—if he was even back in Rocky River. It didn't really matter what I'd say when I got there. Somehow Rainey would twist things so everyone blamed me. I didn't need to speed home for all that.

"Let me get back to cooking, then."

In answer, my stomach growled. Mrs. Cooley just smiled, then turned toward the stove. Mr. Cooley left and came back in with the newspaper in hand. The headlines were huger than I'd ever seen. "Plunderers profit. Merchants Quit," read one. Below that in even bigger letters: "Ohio Guard Moves Into Hough."

"Wanna see my room?" Tyisha bounced up from the chair she must have sprawled in while I'd been upstairs.

"Sure," I said, though what I very much wanted was to read the newspaper. Find out what was going on *really*.

Back up the stairs we went, past the bathroom. She pushed open a door. The room had blue walls and posters of Negro musicians and athletes including the boxer who'd changed his name and dodged the draft.

"That's my brother Wayne's room. He's down south with Grandmama this summer."

"Down south?"

"North Carolina," she explained. "I didn't want to go this year. It's hot and boring. I promised to do all my summer reading and get a head start on work for fifth grade, so Momma and Daddy let me stay."

"You call your parents momma and daddy?"

She squinched her nose at me. "Doesn't everybody? Oh, are you from some other country, like in Europe? You don't have an accent."

"No, I'm just from Rocky River."

"Got it." She shrugged. "Here's my room. She pushed open a different door. I tried not to fall over with envy. It was beautiful. Her walls were periwinkle blue. She had a canopy bed with a white cover that matched the bed-spread.

"How do you keep it clean? My mom would never let me have white in my room."

"I don't know. No shoes? We're not allowed to wear them in the house."

I looked down. Tyisha had on bobby socks. My riot dirty sneakers stood out against the polished wood floor.

"I'm sorry. These are new. It was dirty out there, though."

"You really live in Rocky River?" She sat on her per-fect bed and hugged a teddy bear against her middle.

I nodded while I pulled at my double knotted laces, the dark and light parts separating into a zebra effect.

"Why you on this side of the Cuyahoga River?"

I wanted to tell her it wasn't my first time. That some-times Momma took me to Higbee's downtown.

"My sister wanted to come see what was going on. Walter Cronkite was on TV talking about it. She's really curious like that."

"How old is she?"

"Sixteen."

"My brother's fourteen."

We were quiet for a moment. I gave her a look. She returned it. Then we both laughed.

"My sister Rainey's a pain in the...butt." I'd whispered that last word. This seemed like a house where no one said curse words.

"Wayne teases me all the time," Tyisha said. She shook her head. Lowered her voice. "Don't tell my parents, but I'm loving the summer here without him. Even with the riots."

I wandered over to a bookshelf painted a glossy white. All my favorites were on the top shelf. *Charlotte's Web. A Wrinkle in Time. Charlie and the Chocolate Factory.* So many were familiar. Then I saw a book on the end. I leaned closer to read the unfamiliar title on the spine. *The Island of Blue Dolphins*

"What's that one about?"

"A girl alone on an island."

"What happens? Are there blue dolphins? I thought dolphins were gray."

Getting home to Rocky River suddenly didn't seem so urgent. All I wanted was something to eat and then to be able to curl up and read this one book. There was a pretty braided rug in a corner of Tyisha's room that would be perfect for just that.

"You want to borrow it?" she asked.

"Can I?" I asked. Before she could change her mind, I took it and hugged it like it was my dog. Books were my escape. I didn't have to think about Rainey or anything else when I was reading about Charlotte or Meg or Charlie.

"I don't know if I can ever—"

"Tyisha. Sarah? Breakfast is ready!" Mrs. Cooley called up.

Tyisha ran down the stairs like her butt was on fire. I followed more slowly, trying not to slip and slide in my socks on the bare wood steps. Ours at home had carpet.

The table was already set. Tyisha and her dad were sitting when I finally got to the kitchen, the book still gripped tightly in my hands.

"Sit, Sarah. Sit. What do you want?"

She had a pot in hand filled with some kind of porridge.

"What's that?"

"Grits." When she saw my face, she explained. "It's hominy corn, ground and cooked."

I didn't say that hominy and corn didn't explain more than grits did.

She dropped a heaping spoon onto Tyisha's plate, then her father's. Father and daughter both sliced soft squares of butter from a glass dish on the table and put them on their grits.

"Sure," I said with a shrug.

Tyisha's mother placed a glop on my plate followed with scrambled eggs. Then link sausage. And buttered toast after I said yes to it all.

I followed their lead and put the paper napkin on my lap. Then I took the fork next to my plate and tried the eggs first. They were buttery and creamy and maybe better than my mom's. The sausage was the same kind we had at home. Tyisha and her dad had taken a bite of the grits. After I added butter just as they had, I scooped a little on my fork then got what I could into my mouth before the thick white food slipped through the spaces on the fork. It melted in my mouth. It was really tasty and slightly tasteless at the same time.

"This is really good," I said, then dug in. I hadn't realized how hungry I was. I finished the orange juice that appeared in front of me, then nodded yes to a second serving of everything.

When all the food was put away and all the dishes were in the sink, Mrs. Cooley took off her apron and for the first time sat down.

"It's almost eight. I think you should call now, Sarah. You have the number right?"

I nodded. "Momma made me learn it when I started walking to school by myself last year."

Mrs. Cooley pointed to the white telephone on the wall. The cord was long and dangled, coiled nearly to the floor.

Slowly I got up. I couldn't figure out why I wasn't dying to call and get back home. I'd been scared in the alley but felt perfectly safe here. I'd have given anything to spend a few hours playing with Tyisha. But this wasn't a normal day hanging out at some friend's house.

I lifted the receiver and stuck my fingers in the number two to start, then the other six as the dial came back around. A broken buzz came through the line instead of the ring I was expecting.

"It's busy," I said.

"They're probably on the phone to everyone looking for you. Give it a few minutes."

"What school are you at?" Tyisha said when she was done drying a plate her dad had just washed.

"Goldwood. It's the only school."

Tyisha looked at her dad. "Just one school?"

"It's a small town, not a city like Cleveland," he explained.

"How about you?" I asked.

"Mary B. Martin."

"Is that a real person, like Lincoln or Roosevelt?" I asked.

Tyisha shrugged and went back to drying.

Mr. Cooley turned off the water, then turned toward me while drying his hands on a towel. I tried not to stare because Daddy would never do the dishes or anything he considered women's work.

"Mary Martin was the first Negro woman elected to the Cleveland Board of Education. The school is brand new. Built just three years ago. I hope it survives this here." He gestured toward the front door, but I knew he meant the riots. I hoped so too, for Tyisha's sake. I don't know what I'd do without a school to go to every day. It was the only real time I had free from Rainey.

"Why don't you try again, Sarah?" Mrs. Cooley said. She didn't have to say more. I knew she meant try the telephone. Reluctantly, I made my way back to the phone. Dialed again. This time it rang only once before it was answered.

"Hello?" I asked when there was silence.

"Didn't think you'd make it," Rainey whispered into the phone. "Next time you won't." Then I heard the phone crash to the table. Seconds later, someone picked up the phone.

"Sarah!"

"Mommy," the single word rushed out of me. Then the tears came. I was so relieved to be alive and to know that in a little bit I'd be home.

"You're safe?"

"Yes. I'm with the Cooleys. We had breakfast. I'm fine."

I thought my momma would cry tears of relief like me. Instead, her voice got very low which meant she was very angry.

"Then you're in big trouble, missy. Rainey told us how you hitchhiked down to Cleveland. She's been driving around looking for you for hours."

The food that had warmed me and filled me up good, now set like a giant stone in my stomach. I was going to have to work really hard to convince them of the truth. I closed my eyes for a long moment, feeling the wetness of tears on my cheeks. I feared that I wouldn't be able to do that. Rainey's poisoned lies were impossible to turn around.

8

"In the words of Isiah one seventeen, 'learn to do right, seek justice.' That's it for today. My office door is open if you have any questions or need to run anything up the flagpole," I said. I looked at the clock at the back of the conference room. It was four forty-five...on a Friday. I didn't need to utter a single word of dismissal. Nearly every single one of the twenty-one assistant prosecutors in the room had their pads and pens in hand and were all headed out the door as if the building was on fire.

Friday afternoon meetings weren't ideal, but the only other public servants who wanted to work fewer hours before the weekend were judges. This was the only time the courtrooms were guaranteed to be empty and most of my staff of assistant county prosecutors—available.

When I finally looked up from my packed bag, there was one remaining attorney in the room. I tried to steel myself against the shock of seeing her. It was like a ghost from Christmas past had appeared on my doorstep. All that was missing were the rattling chains.

"Valerie...I guess I didn't see you on the roster," I stuttered out. I should have, though. She was only one of two African Americans on my team. But I'd been so discomfited by my first leadership task, I hadn't been paying attention.

Truthfully, I hadn't so much as glanced at the list of those I was tasked with supervising. I didn't want or need the reminder of everyone who'd covered for me when I was at my rock bottom, or worse, those who'd tried to take advantage. Not a single prosecutor had said anything to me outright about my sudden promotion.

No doubt there were a crap ton of questions as to how I'd gotten the top criminal job when I'd been nearly out the door on more than one occasion. If they'd asked point blank, I wouldn't have been able to answer anyway. It was some toxic combination of Pope love and Brody hate or vice versa. Tom Brody, the son of the previous prosecutor, had used me to hide his nefarious crimes. I suspected Pope, the current prosecutor, had something up her sleeve as well.

"You forgot the rest of the verse," Valerie Dodds broke into my introspection. Bourbon made me self-reflective.

"'Take up the cause of the fatherless. Plead the case of the widow,'" I finished the recitation. "If I were supervising folks in juvenile, I'd have surely done the rest. If I remember correctly, you did a bang-up job in juvy before you left us for greener pastures." I knew my response was passive aggressive, but I didn't care. My thirst salted by Dodds' betrayal of the girl code didn't sit well with me.

The early morning shot of bourbon had long worn off. I'd been edgy to begin with and the whiskey hadn't helped. I'd needed the second bottle, but the department assistant had interrupted that first sip when she'd come into my office to remind me of this meeting. A top up would have to wait until later.

"I need to talk with you about a case that came my way from the assignment pool," she said, her tone professional, matter-of-fact.

Rather than play favorites like some people in my position had, I'd had my assistant spread out the incoming cases on a strict rotation, taking into consideration case complexity and attorney availability. Left to their own devices, attorneys would pick the easy wins and hog the glory of a nearly perfect win rate. I may have played that hand myself once or twice with a naïve and unsuspecting deputy.

"Is it still snowing?" I asked Dodds. She cocked her head as if considering whether approaching me had been a good idea. I could almost see the gears turning inside her head as she realized she had no choice but to deal with me. Whether it was now or later made no difference.

"Last I checked," was her wary answer.

"Let's get out of here, then." I didn't wait for her acquiescence, but made for the conference room door. "I'll meet you at the Tipsy Jurist in twenty," I said before I click-clacked down the hallway in my block heels. I'd ignored the face she pulled. Yes, I was a sober woman ready to walk into a bar. But I didn't want to say what needed to be said to her in the office where anyone could overhear. Supervision took finesse and discretion.

Ten minutes later, I was seated at a booth in the nearly deserted establishment where defense attorneys gathered. The people on our side of the aisle went to the Side Bar. I'm sure at least a dozen of them were there now complaining about me. I thought it best to skip all that scrutiny. They'd need the time to vent anyway.

I sidled up to the bartender and ordered two drinks, a seltzer and cranberry with lime as well as a finger of whiskey. I downed the second and handed the glass to the bartender before taking the first back to the booth where I'd left my coat and briefcase. Unless there were cameras in here, that little tipple would fly under the radar. Looked like all but the most diehard defense attorneys had braved the snow to get to their cozy homes filled with embracing spouses and cherubic children. I had no one to greet me at my Lakewood condo, something for which Valerie Dodds was directly responsible. Now was the perfect time to hold her to account.

Though Dodds couldn't see me, I saw her. She came in, waited for her eyes to adjust to the dim room, then scouted for me. I raised my hand, virgin drink in hand. Haltingly, she stepped down the two wooden steps into the main area and came my way.

"I have to admit, I'm surprised that you wanted to meet here." As if she were going to run, Dodds stood there a long minute. With my empty hand, I gestured for her to take off her coat and have a seat.

"Apparently my former reputation proceeds me. That said, I'm your boss now, so there's that."

Dodds finally acquiesced and made a place for herself on the other side of the high booth. Valerie hadn't been a drinker when I'd met her all those years ago. Her order of ginger ale from the server was an indication she hadn't changed in that one aspect. I hope she had changed in another.

"We used to be friends," Dodds said in opening once her ginger ale was situated on a tiny cocktail napkin next to a bowl of Chex mix. "I'm not sure what happened."

I didn't believe for a single moment that she didn't know the cause of our disconnection. But we'd circle back to that. I had other more pressing questions.

"Why are you back?" I put my question to her bluntly. "You left here and went to D.C. in a blaze of glory." I sat back as the whiskey finally kicked in, mellowed me out, kept me from snatching the hair right from her head.

"I wouldn't exactly put it that way. I had an opportunity to work for the Public Defender Service. It's one of the two most prestigious defender offices in the country." What she said about District of Columbia's PDS was one hundred percent true. Philadelphia was the other. One of those two cities were where a new lawyer went to get Johnnie Cochran good in only three years. Competition for those low paying jobs was fierce.

"So how did you get back into prosecution?" I leaned back, laced my hands behind my head, and settled in. I wasn't going anywhere. I nodded toward the two defense attorneys hunched over their drinks like someone might steal their liquor. "When I picked this place, it was for its discretion. Now I think I hit the nail on the head. You must be right at home having played for the other team."

Dodds must have gotten a Teflon coating in the capital because everything I was throwing at her was bouncing off.

"Lori hired me back in January when the new budget came in. I heard you were away."

Ouch. She'd returned my bitchiness to sender. Time to change the subject and really put her on the defensive.

"How's Michael?" I asked, proud that my voice was devoid of bitterness.

Like a cloud, Dodd's eyes cleared of the confusion that had been hovering there. "Is this what this is about? Michael Fucking Betancourt?"

I didn't want the disbelief in her voice to wound me, but it did. "You took my boyfriend and went down to the district." That was the entire truth in a single sentence.

"He wasn't your boyfriend." Dodd's counter included a deep squint of her eyes as if she were trying to piece together a puzzle.

"Technically." That one had come through gritted teeth.

"In our business, technicalities are everything."

Touché. I wouldn't have to worry about this one. She was going to eat up the defense in the courtroom.

"Have you ever heard of the girl code?" I pressed.

"Are you serious?" She'd omitted the epithet this time, but I could hear it in her voice. "We're over thirty; not thirteen anymore."

When she didn't give me what I wanted, I ticked off the code using my fingers like I'd memorized test answers.

"Don't be a hater. Be honest with your girlfriends. Don't leave a girl behind. Don't share secrets. And last but not least, exes are off limits. That's only five. For someone who passed at least one bar exam, that should have been an easy one for you."

"That's for friends. We weren't friends. You were the star. Tom's baby. Lori's pet. But my girl, never."

I broke eye contact for a second. Turned my head toward one of the other drinkers. He was flipping through a stack of documents and grumbling under his breath. Even in the dark room, I could see Pope's name at the top of some letterhead. The small smile that pulled at my lips almost dried up the tears that had been threatening the dam of my lower lids. I'd wanted to tell her my secret, be her girl back then. But the revelation of my heritage, that I was black like her, had still been too raw to share with anyone except Michael.

I turned back to her. Her gaze was steady. I wanted mine to be.

"Why him?"

Dodds' sigh was long and world-weary. The gracious thing would have been to change the subject again to something polite, acceptable. I didn't care to do that, so I waited. Eventually, her lips moved.

"Look, I don't like to mix work and business. But I'm going to make this one-time exception." She downed the remainder of her soda, flagged the server down for another. Right then I wished she drank.

Dodds continued, "Michael and I had exactly a single conversation about you. One. Because even though you weren't my girl, I do honor the code, okay?" An acknowledgement. Finally we were getting somewhere.

She went on.

"He wanted a relationship with you, but he had a single deal breaker. He refused to be involved with someone in the throes of an active addiction. You refused help. He broke it off. I didn't follow him to D.C. Both of our relocations were purely political. Neither of us could stay here and think we were going to get anywhere in this office." Dodds gestured vaguely to the Justice Center to the north of us. Most of the prosecutor's staff were on five floors of the building.

"Tom had his family connection. You had Lori as your guardian angel. You know how hard it was to even get into this office. You were in juvenile because you were a fuck-up. I was in juvenile because I got stuck there as a black woman butting up against my own glass ceiling."

The urge to tell her my truth was strong. I held back. Now was not the time.

"So why are you here now, then? How did you get up to the eastside apartment in the sky?"

Dodds didn't even crack a smile at my reference to the seventies' sitcom theme.

"Lori's going to be up for reelection. The primary is around the corner and her office...how did she put it exactly...I wouldn't want to get her words wrong. She said it...doesn't reflect the diversity of the population she serves." I'd have been offended at the tokenism, I think. Dodds' tone was matter-of-fact.

"So you're saying this is just...optics."

"Welcome to the real world. It's a good step in my career."

That had to be enough for now. One day I'd get some liquor in her and get the real story on Michael. She had the key to closure, which my ex-boyfriend had refused to provide. He'd been quick to cut me off once the breakup was official. Our short but intense relationship over, Michael had left right after as if nothing...or no one in Cleveland had mattered one bit.

"What did you want to talk to me about?" It probably wasn't about any legal questions. Looked like she had a handle on that part of the job. I almost envied her skill, but I was as good as her or maybe even better when I wasn't drinking.

"I wanted to discuss Libby Saldana," Dodds said.

"Who in the heck is Libby Saldana?" That name sounded vaguely familiar. For a brief second I wondered if Pope had hired someone else I'd have to worry about gunning for my job. Relief flooded through me, shook off my paranoia when Dodds took out a file not much thicker than the one Pope had handed me regarding cases that needed special handling.

Things were getting thin on the ground. I was used to hefty files the likes of which the defense attorney at the other table was paging through. Had the police slacked off on full investigations for some reason? Was there a policy of burying evidence I didn't know about? I'd have to take a look at the reason for that. Evidence was what kept us in business and what kept convictions from being overturned.

"Charged with manslaughter among other things."

"Someone died? Don't think you can handle the case? I can find someone else who'll happily take it."

"That's not the question. I just want to understand the policy around drug charges."

"Drugs? I thought you said manslaughter."

"I put in a call to the police officer. He'd declined to charge. Cleveland police and some other departments don't usually file more than an incident report in these kinds of cases."

"Don't keep me in the dark. What kinds of cases?"

"Drug overdoses."

"Manslaughter for an overdose. Are you sure?"

Dodds turned the file to face me. "Have a look. Saldana was charged with manslaughter, possession, evidence tampering, and corrupting another with drugs. But when I talked to the cop, he said it was a straight-up overdose. The officer said there are dozens of them every weekend. If they can't revive them, they pronounce them DOA on the scene and call the coroner to pick up the bodies."

I took the file from her and paged through everything. I needed another drink because there was nothing worse can being caught off guard. Somewhere along the way, Lori must have changed tack. Up until now, Pope had been all about going hard on violent crime, and leaving drug addicts and nonviolent drug offenders to the misde-meanor courts or diversion. This indictment was the equivalent of throwing the entire library at Saldana.

Then it hit me. This was one of the special handling files she'd given me on day one. That tiny bourbon shot and my boss' sudden appearance in my office a week ago had turned my memory into Swiss cheese. I needed to walk a very fine line. Office policy was one thing. Pope's policy, another. Supervision required authority, though. I'd deflect until I figured out what game I was expected to play.

"Is there a defense attorney on this one?" I asked Dodd. "The public defender?"

"No appearance yet," Dodds answered.

"Don't do anything, then. Let me get the word on what we're doing with these cases. Pope did mention a shift in policy last week on a few test cases of which I think this was one. But she didn't fill the details."

"I'll give it a week, then. Work my other cases. Only a week, Nicole. I'm not sure what you're playing at, but I can't go there with you."

"I'm not the bad guy you think I am, Valerie."

"I never implied that. You're my boss. We have to work together. I'd like to have a good working relationship."

"I think we can be friends."

"I like to keep my professional and personal life separate."

"Why?"

"Part of the reason Michael left was because he could see nothing but issues."

"What issues?"

"You've always been on the fast track. If you'd become his boss, what would have happened to his career? He couldn't risk it stalling because he made a mistake."

"A mistake?" I tried to figure out what I could have done. I'd practically been a Girl Scout since I landed in Cleveland. "What mistake?"

"The one I'm trying to avoid here...mixing professional and personal, like I said."

"Why don't you drink?"

I could see that my question had thrown Valerie off her rhythm. It was something I'd always wondered, though.

"I've seen people let alcohol control their lives. I'm not going to let that happen to me. Sobriety is sanity."

Obviously her life had been a walk in the park if she believed that.

"I think there's something you need to know about me," I started.

"I look forward to working with you, but I want to be clear—"

"I'm a lot like you," I finished. I wasn't going to let her get away this time without her knowing that we had a certain solidarity. Without her knowing the truth. I needed all the loyalty I could get from my staff no matter how I got it.

"How, Ms. Long, are you like me? Let's be frank here. I'm a black woman in a job where I'm the only one. Maybe there's another one of us down in juvy. Probably. I haven't been back long enough to get a lay of the land on that.

"Kevin is the only other black face in Major Crimes. I don't come from money like you. I didn't go to fancy schools like you. So I'm going to guess we don't have too much in common outside of starting this job at the same time. And from where I sit, you've been more successful than me despite your...probationary periods. So you're going to have to excuse me when you do that, 'pseudo feminist, we're all in this together dance.' At the end of the night, I always end up solo."

Dodds stood, gathered up the file, and put it in her bag. I was losing her, and it was scaring me. I didn't quite know why I was so important that I keep here there.

"I need you to know that I've got your back, Valerie." At least as much as I needed her to have mine. "I'm a black woman just like you."

"Wait? What?" She plopped back down in the booth like an anchor had weighed her down.

"It's a story as old as this country. My mother is the housekeeper."

"Are you passing?"

"Maybe?" My shrug was big. I didn't want to talk about that. Race was a construct. How I'd thought of my-self for twenty-plus years was hard to shake. The other reason I didn't want to talk about it was because it would reveal the advantage I had over a woman who looked like her. "I don't need to give anyone any more reasons to make my life here difficult. You already know how hard it is."

"Why did you want to tell me this?" she asked. My revelation hadn't brought about the instant solidarity I'd seen her have with the aforementioned Kevin. With me, there was just...more mistrust.

"I think us women, women of color, need to stick together. Lori isn't as...nice as she seems. I think she would stab any of us in the back in a hot minute. Even more than that, though, I need you to know that I have your back, and until that new prosecutor gets elected, I think you're gonna need it."

9

"I can't believe the news. How are you holding up?" I asked.

I turned toward Tyisha and away from the television broadcast which was showing one special report after another. No matter whether it was channel three or five or nineteen, the images were all the same. First it was Martin Luther King, Junior marching in Alabama or somewhere in the South, then him in D.C. giving a speech five years ago, or the front of the motel in Memphis.

"Is it okay to ask that? I don't know exactly what to say. Or if I should say anything. Sorry. I'm so sorry." Those were the only words I had.

Tyisha swiped at her eyes and looked back at me. In the two years we'd been friends, I'd never seen her cry. Even with the tears leaking, she held my gaze. I really admired how strong she was. Tyisha never shied away from anything—from racing bikes downhill to talking about her feelings. I only wished I could be so brave.

"Sad, I think," she finally said after pausing to think about it. Tyisha never rushed her words. "Feels like nothing will ever change."

"Do you want me to ask Momma to drive you home?" She'd only been here a few hours, and God knows I'd never bother Momma for a spur-of-the-moment ride to the city, but this was different. Maybe my friend needed to be around her own family.

"No, we planned this for weeks." After the really weird way we'd met during the Hough riots, Tyisha had become my best friend. Unlike Rainey or any of my school friends here in Rocky River, she understood me. We could talk about everything. And we did on the phone when my parents weren't yelling at me to get off.

Tyisha wanted to talk about books and how annoying her brother was and lately, boys. I didn't quite get the last one, but Momma said I was probably going to be a late bloomer, so I'd understand *all that* when I got a little older.

"Right." Even though the anchorman was still talking and showing pretty depressing looking film footage, I was pretty happy inside. I'd get hours with my friend. It would be the best day of the week. I did all I could to sound serious. "What do you want to do? Did you finish *The Outsiders*?"

She'd called me two weekends ago and told me to get the book. Fortunately, Momma didn't think reading was as geeky as my friends did, so she'd taken me to the library right after Girl Scouts. The book had been right there, still glossy with the cellophane wrapping, standing up by the checkout counter. The librarian had let me take it right from the display. Then she'd told me the most incredible fact about S.E. Hinton.

"I loved it," I gushed. "Did you know the author was a girl?"

"Yeah, I forgot to tell you that on the phone." Tyisha's eyes went as wide as mine probably were. I didn't think a lot of women wrote books. She continued, "My dad has some college friend from Tulsa who said he met her."

"Wow. That's amazing." I fantasized about what it would be like to meet a real live author in person or even *be* a writer. "You think we could write a book someday?"

I could practically feel Tyisha's energy coming off her. She was getting as excited as me. That's what was the best thing about her. She got hyper about the same things, and she never made fun of me. Momma mostly didn't think my ideas were crazy, but she did say I should keep them to myself. I couldn't say the same for Daddy or Rainey. Those two acted like I was one step away from a place in the looney bin.

"Maybe we should try one together." I could practically feel the blood pumping in my ears. That would be seriously so fun, and I knew that she was dead serious. Tyisha didn't joke about stuff like that. I started thinking of whether Momma would let me get her typewriter out of the attic. Then I remembered Rainey had taken it to college.

"I don't think either of you have enough brain cells between you to write the back of a cereal box."

At the sound of my sister's voice, my stomach plummeted to my knees. For a long second I wondered if I'd conjured her up just by thinking about the typewriter. Since Rainey had gone to college, she'd been around a lot less, and in the last nine months, my life had gotten a whole lot better. Bowling Green was a long way from Cleveland. Though not far enough, apparently. I looked up and there she was standing next to the TV, her arms crossed and her hip against the set's brown wood frame.

Tyisha's manners were much better than mine. My best friend sat up straight, fixed her shirt, patted her hair, then spoke to my sister as if they were equals.

"Rainey, it's good to see you," Tyisha started, her voice strong and clear. "How are you enjoying college? I hear you pledged Phi Mu. How do you like it? My mother really enjoyed her time in her sorority."

My eyes snapped to my friend. How did she do it? I'd have stuttered and practically peed myself before I'd have had the guts to ask Rainey all those questions.

"*Your* mother went to college?"

"At Hampton University," Tyisha answered, as if she hadn't heard the insult. "It's where my parents met."

"Where's that?" My sister practically spat out the question. "*I've* never heard of it."

"It's in Hampton, Virginia." Except for my friend balling up her hands, no one who didn't know her would suspect Tyisha was about to be annoyed.

"Is it a *real* college?"

"Of course. It was established in the eighteen hundreds, about forty years before Bowling Green, I think." Tyisha had burned Rainey without raising her voice. I admired her a whole lot for that.

Seeing she was losing, Rainey changed the subject.

"Were you guys watching the news?" Her voice was sugar and spice and anything but nice.

"There's a manhunt for James Earl Ray." Borrowing some of Tyisha's bravery, I answered this time. "No one can find him."

"Maybe it's best he got away. Maybe he did a service for the country."

"Rainey!" I screamed. I wanted to get up and put my hands on Tyisha's ears. "That man was assassinated! You can't say that. He was making things better for America."

"He was causing a lot of problems. If it weren't for him, maybe we wouldn't have had riots."

Her eyes were squarely on my best friend now.

Even though my knees were shaking, I stood up in protest. "That's not fair—"

"No, it's okay." Tyisha came to her feet slowly. "I've heard it all before." Her sigh sounded like it had come from my dad after a double shift. "You want to try on outfits? Are you going to that dance?"

Rainey made me do that...forget about the stuff that really mattered to me. My school was having a dance. There was one every year, but only the sixth graders— the oldest kids in the school—were allowed to go. I was super excited to dress up. I kind of wished my best friend were going with me, but even I knew that would be one step too far. Instead I tried to focus on the boys every other girl in my grade was excited about.

"Yes! Scott's going to be there," I blurted. "He told John who told Paul."

"I thought *Paul* was the cute one," Tyisha challenged. I'd forgotten I'd told her Paul was my crush. None of them were, but I wanted her to think I was like her and everyone else. That I was normal, even though a lot of times I didn't feel like I was.

"The problem is that he knows that he's cute," I said, mimicking something one of my classmates had said.

"Why is that a problem?"

I didn't have an answer to that. And the girl who said it wasn't around for me to ask. Wildly, I cast around for something else to talk about. Something Rainey wouldn't criticize.

"You hungry?" I asked. "Let's see what's in the fridge." I pushed in the TV knob, silencing the chatter and made for the kitchen.

"You guys want some fries?" Rainey asked.

"Are you making them from scratch?" Tyisha asked. I knew my sister had hooked my best friend with that offer. That girl loved potatoes. Her dad would fry them when we were at her house, and she'd cover them in ketchup and some kind of hot sauce. They were good, but I didn't love them like she seemed to. My latest favorite was that frozen chicken pot pie Momma had started buying a year ago. I almost suggested that instead. One look at Tyisha's face and I decided that I'd go for the French fries.

"One of the girls did it in the sorority house," Rainey said, her voice suddenly sunny and bright, a warning sign if there ever was one. "They're almost as good as McDonald's."

"Those fries *are* good. You don't mind sharing?" Unfortunately, Tyisha couldn't hear the bells going off in my head.

"Anything for my favorite sister."

Clang. Clang. The bells got louder.

I didn't say a thing because Rainey or Tyisha would have said I was crazy. Instead I was quiet as all three of us worked to cut the potatoes into shoestrings and get the fat going in a big heavy pot. When it got to the hot part, Rainey took over. She dropped in a single potato to test the lard, and when it bubbled to her satisfaction, she took that one out and dumped in the rest from the cutting board.

Tyisha and I both stood in wonderment as the potatoes turned from white to golden brown. They did look just like the fast food ones. Maybe my sister was playing it straight for once. My stomach started rumbling as hunger replaced fear. I got the ketchup from the fridge so it wasn't so cold when the food was ready. I went back to stand next to my best friend and watch the magic.

Rainey took out the first batch and sprinkled salt everywhere on them. Then she put in the second batch of potatoes before she went to the sink to start cleaning up. Momma and her still didn't see eye to eye, but they got along better than they had a couple of years ago once Daddy had finally convinced Rainey to do some chores. Wet up to her elbows, Rainey threw a look over her shoulder at me.

"Sorry, turn them over."

Though my shoulders went up around my ears, I didn't say anything about the nickname. I only hoped Tyisha hadn't heard it. My sister said it in such a way that my parents always believed her when she said she'd used my real name.

"How?" I asked because I wanted my best friend to get her favorite treat even if my sister was a jerk to me.

"You see that spoon, the one with the holes?" Rainey pointed the sponge toward the spoon rest on the counter.

"Yeah?"

"Just flip them around until you don't see any pale left. Can you do something as simple as that?"

I wanted to point out I was twelve not five, but kept my attitude in check like Momma told me to around Rainey.

"Of course."

I picked up the big spoon and moved closer to the stove. The hot fat looked pretty scary, but the spoon had a long handle. Normally, I'd be afraid of a situation like this, but with Tyisha here, I was pretty sure that I was safe.

"Tyisha, come here. I think you're going to want to see this." Only I could see my friend rolling her eyes, but she minded her manners and heeded my sister's call to come out into the little mud room by the kitchen where Momma kept some extra pantry stuff.

"What did you want to show her?" I called over my shoulder. "I think these are done."

"I think you're done." Rainey grabbed me, one hand on my shoulder, the other gripping my hand. I dropped the spoon, but before I could bend to retrieve it, she pushed my elbow down into the fat. One minute I was turning off the fire. The next my arm was on fire.

"I wonder if you'd taste good fried," she whispered only loud enough for me to hear.

"Rainey. Stop! Please. Tyisha is here." I jerked my arm from the fat, rubbed at it with my hand which promptly started burning as well. I tried to reach for a towel or dishrag or sponge or anything to cool the heat, but my sister kept me still with a steel grip.

"Better you than Oreo, right?" she asked, as if I hadn't said anything at all. "The Chinese eat dogs. Maybe they're good."

That scared me silent. I loved our family's little dog. I looked over my shoulder to see Oreo huddling in the corner as if he sensed danger.

I'd learned to hold in my screams, but this time I couldn't. Not when the smell of my own flesh filled my nose. The dog and cat ran out when the sound of an animal in pain bellowed from my mouth. Tyisha ran in. My arm was out of the lard and Rainey was back with a towel in her hand, wrapping it around my skin.

"Oh my God, Sarah! Are you okay? The grease splatter on your elbow? You have to get it in water or something. Stop the burning."

Silently Rainey followed my friend's advice and pulled me over to the sink. The cold water stung worse than the fat had. Tyisha ran between the stove and the sink. "I think we have to call that new number…oh my God, what is it again?" she panted. "I know, I know. 911. It's supposed to get you whatever help you need."

My best friend ran to the yellow phone on the wall and lifted the receiver all the while I stood at the sink wondering if I was going to lose my arm. At the pantry door, Rainey stood, her shoulder leaning against the jamb as if she were watching a bad performance on the Ed Sullivan show.

I knew right then, my big sister would one day succeed and I'd be dead.

10

"Who is the judge?" Libby Saldana asked. We were stand-ing on the twenty-second floor of the Justice Center. Each of the four courtroom doors were closed. The benches were empty. My client was pacing again. I was trying not to be infected by her anxious energy.

"Judge Essie Cox," I answered. My voice was deliber-ately anchorman neutral.

"Have you had other cases in front of her? It's a girl, right, this judge?"

I was starting to feel old because Essie was a familiar name to me, but obviously out of fashion for Saldana. After Casey, I'd gone back on the dating market and hold-ing a conversation with twenty-somethings like Saldana was a bigger challenge than I'd imagined.

"I had a murder case in December," I answered.

"Last December? Like three months ago?"

"Yep."

"Did you win?"

"Absolutely," I said. I'm not sure that was exactly the truth. But it wasn't a lie, either.

"Justin! Imagine running into you here. Are you back in front of Judge Cox?"

I knew that voice. To Saldana, I said, "Speaking of the devil. Casey here was my co—"

The rest of whatever I was going to say died on my lips as Casey moved from my peripheral vision to standing in front of me.

She was *really* pregnant.

Like no denying there was another human inside Casey. I knew her due date was April, but if I didn't know there was a whole month left, I'd have assumed it was possible that she could go into labor right here in the hall.

"Congratulations! You must be so excited," Saldana exclaimed peering at Casey's belly as if she had X-ray vision. "Are you having a boy or a girl? You're carrying high. A boy, right?"

"I don't know." Casey paused. "I'm planning to be surprised."

"Libby, please excuse me. Ms. Cort is an attorney I've worked with frequently. Since we're waiting, I'd like to talk to her, if you don't mind."

Saldana—not frenetic for once—took a seat and flipped open a phone she took from a pocket.

Casey looked between me and my client, obviously confused. "Justin…what—"

I put my hand on Casey's arm and steered her toward a quiet corner of the cavernous waiting area.

"You're…really pregnant."

"This is how all people are created, Justin." Her hand swept up and down indicating her swollen frame.

I knew I shouldn't...ask. That I'd given up the rights to this conversation, but I suspected the truth was something different than what we'd all tacitly agreed. Then I did...ask.

"Are you going to get him or her tested?"

"For what?" Casey's squint was fleeting. "Genetic abnormalities? We're all clear there."

"To find out who the father is."

"There's no need, Justin. I really can't see any reason to do anything like that." She flashed the diamond on her left hand. "We're engaged. As soon as I'm not as big as a house, Ron and I will plan a wedding. Get married. He's going to sign the birth certificate as the baby's father. You made one decision, Justin. I made another. Now that everything is settled, I will not upset the apple cart. What's best for me and my relationship and my baby is certainty. For once in my life, I have that. I will not lose it."

"When...are you due? You look very pregnant."

"Nothing's really changed. The doctor thinks sometime in the last full week of April. But babies aren't airplanes. They don't arrive on schedule. I'm prepared for anything from mid-April to sometime in May I guess. I'm officially going on leave in three weeks, though. You know what? I need to stop talking. I don't know why I'm telling you this."

"I asked."

"Discretion would have served me better." Her usually open face, closed. Her tone serious. "What case are you here on?" Her pivot was so smooth, I couldn't think of any way to get back to what I really needed to know.

Instead, I decided to take advantage of the fact someone with better "boots on the ground" knowledge in criminal practice was standing right in front of me.

"Weird case." I tilted my head slightly toward Saldana who was still immersed in her phone.

"Tell me. Maybe I can help."

I explained the overcharging of my client plus near silence from the prosecutor's office.

"That's new," Casey said, her face gone pensive.

I was relieved that I hadn't made some blunder in my assessment. Saldana should be home with her family, maybe in some kind of outpatient drug treatment program that would rubber stamp her attendance. Jail...prison made no sense here.

"New policy?" Her question was rhetorical. From working with her, I knew there was more. I waited. Thinking out loud, she continued, "Or legislating from the prosecutor's office? Could be either. Talked to the APA yet to figure out which?"

"No, today will be our first time. Just got the three sheets of paper they call discovery. Otherwise, the office has been completely unavailable. Not even a call to see if my client would plea."

"Curiouser and curiouser? There's more to this story than what's on the surface. I'd be careful on this one. Who's the judge? Tell me you're not back in front of Cox?"

"I wish I could tell you that. She seemed fair. But that last case was obviously a whole different kettle of fish for a whole different bunch of reasons."

"Kettle is better than school, maybe?"

Just that reference to our old standing joke about the *Book of St. Albans* made me want to pull Casey in for a hug. Ask her to join me on this case *and* on Sunday nights in my bed like we used to. But all that was gone. Long gone. If she partnered with anyone in the future, in work or in love, it would be Ron. Although I was starting to think maybe I could help her with the first.

"What's going to happen to your practice while you're on leave?" I asked, ready to lend my help with keeping her existing clients happy. I never got to make that offer because in the next second I heard a shout from in front of Cox's courtroom.

"State of Ohio versus Saldana. Justin McPhee for the defendant!"

I raised my hand, then waived a little to let the court officer know that we were present and accounted for. With a bit of a waddle, Casey walked back toward the courtroom doors with me.

"Can you come to the back?" That was from the bailiff. The fact that he'd shouted for me in the hall meant the judge wanted to bash my head against that of the prosecutor to get one or another of us to see sense. Outside of fundraisers, judges weren't a chatty bunch. They usually let us lawyers do the dealing and come to them when everything was ready to be finalized.

"Casey, great to see you." I didn't know if I should kiss her or shake her hand, so I did neither. Waved awkwardly instead. Wanted to snatch my flapping hand back, but it was too late. I turned back to my client, my work, my solace. "Libby, please take a seat in the courtroom. The judge wants to see the lawyers alone."

"What does that mean?" My client looked scared. I wanted to reassure her, but stopped when I caught Casey's eyes from the corner of mine and like we used to— read each other's minds. My former co-counsel nodded, confirming my suspicions. I took her cue and gave Saldana the lowdown.

"It only means the judge wants to talk to us. But it's not bad news by any means."

Casey's slight head shake had kept me in check, and I didn't promise anything more. Either way, as far as I could see, it *was* good news. The judge wasn't ready to put her in jail if there was time to talk. Without Casey around to hear me be too optimistic, I'd probably have promised Saldana that she'd get probation for sure. Partnering with Casey had always been good. She'd always had street smarts I could only hope to get one day, hopefully soon.

"I know it's not my place to say anything, but you should tell her," Saldana said when Casey was well out of earshot having gone into a courtroom across the way.

"Tell who what?"

"Tell that pregnant woman that you're in love with her."

"I'm—"

My client's sharp head shake stopped my protest in its tracks.

"The reason I'm here is because my best friend died too early. Life is short. You have to go after what you want. That's all."

After I got Saldana situated, I cut across the courtroom to its back door concealed by the hideous seventies-style slatted wood paneling.

The courtrooms of the justice center were like a mullet, the business in the front was nothing like the back. The front was all wood, a high bench, jury chairs, and formality. The back was a workhorse of a space with few frills. Just government issue furniture and civil service workers.

"Good, you're here," the bailiff said after the court officer handed me over. "I'm sure you know Valerie."

I squinted because for some reason I think I did know her. Though here upstairs in General Division she was woefully out of context. I held out my hand, and she politely shook it.

"Juvenile court," she said before I could ask the question.

My mind had to scramble to make sense of it. Then it hit me.

"Right. You worked in abuse, neglect, and dependency." *For years* remained unspoken between us.

"Left for D.C. for a bit. I'm back," Dodds explained.

"And in Major Crimes." My eyebrow raise was deliberate. I wanted the backstory. She ignored my subtle ask.

"That's right," was her non-answer.

"Judge is ready for you," the bailiff announced. I could see I wasn't going to get the tale of the meteoric rise of Dodds. There was a story there, for sure. The inner workings of the county prosecutor was on par with a Spanish telenovela. Unfortunately from my position on the outside, I only got to see the equivalent of one episode a month.

I took the open invitation and stepped into the judge's chambers after Dodd.

Judge Essie Cox was dressed in a bright blue suit. Her empty black robes were on a coat rack in the far corner of her chambers. The judge's floor-to-ceiling windows had an excellent view of both the new football stadium and Lake Erie. Maybe I'd take my settlement money and upgrade my office. I'd always envied Casey's full on lake view. I shook my head. I needed to stop thinking about Casey and get my head back in the game. Saldana's charges couldn't be any more serious.

"Okay, close the door," Cox ordered. Her bailiff scampered out faster than a rat on the RTA tracks.

"Your honor, I'm Valerie Dodds from the prosecutor's office." Opposing counsel stood stiffly as if she was in the service. A salute wouldn't have been out of place.

In the silence was my cue.

"Your honor, I—"

Judge Cox sliced a hand in the air.

"Mr. McPhee, no need to introduce yourself, you were in here just a few months ago. On a case we're still talking about back here. You and your co-counsel did a hell of a job."

"Thank you, your honor." I tried to keep my chest from inflating too much. She invited us to sit. I accepted. Dodds did too, though reluctantly.

"So, Ms. Dodds, I have a big question I'm dying to get an answer to." Judge Cox leaned forward.

Dodds leaned back from the judge's intense scrutiny. "Yes, your honor?"

"What in the hell happened where you're charging Ms. Saldana for…excuse me, I need to read this one more time to be sure I got it right."

With a dramatic flair, Judge Cox pulled some turquoise reading glasses from her desk, shook open the temples, and slipped them onto her nose.

"We have tampering with evidence, possession of heroin, corrupting another with drugs, and the cherry on top, involuntary manslaughter. Now I had a look at all of this, then started looking at my calendar because surely someone charged like this is in jail and itching to get out of her orange jumpsuit and get to trial.

"Imagine my surprise when I open the file and find this woman made bond because Judge Marsh didn't think this Libby Saldana was a drug cartel kingpin. She's merely a nursing student at Tri-C. So, please tell me what I'm missing. Why is this woman facing twenty-three years in the care of the Ohio Department of Correction? Ms. Dodds?"

That was my exact question in a nutshell. It was more or less what had put Saldana into my crosshairs. Legal Aid didn't send over everyone who was working poor. But those who really needed help got a swift referral.

Despite the dressing down from Judge Cox, Dodds didn't even flinch. I'd have been cowering under the nearest piece of furniture if that had been directed my way.

"As you already know, Ohio is in the grips of something we've never seen before. Deaths from heroin overdoses had a sharp increase in 2006. The legislature hasn't done much so far, so Ms. Pope has decided that in this year, she's going to put a dent into this before we have an epidemic on our hands."

Dodds rattled a stack of papers for effect. I didn't remember her being as self-assured when we'd last gone up against each other. I wanted to butt in, to cough, "reelection" into my cupped hands, somehow slow her momentum, but I couldn't think of an *appropriate* thing to say, so I just watched and learned.

"These charges," Dodds continued, "are commensurate with the harm involved. I'd like to, your honor, point out that someone lost their life. That someone is a woman named Grace McNeill. Was a woman, *was*, your honor. Ms. Saldana isn't some hero. She saw a woman who was an addict. Rather than give her help at best, or leave her alone at worst, she put the killer drugs in Grace's veins."

"There are three salient facts counsel seems to be ignoring, your honor," I shot back, a sudden fire of indignation burning in my belly. Though I was skirting the edge of politeness, I couldn't help myself and started ticking the facts off on my fingers. "First, Ms. Saldana is herself an addict. She may be six months sober, but at the time, she was as impaired as Ms. MacNeill." Another finger went up. "Two, Ms. MacNeill consented to the drug infusion." By the third finger, I was in a groove. When I peeked over at Dodds, she didn't look very happy, but Judge Cox didn't say anything, so I kept going.

"Three, the very skills that have pulled my client out of addiction, and poverty—her nursing skills—are the very ones that put her in this position. Everyone asked her to get them high because she knew her way around a clean needle, kept them clean, and there was little possibility of shooting in an air bubble, or worse, HIV."

The judge took off the cheaters, then leaned into her high-backed swivel chair, a near carbon copy of the one in my own office. Money could buy the look of prestige, if not the thing itself. Cox rested the temple tips against her mouth. She looked deep in thought, as if she were doing a math equation in her head without the benefit of paper.

"So, in fact, Mr. McPhee," Judge Cox said, "Libby Saldana...she saved more lives than she ended, if your facts are to be believed." The judge cast her gaze on the assistant prosecuting attorney.

"That's certainly one way to look at it, your honor," Dodds conceded.

"What are you preauthorized to go down to?"

"Your honor?" Dodds' intonation pretended misunderstanding where it didn't exist. In the world of negotiation, the prosecutor's office was no different than any other law firm. Everyone had a bottom line. It usually took longer than this to get to it, some pretrial conferences, trading of discovery, maybe some plea negotiations. Cox was short circuiting all that in just moments. When Dodds didn't answer right away, the judge continued.

"There are three branches of the government," Cox lectured. "I'm the third branch. My job is to interpret the laws, not to make them. If Lori Pope wants to make a stand or make some laws, then she needs to drive one hundred forty miles southwest and plead her case in front of the legislature. This"—Cox's glasses took in her chambers—"is the wrong forum."

"The law is a lagging indicator," Dodds countered.

I looked between Cox and Dodds and kept my big mouth shut. The judge was pleading Saldana's case in a better fashion than I could. For too long a moment my mind wandered to Casey and what my life would be like right now if I'd said yes to her. Maybe we'd have gone in to business together and she would be standing next to me right now filling in the gaps I'd probably left in my argument.

"So, Ms. Dodds, I ask you again, what's your best offer?"

"I have no room to deal."

Cox looked at Dodds. Squinted. I imagined the judge rarely heard that answer.

"Do you want to call your bosses?"

"I asked before I came here. Twice." Dodds held firm. "There is no wiggle room."

"Well, then, Ms. Dodds, Mr. McPhee, it looks like we're going to trial."

That stopped any thoughts I had about Casey or my life outside of this courtroom dead in their tracks.

"Can you be ready by the last full week of April?"

I wanted to say something about having a baby due, but I didn't really have anything happening in *my* life that week. All of that was going to be up to Casey and Ron. Not me.

"Mr. McPhee. Don't you need to check your calendar?"

The bailiff was back in the room. Dodds had her planner open on her lap. Obviously a good few moments had passed. I looked down, trying to remember where I'd set my briefcase.

"Your calendar is in your right hand, Mr. McPhee." Cox pointed toward me. "Perhaps you'd like to open it."

I took a deep breath and tried to bring all of me back into the judge's chambers. I knew my calendar was clear. Had dialed down the number of clients I'd taken on when I'd finished handling the toxic tort case that had led to the huge payout. The one that allowed me to pick and choose what I'd take on. I wet my index finger and flipped the pages as if I were thinking hard.

"I can be ready, your honor."

"We're set, then."

Casey had been right this time, like she'd always been. I'd have promised Libby Saldana the moon. It had looked good when I'd been walking into chambers. Now I had to deliver the worst news of Saldana's day, year, or maybe even lifetime. Braced myself to tell my client that she was facing a jury in a month. I'd have to break the news that if twelve of her peers found her guilty of manslaughter, she may not be able to go home until the cusp of her fiftieth birthday.

11

"Does your mom want to come in?" Mr. Cooley called from the front door. "She's more than welcome."

The words were spoken mostly out of politeness, I thought. Momma had never turned off the motor when dropping me off at Tyisha's Hough house. Before we got off the expressway, Momma made sure I had my bag on my lap, and kept one of her feet on the clutch and the other on the brake of her Mustang. Since she let me come all the way over to the east side, I didn't make any noises about her leaving like she was driving a getaway car from a bank robbery.

I turned away from the open passenger window to look over my shoulder to see if something had changed. To see if Momma had turned off the car or opened the driver's side door and stepped foot on the Cleveland asphalt.

None of that had happened.

Instead, she was easing away slowly, her eyes focused on the windshield. I didn't even bother to shake my head at her rudeness. Tyisha was the only friend's house where I didn't get escorted to the door. I didn't know why, though I had a guess. As best I could, I hoisted my bag, then put the crutches in my armpits.

In a fraction of a second, Mr. Cooley was down the walkway and helping me with the satchel that held a change of clothes and more books than it should. *His* manners were always perfect.

"How'd you break your leg?" Mr. Cooley asked. He was holding the door open as I crutched my way up the four front steps and across the porch.

"Clumsy is all," I said, keeping my eyes down on the painted planks. I was bad at lying.

"How's your arm?" he asked as I did my three-legged thing past him.

"Better. It wasn't as bad as Tyisha said, probably." Of course she'd have told her dad about the French fry accident, even if I'd hoped she wouldn't.

"What's good about a burn?" He'd dropped my duffle on the shiny wood floor and was now squinting at me. Mr. Cooley's head was tilted sideways, like our dog did when he heard something far away. I wanted nothing more than to throw my friend's father off the scent. He was the kind of person to actually try to do something. In my situation, there was nothing to be done.

"It was only a second degree burn. The doctor said it's all healed. It didn't even hurt that much. More like my skin felt tight and weird."

Mr. Cooley was silent for a long moment while he chewed his bottom lip. Then he looked up at me, his eyes clearing of concern. Suddenly a smile split his face.

"Guess what?" he asked. "Mary made your favorite for dinner."

"Chicken fried steak?" I could feel my mouth water. Tyisha's mom's food was out of this world and nothing like what my mom made. Last night Momma had opened a can of Campbell's cream of mushroom soup and come up with tuna noodle casserole. It had taken a lot for me not to pitch it in the garbage. Whoever in the world had thought up hot tuna should be left outside in January lake effect snow.

"With country gravy?" I asked. That's how she'd made it that first time, and I loved the oddly thick milky concoction.

"Biscuits, too. It's why Tyisha and I like to have you over," he whisper-shouted as Mary came out of the kitchen wiping her right hand on a flowered apron. "Mary likes you better than us."

I accepted a hug from Tyisha's mother. It warmed me to the core. I had to push away the wish I sometimes had that my friend's family was my own. The way Momma and Daddy talked we were way better off in Rocky River. I mean, we didn't have riots out there or anything. But I'm not sure the crime from Cleveland was worse than Rainey at home.

"Sarah!" Tyisha squealed as she slip-slided down the stairs in her socks. "Nobody told me you were here." Evil glances were shot at her mother and father. I heard something upstairs. Turned my head, but didn't see anything.

"Is Wayne here today?" I hadn't seen my friend's older brother in a while. She claimed that he was a pain in her butt, but he was much less a pain than Rainey. I'd have traded siblings any day even if it came with daily noogies from him.

"He's happy *you're* here." Mr. Cooley wiggled his eyebrows. I could practically feel my friend's embarrassment fill the air.

"Let's go to the family room," Tyisha practically pushed her father out of the way. If I hadn't been on crutches, she'd have dragged me to the TV room. Instead, she poked at me with her dark brown eyes. It didn't take a mind reader to figure out she wanted her parents to do a disappearing act.

"Should I say 'hello' to your brother?" Momma had always insisted everyone in a house you visit should be greeted if possible. Not so much out of politeness, but not to startle them. She hated when Rainey surprised us with friends who came to greet my parents from upstairs instead of through the front door.

"No need. He's in the shower. He'll be in there for hours. Apparently, he gets very *dirty*." The way she said the last word made me think she wasn't exactly talking about cleaning, but I couldn't quite put my finger on what was going on when I looked between my friend and her parents, whose faces had gone from smiling to stern.

"Tyisha," Mrs. Cooley scolded. "We don't discuss bathrooms in polite company."

"Let's go see if there's a movie on TV," my friend said. Finally, I hefted the crutches and followed her to the family room with its brown corduroy couch and orange shag rug. It was one of the most comfortable rooms I'd ever been in in *anyone's* house. Sometimes I just wanted to curl up and sleep there. If Mr. Cooley hadn't unfolded a cot in Tyisha's room when I visited, I would have done just that.

While we were arguing over whether the *TV Guide* description *Cinderfella* made it sound any good, Tyisha's brother, Wayne, bounded into the room. He was never quiet. Daddy and Uncle Phil would never have taken him deer hunting in Coshocton County. They already said that girls were too loud. Her brother was noisier than us by a factor of a thousand.

"What's wrong with you now?" Wayne poked a tube socked foot at the rubber tip of my crutches.

"You ain't blind," Tyisha retorted. "She got a cast on her leg."

"If Daddy heard you talk like that, you'd be in your room reading and not down here looking at the *TV Guide*."

"Well, it's a great shame that he didn't get a chance to take in my spectacular oratory skills."

I had to laugh. I loved how Tyisha could sound like three different people. When she talked to her parents it was like she was in school or church. But when she talked to her brother or her neighborhood friends, she had a whole different way of talking that was kind of hip. Then with me, I think she was most herself.

"Oooh. Momma bought some new snacks," she said, completely switching subjects. "She only does this when you come. Lemme go see if I can sneak something out of the pantry." With that, my friend ran out of the room to get some contraband food. I was hoping whatever her mom had bought wasn't too good. I really had to leave space for dinner.

"What did your mom make for dessert this week?" I was starting to wish I'd skipped breakfast and not just the tuna sandwich lunch. Momma really had to get away from fish in a can.

"Seven-up cake."

Oh God, I had to figure out how I wasn't going to overdo it today. A few months ago, I ate two servings of everything: fried chicken, macaroni and cheese, and even two slices of coconut cake. But I felt so sick after dinner that I had to lay down. Then when everyone was asleep, I'd run to the bathroom and made myself upchuck.

It had been so embarrassing when Wayne came in that time. I knew I liked him better than Tyisha did when he kept that a secret. Rainey would have found a way to take a Polaroid of me, develop it, and then put it on the fridge for everyone to see. Wayne had given me a wash-cloth and mimed a zipped lip.

"Seriously, Sarah, what happened this time?" I could see in Wayne's brown eyes that he didn't believe a word I'd said either today or the other times before.

"You know how clumsy I can be." I had to look away from him because I was starting to feel like he could see right through me. I dug my hands in the carpet fibers and squeezed as hard as I could. "I just fell down the steps at my house," I said to the shag.

"You never ever fall when you're here. You never burn yourself. I'm just going to say it, Sarah. I don't be-lieve you."

Raised voices trickled into the back room. I was never so grateful to hear a parent's scolding voice. Maybe Wayne would forget that I wasn't making any sense.

"Your mother found Tyisha in the pantry."

Wayne laughed. "She was probably too noisy. I'm bet-ter at sneaking than she is."

I doubted that while looking at his feet. They were huge. He looked like a puppy with too big paws.

"I'll be okay," I whispered into my chest. "Really."

"Will you? Is it your dad that's hurting you? People say cops are angry at home as well as on patrol."

"Do you know someone in the force?"

"After the riots, they added some colored people." His hand came to rest lightly on my chin. He titled my head up so I couldn't avoid his eyes any longer. "You didn't answer me."

"No, it's not my dad." I blinked rapidly. Tears were coming if I didn't do something to keep them back. I swiped at my eyes with the back of my hand.

"If it's not him, then you're really saying it's someone else. Your mom?"

"Wayne. I really shouldn't talk about this."

"Why not. If it's not your dad, then you should tell your dad. If it's a neighborhood kid, I'm sure he'd square it away for you."

"I wish it were Josh Anderson."

"Who's that?"

"The local bully."

"Tell me. If it's not this Josh Anderson or your parents, who is it? You have to want to get it off your chest."

I did want to tell someone. Very much. I'd tried telling Momma once and she'd just given me a speech on getting along with Rainey. How I had to be kind because she didn't have a mom. Daddy felt even sorrier for my sister. Siblings fighting is how he and Uncle Phil had learned to get along with others, he'd said. I'd said that Uncle Phil had probably never tried to kill him. Daddy had smacked me in my face after that. Said I was ungrateful. Promised he wasn't getting in the middle of anything ever. That

Rainey would make me tougher so that people didn't take advantage of me when I was an adult.

I think the lesson I'd learned was to keep my big mouth shut. It was hard, though. Getting harder with Wayne's kind eyes boring into mine.

"It's my sister," spilled out of me. "My *half*-sister, Rainey. I think she blames me for her dad marrying my mom." The words rushed out so fast, I half hoped he didn't understand a single one. The other half of me hoped that he understood every single one.

"How long? How long has it been going on?" There wasn't a trace of the sarcasm or humor he usually heaped on his sister and me. Wayne sounded far less like a kid and more like the adult he'd be in a couple of years.

"Ever since I can remember."

"Do your parents know?"

I shrugged. Every single night while I huddled in my bed, I wondered the same thing. I figured either they knew the real truth, not what Rainey fed them, and didn't care—which made me want to kill myself. Or they didn't want to really know, which killed me in a different way in that they couldn't see how much she truly hated me for being born.

"They just say I should try harder to be nice to her."

"*You* be nice to *her*?"

"Well, her mom doesn't want her and that has to be hard." I parroted the excuse I'd heard a thousand times.

"What happened to her mom?"

"No one ever answered me when I asked the question. I think, though, I overheard my parents one night saying she was a junkie. So maybe drugs or something?"

"Whenever we pass people on the street who are strung out or begging or something, Daddy always says it's sad, but not our fault nor ours to fix."

I was about to ask him what he meant when Tyisha stomped back in, a bowl of peach slices in hand.

"If we're so hungry, we can have these," my friend sing-songed in a near exact imitation of her mother. She shoved the bowl towards us.

I had never been so happy to see fruit. I'd dodged the part of the conversation where Wayne made me promise to do something. I could already see that intention in his eyes.

"Let's divide it. Wayne you take half and each of us will have a quarter."

"Why?"

"Because I don't want to jinx the possibility that she won't give us dinner."

They took Mrs. Cooley more seriously than I did and fell on the yellow fruit like hungry dogs. Even though they were used to their mom's cooking, no way were they going to make an enemy before a special Saturday night meal.

Wayne shoved the fruit into his mouth like it was a Japanese hot dog eating contest. I watched as he considered wiping his sticky hand on his pants.

"Gotta go wash this before…" He didn't finish before he left the room. Tyisha sighed in a kind of relief.

"Thank God. I thought he'd never leave. He wants to see this stupid new Star Trek show."

"Not the Mod Squad?" I shook my head, happy to be talking about something so normal and unimportant. "Boys have no idea what's good."

After the peach, my own hands were sticky. I wasn't so much worried about Momma Cooley getting on me, but having green rug hair on my hands. I excused myself, lifted up on the crutches, and started padding down the hall while Tyisha promised to get the antennas perfect. I stopped when I heard voices.

"Dad, don't you think we should do something?" Wayne asked that.

"Her dad's a cop. Who exactly can we tell?" Mr. Cooley answered.

"Some other authority? There are lots of social workers in Hough keeping an eye on kids here. There's not a day goes by I don't see one of those ladies driving through the neighborhood."

"That's our neighborhood. I don't think anything similar is happening in Rocky River."

"Maybe there should be."

"Inequity and unfairness is one of the reasons there was a riot, and why the Kennedys are so popular right now. That's another discussion for another time, though. About Sarah, let me think about it."

"You'll do something, though, right? She's a really nice girl."

"I promise, son. I'll think of something."

I closed my eyes and rested heavily on my crutches. I dreaded the day Mr. Cooley came up with a solution. I couldn't see how it could do anything but make it all worse.

12

"Are you ready?" I clapped a stack of files on the conference room table. I was glad when Valerie Dodds jumped a little.

"I don't *want* to be ready," she said. Dodds started putting stacks of papers into brown banker boxes. She stood and unfolded the little hand truck we used for court, loaded the boxes on, then bungeed the whole thing together for good measure. I could feel my face heating in mortification at the memory of the last time I'd rolled that same hand cart.

I may have overindulged during my last trial. I'd forgotten to check the bungee cords and files had gone everywhere in the courtroom. If the defendant hadn't been a very bad guy and his counsel not much better, I'd probably have lost the case.

Thankfully, Dodds speaking brought me back from that memory. She said, "Looks like I have no choice. Unless something has changed."

"Did you forget how the job worked while you were gone? Prosecute crimes. Put the perps behind bars. Celebrate the victories. Maybe the district rattled your brain into inaction."

"I was talking to some of the other APAs and they all say this case is a departure from Pope's policy."

"It is."

"What gives?"

"I don't know, Valerie. Honestly, like you, I asked. I may be your boss, but she is *the* boss. So we follow her lead. It's not as if the defendant didn't do what she was accused of. Justice isn't always doled out evenly."

"I feel uncomfortable being a part of that system."

"But not the whole system. I don't think any of us can say it's entirely fair to those who are black and brown like us or those who are poor, either."

I ignored her raised eyebrows, which I knew was meant for including myself in the black and brown group. Instead, she shrugged.

"Hazard of the job. Are you coming to observe? Is that why you're here?"

I nodded, hoisting a to-go coffee cup in my hand.

"Part of supervision."

"Can you carry something?"

I shook my head. "That's not part of it. I'll see you up there." I took my files and my coffee to my office. It would take her a good hour to get up to the courtroom, go through whatever rigamarole the judge had in store, and get to the actual meat of pretrial motions and jury selection. I didn't need to be there for that. Instead, I closed my door tight. It had taken a few weeks to get the message across that an open door policy did not mean walking through a closed door without an express invitation.

Comfortable that I'd be alone for the next minutes, I pulled open my bottom drawer. Inside was a large wooden box that I'd gotten at a headshop in Lakewood called Daystar. Turns out people who wanted to be discrete about their pot consumption had a number of intricately carved wooden boxes for sale. Mine had some kind of Egyptian or Greek god on it and opened with a little key. It wasn't enough to discourage a serious thief. But I couldn't imagine Lori or one of my coworkers prying it open, and that was enough.

After locating the little key on my ring, I twisted it in the box's lock and popped open the lid. Took out one of the small bottles and poured it into the space I'd asked the barista to leave for cream. As I sipped, I reviewed the book we were throwing at Libby Saldana.

This woman was going to prison and there wasn't much to be done. I pushed the file aside. I'd think about that when I got upstairs. I took the next hour to review everything else that had come across my desk. Most were requests for approvals of plea deals. Though Pope had pulled my discretion in Dodds' case, true to her word, she hadn't interfered in any others.

I was able, in this small way, to shape the Major Crimes division how I wanted. Slowly, I was able to mold the office into what I wanted, which was to max out prison sentences for rapists. There were no deals on sexual assault. Everything else was open to negotiation. When my coffee was done, the papers were cleared.

I stood and got ready for whatever shitshow was waiting for me in Judge Essie Cox's courtroom.

On television, courtrooms were regal. Defendants—whether they were smarmy or smug—always oozed confidence. Neither was true in real life. Cox's courtroom was a near carbon copy of all the others in this building, which could only be described as serviceable.

From my angle at the seat I took behind Dodds, Libby Saldana looked like she was going to pass out. She was so pasty and sweaty that I had to curb my impulse to summon paramedics. Her counsel, Justin McPhee, looked better, but not much. In the case I'd had against him last year, his co-counsel and my nemesis, Casey Cort, had done much of the talking. I had no idea if he had the gravitas to pull off a win for Saldana. I was guessing we were all about to find out.

"Ms. Dodds, Mr. McPhee, with the preliminaries out of the way, are you ready for me to bring the jury in?"

I looked between the prosecutor and the defense attorney. Both had grim smiles plastered to their faces. Both nodded, then affirmed their readiness out loud for the record. I'd come up too early because it took a full seven minutes to get twenty-plus potential jurors into the courtroom and situated. The first twelve took seats in the box. The remaining took up seats on either side of me and behind me in the first two gallery rows.

Dodds' questions were by the book. Did they know police officers? Had they been victims of crime? There was no worry about having either cops or attorneys on the jury. Both were exempted from service in Ohio.

McPhee's questions were softer. He probed for people who'd been wronged in one way or another. Those who'd hit their own rock bottom and had risen from it. Jurors who believed in redemption and second chances. In about an hour, a jury was seated. Cox called a lunch recess. Something told me Saldana wouldn't be eating much.

"Good job out there," I said to Dodds once the jury had left.

"I've done this a lot over the last years."

"Right. There weren't any juries in juvenile, though."

"Hopefully this is your opportunity to see how much I've grown since those early days."

"Right. What's the plan after lunch?"

"The usual. Get the statutory facts on the record first through the Cleveland police detectives. Then get Mac-Neill's daughter on the stand to testify about her mother's last days before the jury gets bored. Coroner. One or two other witnesses. I'll have to do a sobriety check. The first two this afternoon. The rest tomorrow. It's not complicated, so we should have a conviction by Wednesday at the latest.

"Do you want to go out to lunch? No work talk."

Dodds produced a brown paper bag from a banker's box. Held it up. "Going to prep in an attorney room. I don't let anything slip through the cracks, no matter how much of a slam dunk."

It was a wise choice. Probably the right answer. I'd have had a lunch of liquid courage. To each their own, I guess. I was on my way out to find sustenance of a liquid or solid variety, when my Blackberry nearly vibrated itself out of my blazer's tiny interior pocket.

It was a 911 text from Pope. She wanted Dodds and I to meet in her office ASAP. My stomach gurgled. I'd have to ignore that and any other craving. When I got back to the prosecutor's office, Dodds was already outside, pacing in her low-heeled pumps. TV prosecutors had better wardrobes.

"Did you tell Judge Cox that you were up here?"

Dodds nodded. Pissing off Pope was one thing, pissing off a judge was another. Neither was good. Walking between two powerful women who could make our lives easy or difficult was the work of a tightrope performer, not an attorney.

When we were finally allowed to broach Pope's office, each of us took a seat in front of the desk. Neither of us spoke.

"You were right." Pope was soberly matter-of-fact. "This isn't the case for this."

I looked at Dodds. Her face was turned toward mine, probably a mirror of my own perplexity.

"Why are you looking at each other? You need to do your jobs."

"And what would that be?" I asked. "You cut me off at the knees on this one. Said I didn't have the discretion."

"You do now."

"I want to be crystal clear on Saldana. That's who we're talking about, right? Saldana? The jury's been empaneled. Jeopardy has attached."

"I'm well aware of Ohio law, Ms. Long."

"So that's it? Drop the charges?" Dodds asked what I wasn't willing to go out on a limb to find out. Saldana may have been getting a raw deal, but in this dog eat dog world, protecting myself was the first order of business.

"Not drop, Dodds. Convict her of possession. Offer probation. That seems fair."

"What about the whole idea of using our office to put a stop to this thing you say is going to become the biggest crisis since crack cocaine?" I asked. Balancing policy, justice, and internal politics was a juggling act I was working to master.

Pope sighed. "Use your discretion. This is what I'm paying you to do. You're professionals. Go out there and do your job, Dodds."

Her use of my colleague's surname meant the junior prosecutor was dismissed. Valerie Dodds would have to go downstairs eating crow and make the best of the bizarre situation. On the upside, almost everyone would be happy. Saldana would go home. McPhee, if not a win, at least wouldn't have a major loss in his column. The jurors would have completed their service without missing more than a day of work. The judge could get back to her docket. Despite all of that, I felt unsatisfied and unsettled somehow.

"Close the door," Pope insisted the moment Dodds was out of earshot. I did as I was told. When I turned, Pope's desk was clear except for one single file folder. I was starting to hate oaktag. It presaged doom.

"Saldana was a mistake."

"Mistake?" The question popped out before I could think better of it because I was so surprised to hear an admission of wrongdoing from a woman covered in Teflon.

"Wrong defendant."

Again, I wanted to commiserate in solidarity. But I didn't. At least I wasn't the only one making mistakes here.

"If Libby Saldano comes through the system, throw the book at her."

"Saldan-*o*?"

"Exactly what I said."

My mind flew through all the possible permutations of what could have happened and landed on the simplest one: clerical error. She'd thought Saldan*a* was Saldan*o* and had acted accordingly. I couldn't decide if the defendant sitting downstairs waiting for a judge and jury to decide her fate was very lucky or extremely unlucky.

Not my problem, so I pushed it out of my mind. Was a question above my pay grade. I wouldn't give it another thought. To keep my job, I needed to do what I was told, not go asking a shit ton of questions no one wanted the answers to.

"Well, I guess I'll go upstairs to Cox's courtroom, and make sure Dodds doesn't give away the farm."

"No need. She can do whatever she wants. I'll approve it."

I wasn't dismissed. So I waited. Tried not to let my leg jiggle. The one part of my body that could admit I needed a little nip to get me through the rest of the afternoon. While I was trying to still my body, I almost missed it, my boss tapping at the file.

"*This* is the case we're going to ride the horse of prevention on." Her voice had gone from laconic to fiery with conviction.

"Am I going to be on this case?" I asked. Having to supervise Dodds through Saldana had left me feeling distinctly impotent.

"I hadn't considered it." As I sat, Pope slipped the file from her side of the desk to the far side near me. "Now that you mention it, though, I think you'd be an asset."

"What's the story this time? Is it a cold case?"

"Cold? You could say that. But this time there's no mistake."

"Good."

"Here you go." Pope walked around the desk toward my side, picked up the folder and thrust the paper toward my chest. If this hadn't been an office, I'd have thought the movement unnecessarily aggressive. "It's a murder case."

I accepted the file, all the while waiting for her to say something about my last murder case, where *I'd* indicted the wrong defendant.

When she remained quiet, I flipped it open because it was another one empty of the usual heft, murder photos, detective investigative notes, autopsy report. There was only a single sheet police report. There were a few other pages at least. I'd peruse those when I had a moment alone, after I'd taken a drink.

"Where's the re—"

"That's it."

I shouldn't have been surprised. I was discovering when it came to me, Lori was all about low information for low accountability.

Like the Saldana/MacNeill matter, there weren't more than a few white sheets of paper between the file's folder tan leaves. It was another overdose. I skimmed the anemic police report for information. It was almost as paltry as the last had been. Pope's face said she was waiting for me to figure it out. So I ignored my stomach's loud protest and took my time reading the sheets from top to bottom. When that didn't yield anything, I tried again. On the third look, I got it.

"Is Sarah Rose Pope related to you?" I asked, though the dread mixing with the stomach acid was giving me my answer.

"She was my very precious, very favorite little sister."

I closed the file and held it as close as she had thrust it. The only thing worse than a prosecutor with an agenda was one on a personal crusade.

"Anything more than what's in here that you want to share?"

Pope shook her pointed finger at me with some vehemence.

"There can't be a single whiff of impropriety on this one. I suggest you find the best detective you can, then figure out how to bring the murderer to justice."

I stood and left her office without being dismissed or any of the other usual formalities. Something told me it wasn't going to be that simple.

13

"You got the typewriter?" Tyisha's eyes went wide. My best friend knew I did everything I could to avoid upsetting my sister. Even though the typewriter was really Momma's, Rainey had been dragging it back and forth to college along with her dirty laundry.

"Shhh. Rainey hasn't noticed it's missing, yet." I held one finger to my lips and another to hers emphasizing the importance of us both keeping quiet. "But it'll make it a lot easier to write our book."

"Wait a second." Tyisha got up and closed my door. I'd forgotten about how much noise the machine made with its tapping and bell ringing at the carriage return. She then skipped to the overnight bag she'd stashed in the corner of my room. From it, my friend pulled out a big stack of notebook paper that she'd clipped together with three of those brass things that looped through the holes.

"So how do we do this?" I asked. "Do you want to tell the story out loud and I do the typing? According to Mrs. Meyer I'm the fastest typist in the class. I'm up to forty words a minute," I boasted.

Tyisha's frown was unexpected. "Daddy wouldn't let me take typing," she said.

"Why not? Momma had said it would probably be the most useful class I ever took in school."

"Daddy says it's an easy way for someone to stick me in a secretary job."

"Why is a secretary job bad?" I searched my brain for negatives. I loved seeing the women in movies, all starched shirts tucked into their skirts, taking dictation and typing efficiently.

"I don't think it's bad. He just says that after I go to college that I shouldn't let my talents go to waste."

I tried to think of what jobs Negroes had in Cleveland, but came up blank.

"I'll do the typing, then, I guess."

Tyisha flipped through the papers slowly. When she was done, she looked me squarely in the eye and said, "So, we have a total of twelve chapters. Should we start at the beginning?"

By now we'd been friends for years, so I'd seen Tyisha all times of day and in a lot of different ways. For some reason, though, when she was looking at me now, my stomach was going all topsy-turvy. I kind of wanted to hug her and run out of my room like my hair was on fire at the same time. I swallowed hard, but the feeling in my stomach didn't go away.

"I kind of want to write the part where the second mate finds out Julienne Prentice is a stowaway."

Our heroine was escaping from awful relatives somewhere in the wilds of England. She'd overheard that life was better in America.

"He's going to report her," Tyisha said, her own voice rising in anticipation.

"But then he falls in love with her!"

"It's so romantical," Tyisha cooed.

"Oh my God." I knew rolling my eyes was rude, according to Tyisha's mom. But I couldn't help myself. "You're still talking like that redheaded girl."

"Anne Shirley from Green Gables...from Avonlea." My friend practically hugged herself. "I just finished *Anne's House of Dreams*."

"How many books is that?" I tried not to be too exasperated at her love of these books. It was one of the first times we'd disagreed on anything. I'd tried that first book, but the writing had been boring. And the plucky girl who bounces back from every possible hardship didn't ring true. I knew firsthand that when things got hard that no sane person's first reaction was to smile and get everyone to fall in love with her.

"It's book number five." She held up her hands, her fingers spread wide, the light side of her palm facing me. "The librarian said she'll have the next one put aside when I bring back the last."

"Well, that one's already written. If we want to be in the library one day, then we really need to write ours."

And for a good half hour we did that. She told me what to say and I typed it out. When we got to the end of chapter one, I stood up.

"Let's take a break." I cracked my knuckles. "My fingers are starting to hurt."

"Maybe you need to do some exercises."

"Exercises?"

"Stretch your arms out."

I put them out in an imitation of Frankenstein. I groaned like Bela Lugosi moving back and forth, stiff-legged, and pretended to lunge toward her. My room wasn't as clean as hers, and I tripped over some tennis shoes. Then I took her down with me when I tripped. We landed on my bed in a tangle of arms and legs.

I'm not sure I'd ever been this close to my best friend. Suddenly, I could feel everything. Her legs in between mine. The smell of Ivory soap on her skin. The smell of something nutty in her hair. I moved my right hand and it landed against her chest. She'd started developing but didn't always wear a training bra because she said they were uncomfortable.

When I felt her flesh there, it lit my palm on fire. I knew I should take my hand away, but I couldn't. My stomach went sideways. I couldn't breathe. Then I did something I knew was wrong in every sense. I moved my other hand to the gap between her shirt and her jeans. Touched the warm brown skin there. Then I kissed her like we'd practiced against pillows. In her dreams, she was kissing boys. In mine, I was kissing her.

I practically held my breath as I waited for her to push me away. Leave my house. End our friendship forever. I was weighing whether the pure pleasure was worth the trade-off, when my door slammed open. Tyisha and I jumped apart as if we were repellant magnets.

"I told you not to touch that typewriter!" Rainey yelled before her tirade came to an abrupt halt. We hadn't moved fast enough and every part of my body felt like lead as I saw her take in what my best friend and I had been doing.

"You little pervert. I always said there was something not right about you. Now I know exactly what it is."

"Don't tell Momma and Daddy," rushed from my mouth.

A quiet Rainey was a scary Rainey. First she ripped the last typewritten page from the platen. She dropped it, so it floated like a fallen leaf to my carpet. Then she put the top of the typewriter case on. First she loudly snapped one clasp, then the other. Tyisha, who was normally unafraid of my scary sister, didn't move a muscle.

Rainey stood there, swinging the heavy typewriter from its chunky plastic handle, back and forth. If my friend hadn't been there, I'd have worried that she was going to wallop me with it. My friend was the perfect buffer. For once I wished for the hit because this waiting was so much worse. Rainey looked from me to my best friend and back again. Without saying a word, she walked through my door and closed it softly behind her. The snick of the doorknob chilled me to the core.

14

"Nicole. I didn't expect to see you." Darlene Webb's face was the very definition of surprise. My prosecutor's ID had gotten me past the front desk and into the detectives' offices without any trouble.

"Returning the favor." I arched a brow as best I could, then placed my briefcase squarely in the middle of the desk the detective was occupying.

"What...favor?" Webb's voice was hesitant. I could practically see her searching her memory for the substance of our paltry interactions.

"This past October, when you showed up at my condo, unannounced. On a Saturday," I explained. She'd heeded my warning. There hadn't been anymore impromptu visits. But that one and only had left a bitter aftertaste in my mouth.

"Right. The Walker case. Well…how can I help you today?" Webb stood so that we were nearly eye to eye.

"Where can we speak…privately?" I asked. The room around us was mostly empty on a Saturday morning, but not quite. Another two officers sat at desks not doing anything to hide their interest in my unusual visit.

"My lieutenant's office? The interrogation room is full."

Following her lead, I walked in the door she opened, pushed past her, and took her boss' chair. Flustered, she took one across the desk. No doubt her usual one, I figured, so she should be comfortable.

"I have a case that needs investigating." Plain spoken was best here. The way I'd figured the calculus, she owed me. No need to butter her up.

"Am I assigned to it?" Webb made as if she were going to get up. "If you give me the name, I can go get the file."

"There's no file to get." I waved her back down to the guest chair.

"Then…" She looked around as if a thick file of papers were going to materialize.

"This is an off-the-books case that Lori Pope's assigned to me."

"I, uh, heard about your promotion." There was an awkward pause before Webb offered the expected polite response. "Congratulations."

"Thanks."

For another beat too long, we sat in silence. If I hadn't been scrutinizing her, I'd have missed her small shrug of acquiescence. I reached inside my black leather bag and extracted the still thin oaktag folder.

"What kind of case is it?"

"Homicide."

"It was here in Cleveland Heights? If I'm not on it, then Russ Banks or Sheldon Gomez would be on it. It's not like Cleveland over here. We don't have more than a handful of murders in a year."

"It's a cold case. Wasn't classified as murder in the first place."

"Not murder, but have some facts come to light now that put it in the murder category?" she asked.

When Darlene Webb leaned forward, I knew she was as good as enlisted. A handful of murders and her being the lowest detective on the totem pole meant that the interesting cases weren't coming her way.

"What's the story?" Webb's voice was an octave higher, her words coming out staccato. "Isn't that what you asked me on our last case? That there has to be a story for a jury."

"I don't know yet." It was my turn to shrug. "I only have the victim and some random facts."

"Hand it over." Webb did the gimme thing with her hand.

"What?"

"That folder you've been clutching like it's a middle schooler's diary."

I'd forgotten I'd retrieved it from my bag. I extended my hand, but snatched it back the moment Webb's hands made contact. "This is confidential, until it's not. Can you do that?"

She waved her hand. Made no promises out loud. Took the three pages I'd been given. Read them slowly.

"Sarah Rose Pope? Any relation?"

"Direct relation. Sister."

"Je-sus." Webb breathed both syllables.

"That's already been solved. I heard Pontius Pilate was on the hook for that one."

Webb ignored my attempt at humor. Used her unpolished fingernail to peruse line by line.

"Says overdose. You know the policy on those. Pope was the architect of that policy. What's changed?"

"Family?" I speculated.

"So was it an overdose? Is there an autopsy? What happened?"

"That's where you come in." I made sure my look at her was pointed. I was a lot of things, but I wasn't a woman with a badge and a gun and the power to use both.

"A perpetrator, suspect? Something?"

"She doesn't want to corrupt the investigation. Should it come to trial. I think we're going to have to do this on our own."

"We?" She asked, as if I were the Lone Ranger leading Tonto into danger.

"We."

Webb checked her watch. "It's ten-thirty. If the doer doesn't think they're getting caught, they're not hiding. How much time do you have?"

"I have all day." The best part about being a deputy was that I could do that…clear my schedule on a moment's notice. Not that my Saturdays were busy with work.

Webb rose and closed the door to the office.

"We're going to need to switch seats." She gestured toward the computer and monitor facing me.

"Fine." I stood and walked behind the seat she came to occupy.

Webb tapped at the keyboard, waking the computer from slumber. Next she typed in a username and password.

"What's the police report number?" Her eyes pierced me over her shoulder.

I read off the twelve-digit number, the first six the month and year it was filed. She typed it in. Looked at me again with a squint but didn't say anything. Instead, she turned back around and clicked the print icon, then disappeared from the office for as long as it took to retrieve the sheets from the printer.

The police reports available to the public and those available to cops were an entirely different affair, the latter having far more detail and no redacted parts.

She waved me back to the front side of the desk and took a seat. I took the other.

The first pages were no different than what I'd already seen. A description of the scene where Sarah Rose Pope's body was found. That it was a single family house in the part of Cleveland Heights that abutted East Cleveland. She was found dead on arrival. The paramedics' attempt at revival having failed. The coroner had been called. Sarah's body moved to the morgue. Following those descriptive pages was a cursory report. It confirmed the suspected overdose. The post-mortem drug testing revealed high levels of oxycodone, heroin, and not an insignificant amount of methamphetamine. The body hadn't received a full autopsy as was the overdose policy of confirming cause of death, but not expending the county's resources on a full examination when unnecessary.

With half the pages turned facedown, I locked eyes with Webb. Her nod confirmed my thoughts. So far, nothing out of the ordinary. People did drugs, were junkies or addicts or whatever the politically correct term was of the moment. Polysubstance abuse was a term that had been tossed out during some continuing education session. Somehow, addicts couldn't stop at just one. Too many chemicals put a strain on the human body. Sometimes the organs couldn't handle it all.

"It's a tragedy, not a crime." I shook my head. I had no idea what Lori was going for here.

"Tragedy?"

"That's the addiction part," I explained. "I think it's trauma meeting epigenetics."

"Well, that's a lot of woo-woo and multi-syllable words I don't understand. *My* job is to put criminals in jail."

"So the question Lori Pope would probably want the answer to is, why is no one in jail for this? What are the other pages?"

We both craned our heads to have a look at what else was involved in the younger Pope's death.

"It's just a list of the other people in the residence, their rap sheets. Other stuff found at the scene."

"Who else was there? Was this a house just for drugs or did someone live there?"

"Not a drug house or abandoned property. Tyisha Cooley, and some Ja Roach guy were there."

"Ja Roach?" Sounded like a nickname a weed dealer would have used. "Alias?" I asked.

Webb looked down again. Flipped a few pages back and forth.

"No alias. His real name, I guess."

"The usual assortment of people who wouldn't know each other if it weren't for the drugs, sounds like."

"There were needles, baggies, foil, takeout containers, and a couple of duffle bags full of clothes."

Webb pushed the papers over to me and got up to go back to the computer on the other side of the desk.

"Let's start with the known associates of Pope. No one gets this far down the addiction rabbit hole without a few dings."

I fed her a couple of names, she typed, then printed one by one. Though she didn't retrieve anything from the printer, she skimmed and flagged anything potentially interesting. There wasn't much. One of the women had been arrested for prostitution, no doubt in connection with trading her body for money to buy drugs or just an even exchange with a dealer. The men had low-level, misdemeanor possession charges for meth, pot, crack, and opioids in various combinations.

"Give me the address," Webb demanded.

"Nine sixty-one Brunswick Road."

"Five bedroom. One bathroom. Purchased for about forty thousand dollars eight years ago. The owner is one Tyisha Cooley."

"Same name as one of the people on scene, right?" I scanned the papers. "Tyisha. Husband, parents, siblings? Are the taxes up-to-date?"

"Nothing amiss there. Someone's paying Cuyahoga County nearly twenty-four hundred on the half year for the place."

I looked at my watch. "Let's get lunch, then pay a visit to the house. Something tells me that someone will be at home."

15

The moment I heard the honk, I tore through the front door. Tyisha was there as planned. It was a few seconds before she lifted the door handle and got out of her sixteenth birthday gift.

"Happy birthday!" I couldn't help screaming. "Oh my God, I can't believe it. Is it new? It's yellow!"

"I know!" Tyisha's voice was as excited as mine. She ran across the driveway and we hugged and swayed a little. "I wanted red, but now I think this is better."

"It's so cool," I agreed, then rubbed and patted the round bonnet-shaped hood for good measure.

"So this is the trunk, right?"

"Yeah, it's backwards," my best friend confirmed. "The engine is in the back."

"Is it a German thing?" I asked. Foreign cars were starting to appear in Cleveland, slowly infiltrating the near monopoly Detroit had on our Midwest city.

"Maybe? I don't know." She shrugged. For a second we just stood. I hated the awkwardness I'd put between us. It didn't come up all the time, but every once in a while.

"So, do I get a ride?" I tried to smooth things over.

"Let's go now," Tyisha said. She jingled the new key ring in her hand. "It's a school night. Daddy made this one-time curfew exception."

"Let me run in and tell my mom. C'mon, I want to show you the book I got early. It'll only take two minutes. Then we can drive along the river. The rain has let up and it's really warm for spring."

"Should I lock it? Daddy said—"

"Nah, it's Rocky River."

We ran upstairs to my room. My parents were outside walking the perimeter and talking about building either a barbecue or gazebo in the backyard, so I didn't feel obligated to interrupt. On the way out, I promised myself.

"Look what I got!" I picked up the hardcover with two hands and thrust it toward her.

"*The Exorcist*? What is this?"

"I haven't slept in two days," I admitted. The first night was because I couldn't stop reading. The second night was because I was deathly afraid. "I finished it already. It's really creepy, weird, scary. I don't know. But you can have it. It's half of your birthday gift. The other half is here."

I picked up the present I'd spent weeks fretting over. I told my mother it was taking so long to pick the yarn because it was my best friend's sweet sixteen. Only I knew the real reason. I loved Tyisha in *that* way and wanted something that would be perfect.

"Here. This is for you." I thrust the package at her before I lost my nerve, wishing I'd used a box like my mother had suggested. The paper was wrinkling by the second.

"What is it?" The paper crinkled some more as Tyisha turned it this way and that.

"You'll have to open it." I could barely stand still as I waited.

"Should I open it here or when I'm at home?"

It would probably be better manners to have her open it at home. Momma said making people open presents in front of you forced them to say they liked it even if they didn't. But I wasn't worried so much about that between us.

"Here." I knew we didn't have much time, but I couldn't let her get all the way home. I wouldn't have been able to stand the anticipation of waiting for her phone call letting me know her opinion.

She lifted the large wrapped package. When her finger went through the blue wrapping paper, I cringed.

"I should have put it in a box. I'm so sorry."

"I was going to open it just the same. I like the paper, though, blue is my favorite color."

"I hope you like it." Biggest understatement ever.

"I'll like whatever you give me." Her eyes met mine, and I almost passed out even though I knew in my heart she wasn't looking at me in the same way I was looking at her. "You know that."

She tore through the paper. I was glad I'd at least wrapped a silk bow around the afghan I'd crocheted.

"It's a blanket in shades of blue," Tyisha said while she turned the folded yarn this way and that.

"You don't have to pull the bow now. It'll be easier if you keep it folded."

"Where did you get it?" She rubbed it against her cheek. "It's so pretty and squishy soft."

"I made it."

"What? Seriously. No kidding?"

"In home ec. We learned some basic knit and crochet stitches. Momma took me to a store way out to find just the right yarn and pattern. I made it for you."

"Oh my God. That's so amazing. You're so good with your hands." The long hug she gave me made the weeks of late nights and cramped fingers more than worth it. I pulled back before I went too far. I had a hard time keeping from touching her when she was around.

"Okay. I know we're running out of time. Take this and the book. Happy sweet sixteenth. I'm so glad that we're best friends."

"Are you coming to the party?"

I shook my head.

"I can't. It's Rainey's graduation. Daddy's having a party here. There's no way they'll let me go."

"But you don't even—"

"Shh. You know that we don't talk about that. Speaking of, we have to get back downstairs and get that ride in. Okay?"

"We'll miss you. Wayne especially."

"You know I don't like him like that. And you know why."

We went down and made small talk with my mom and dad. It was a rare night when my dad was home.

"I'm just going to be out a short time."

"Be careful," was all Daddy said.

Rainey was standing by Tyisha's car when we got outside. I hadn't seen my sister come out. She hadn't been downstairs when I'd been asking my parents' permission to go for a quick ride.

For a moment I wondered if she'd tampered with the car, like cut the brake lines or something. But that was just how it worked in the movies. In real life, my sister wouldn't have a clue as to how to do that. Rainey wasn't even hiding some kind of big knife behind her back, which a film would have done a quick cut to. Her hands were empty, hanging at her sides. I let my shoulders down from my ears.

"Nice car." The way Rainey rubbed at the paint made the hair rise from my neck. Goosebumps prickled my arms. I rubbed at them to warm up.

"Thanks," Tyisha said, her voice coolly polite.

"How'd your dad swing this?"

Tyisha, well used to Rainey's not-so-veiled barbs, only shrugged. I wish refusing to speak worked when Rainey got me alone.

"I really like it," I heard my friend say as I tried to shake a sense of gloom that was laying on my skin like a wet blanket. "I can drive myself to school and even help my mom out with errands."

My friend turned her back on my sister and leaned down to unlatch the trunk. The hood flipped up.

"Oh, that's where the spare is. Cool," I said. Behind the tire, the trunk was completely empty. She popped in my blanket and the book.

"Okay, let's go."

"The engine is in the back, then?" Rainey asked.

Tyisha nodded. Cool as a cucumber as always. Then she turned her back on my sister, done with that conversation. She looked at me as if I'd asked her the question. "Yeah. Daddy's going to show me how to do basic maintenance like change the carburetor and put water in the battery."

"Water?"

"Keeps it cool, I think."

"Keeping it cool seems very important with a hot engine," Rainey interjected, then sauntered over to lean against the roof of the car.

"So, car maintenance is okay, but typing is not?" I asked Tyisha. It was a genuine question. The Cooleys were very much into higher education. This stab at doing something with her hands was a huge surprise.

"He said he wants me to not have to rely on a guy for help. He wants me to be able to care for the car on my own. Especially if I take it to college."

"Well, hopefully it won't overheat today." Rainy stopped leaning on the car and casually walked back into the house. She looked back over her shoulder and gave us a smile. I didn't think she was wishing us good luck.

I didn't ask for my friend's permission when I opened the passenger door and got in. I just wanted to get away from the house, if only for a few minutes. Rainey was going to be home the whole dang summer. It was going to be difficult to ignore her for two and a half straight months. Even this small break would be a relief.

Tyisha slipped into the driver's seat and fired up the car. I pointed and we backed out of the driveway and toward the street. Soon we were on Wager Road, which was a straight shot to Wager Beach on Lake Erie.

"Do you smell something?" I asked. There was a weird odor coming from the car.

"I think it's the motor. The car was sitting in some old lady's garage for two years. Daddy says it's going to take time to get everything working smoothly again. Engines are meant to run. It's why he's letting me drive out here, I think. To give it time to get oil everywhere and stuff."

I shrugged and watched the scenery roll by. The sun was starting to peek out and I'd stopped being cold. Instead, I was getting that warm feeling I'd started to associate with not only the Cooleys, who treated me like one of their family, but with Tyisha as well.

After that time Rainey had walked in on us kissing, I'd never had the guts to do it again. But every time I saw her, I wanted to—really bad. I was pretty sure she didn't feel that way about me. But not entirely sure. She'd stopped talking about boys around me. I didn't know if it was because she didn't want to hurt my feelings or if it was even a tiny bit possible she had the same kinds of feelings for me. Whenever I thought that, hope bubbled up in my chest and my mind spun off in daydreams of us walking off into the sunset by the water.

When we got to the brick arch that led to Wagar beach, I worked hard to bring myself back to the present. Tyisha turned off the car.

"Want to sit on the sand for a minute?" I asked.

"It's cold."

"We have a blanket." I opened my door and she did the same.

She opened the trunk again, and we took out the blanket. Found a grassy spot that we could agree on, not too near the cold water, and sat down next to each other. She undid the bow and spread the wool out so it covered both our legs up to our waist. I turned to her.

"Sixteen, huh? And a car. That's so cool. Happy birthday," I said for probably the fifth time.

"I was pretty surprised. I woke up this morning to the tiniest box sitting on the kitchen table. I thought it was probably a necklace or earrings or something. But when I opened it, it was a key."

Tyisha fished it from her pocket to show me.

"See how the 'V' and 'W' are in the top part? I just sat there and looked at it for a while. Momma and Daddy were looking at me. Wayne, too. He's home from Howard. I felt stupid, like I was missing something. So finally I asked, 'What's this key for?' They all laughed. Then Daddy said I should get my shoes on and come outside. The minute I saw the car, I knew. I probably screamed loud enough to wake up the whole neighborhood."

"Did Mrs. Greer come outside?"

"You know it. That woman is just so nosy."

"Where was the car?"

"Parked right in front of the house. Daddy drove straight to the Bureau of Motor Vehicles for my driver's test. I passed!" My friend lifted her butt and pulled her newly laminated license out of her pocket. I took the small rectangle of plastic and turned it to and fro. It was such an adult thing to have. I handed it back, and she stuck it and the keys back in her pocket. "He let me drive home," she went on. "I took Wayne out for a few minutes. He got me my favorite Polish Boy. Then I came here."

"I'm glad that I was first," I said, nudging her knee with mine.

"We're best friends."

"Is that all we are to each other?" I asked boldly. After the words left my mouth, I covered it with my hands. It was too late, though. I couldn't grab them from the air and push them back in or take them back.

Tyisha patted my thigh over the blanket.

"I want you to know that you are my very best friend. I know that we met during the weirdest time. But I'm glad for it. Not the riot or anything. I understand that you're different. Not bad or good. That you like girls. Daddy said to me that most girls like boys and vice versa, but some girls like girls. Some boys like boys. But I like boys. I didn't want to say anything, but Ish…Ishmael Gill has asked me to go steady. I said yes. I didn't tell you because I didn't want to hurt your feelings."

"When did this happen?"

"Two weeks ago."

"Oh."

She'd mentioned him once. But she mentioned a lot of people from her neighborhood or from school. I hadn't cottoned on to how important he was.

"I'm supposed to go to his house for dinner in a couple of hours. So I can't stay too long. I wanted to tell you in person. Okay?"

"Can you drive me home?" I wanted to cry alone in the privacy of my bedroom. Not in front of her. I didn't want Tyisha to be the one to comfort me. I wanted to cry even harder when I realized that there was no one to comfort me. Until Tyisha, there hadn't ever been, but I was used to the Cooleys comforting me. For this, they couldn't.

"Do you want to talk about the book?" Tyisha asked. Books and stories were the single thing we could always come back to. Was our common ground from day one. But I didn't have it in me today.

"Which one? You know what? Neither one. I need time to think." I wasn't ready to take the bone she was throwing me.

"We're still friends, right?"

"Sure. Yes. No. I don't know. I just can't talk to you right now. I need a best friend. I need someone I can talk to about how the person I like doesn't like me back. How they're dating someone else."

When our eyes met, I think we both realized we couldn't be what the other needed right now. It was a first that I knew would repeat. I didn't know how I knew, but I did.

"Home, then." By silent agreement we both stood.

She folded the blanket carefully. I wanted to snatch it from her. Save it for someone who really loved me. Instead I tied the bow back like it had been when I was wrapping it in my room that morning. I patted at it.

"Happy birthday."

"Thanks." Her voice was soft. It made me want to cry even more. I turned away and pushed my fists against my eyes to keep the tears away.

She didn't bother with the trunk this time, and instead threw the blanket into the tiny space where a back seat would be. Tyisha tried starting the car, but the engine stalled out. The smell from earlier was a lot stronger.

"That smell is bad. Like hair and meat. Oh God, do you think a squirrel got in there or something?

Once that happened to one of our neighbors after a snow storm."

"I'll check. Daddy showed me a couple of things already this morning."

I waited in the passenger seat, wondering how long it would be before I felt okay again. Before I could spend time with Tyisha and not want to cry. Whether that would ever happen. Whether I'd lost my best friend.

"Oh my God! Oreo!" Tyisha yelled.

Before I could think better of it, I was out of the car and at the back next to her.

My dog was—

Oreo was—

I couldn't look. I put my hands in front of my eyes and slid to the ground. In my mind, Rainey's face came into clear focus. I wanted to pound my head against the pavement to get all the stupidity out. I'd made the mistake again—her smile hadn't been nice at all.

16

"This is it? Nine sixty-one Brunswick Road?"

Webb turned off the motor of the unmarked car. We both turned toward the house. It was as nondescript as its neighbors on either side. White, clapboard, two-story affairs. The three houses stood out, though, because they weren't boarded up. Others on the block had obviously been victim to the latest foreclosure crisis. Cleveland's renaissance, which had been in full swing when I moved here, was long over. If I lost this job, there wasn't another right around the corner. The economic crisis had almost scared me straight. Almost.

We both opened our doors and got out. While Webb locked up the car—and auxiliary weapons—

tight, I stepped onto the sidewalk and had a closer look at the scene of the crime. It was rare the prosecutors got to see crime scenes in person. Our lives weren't much different than the jury's, confined to narratives and photos.

That inexperience suddenly gave me pause.

"How are we going to play this?"

"It's informal. If someone's home, I'll make it a friendly conversation. Unless there's something you're not telling me, this is a fishing expedition. We throw out a bunch of different kinds of bait and lures, then see what swims up to the hook."

I nodded. Seemed reasonable. Webb may have been inexperienced when I first met her, and not much better last year when we had to put together a murder case. But it looked like she'd gained enough confidence to handle the kind of initial questioning this potential case needed.

I swallowed my sigh of relief because I was maybe a little too jittery to take on the whole thing by myself.

Webb strode to the front door in her sensible black clogs, and I teetered after her as fast as I could. She waited for me, then knocked with a kind of authority that couldn't be ignored.

We waited a beat. She knocked again.

Finally, there was stirring inside.

I'm not sure what I expected, but a woman in jeans and an open, button-down shirt over a T-shirt answered the door.

"Can I help you?"

She looked like an advertisement for the Gap. Except for the work gloves. The yellow leather didn't match. She pulled off one, then the other. Waited for us to say something.

"Tyisha Cooley?" I asked. The woman nodded.

"Darlene Webb." The detective badged the woman. "Cleveland Heights police."

"Oh. Oh, my goodness." She held up the gloves to her face in a kind of prayer. "Do you have information? Has the case finally been solved?"

"Can we come in?" Webb blurted her question, probably as surprised as I was.

"Of course. Excuse my manners. Can I call my parents? I think we'd all like to hear this together. Give me a minute."

The woman pulled off her gloves, dropped them, then disappeared to the back of the house into what was probably a kitchen. I heard the sound of what was likely a cordless phone being lifted from the cradle. The alternating low and high-pitched tone of buttons being pressed. Then her urgent whispers into the phone before it fell back into the cradle.

I looked at Webb, deliberately making my eyes wide. Her head shake was barely noticeable. So she didn't know, either. When the detective didn't speak, I figured out we were going with the flow.

"Do you mind waiting? I just want my dad here at the same time," Cooley said when she came back into the room. "I'm so sorry. My manners. Would you like something to drink? Water? Coffee? I put a pot on a few minutes ago."

"We'll take coffee," I said. Putting together a cup of coffee would take time, maybe give us a minute or ten to poke around.

"Come on, then," she said as I expected, inviting us further into the house, her manners winning out over common sense. "The kitchen is back here."

Webb slid me a glance. Then we both got up and followed Cooley through to the back of the house. The kitchen was crowded, with a too big pine table. Cooley took out three bright yellow mugs then filled them three quarters full. She bustled to a fridge and pulled out half and half, then moved various items aside on a counter to unearth a sugar jar.

I took my time doctoring my drink as did Webb. Before we were done, there was a loud knock on the front door. Mugs in hand, we followed Cooley back through to the living room. An older black man with close-cropped salt-and-pepper hair came through the door unannounced.

"Daddy. They're here with news about Wayne. This is Detective Webb. I didn't catch your name."

"Nicole Long." I shook his hand, but left out my job title.

"Let's sit."

Webb took a long sip. Then she spoke, "Tell me about Wayne."

"He was the best brother a girl could have," Cooley said. "He looked out for me and my friends. Treated...them just like they were family. He graduated first in his class at Tuskegee."

"What was his major?" I asked. Tried to smile at her. Not sure I succeeded at being friendly.

"Engineering." Her eyes shifted between me and Webb. "He was working for this place in Independence."

"How did he come to be where he was on the night of the incident?" Webb brought it back into interrogation territory.

"Why do you always ask that?" She turned pleading eyes on her father. "Like it was his fault for being in the wrong place at the wrong time."

"Honey, they're new to it." Her father took her hand, patted it.

"You say that every time, but the latest detectives always ask the same damned questions."

"But they came to us." Mr. Cooley looked between us, and sensing something, nodded in confirmation. "It's different this time, okay?"

"Fine," Tyisha Cooley said as she loosened her tight lips. "He was coming here. To check on...a friend of mine. She was here while I was away. There were a couple of people in the house with her. Probably drug dealers or addicts, I don't know."

"You weren't here?"

"No. I went to a wedding for a sorority sister. It was a four-day thing in Atlanta."

Cooley's dad was patting her hand again. "Honey, you don't need to apologize. You were no one's keeper."

"But if I'd been here—"

"You were saying about your brother coming here to check on someone," Webb interrupted the pity party. "Who was staying with you?"

"Sarah. Sarah Pope. She stayed with me or my parents sometimes when she was in between places. She was having a hard time."

"Because she was an addict, honey," Mr. Cooley added.

Tyisha Cooley shook her head like that wasn't something she liked to think about.

"Anyway, Wayne came by." She told the story she'd probably thought about a thousand times. "I think everything went okay. He'd called Momma and Daddy and left a message on the answering machine saying everything was good, so they could let me know when I called. This was before everyone had a cell phone in their pocket."

"Then what happened?"

The Cooleys gave us a look. Webb's questions were straining credulity.

"To the best of your knowledge," I added to try to smooth out the fact that indeed the questions were going the wrong way.

"Wayne came in." Big shrug. "Talked to her or whatever."

"I'd given him leftovers from Sunday dinner," Mr. Cooley added. "Sarah was looking pretty emaciated by then."

"Then he left. But it was 1988. That was the crack epidemic. The working theory had always been that someone had noticed he was wearing nice clothes or that he was driving that...what was it, Daddy?"

"Audi five thousand CS turbo."

"It was red. Total guy car," Tyisha Cooley continued. "Someone thought he had money and tried to rob him. He would have resisted, and that's how he got shot...dead."

"Tell us more about the woman staying here, Sarah Pope, you said."

"She was my best friend in childhood."

"How did you meet?"

"Long story, but she found herself in Hough after the riots. I think she'd come down with her sister out of curiosity and they got...separated."

A look passed between father and daughter, but neither Webb nor I probed it.

"When Wayne was killed, he was how old?"

"One month from his thirty-seventh birthday."

"Did he and Sarah have a romantic relationship?"

"No." Tyisha Cooley's exasperated sigh let me know other detectives had asked that question before. "She was a lesbian."

I had to work hard to keep my eyebrows from crawling up my forehead. That was an entirely new fact.

"Do you think that was well known?" Webb probed. "Could there have been some kind of jealousy thing?"

"I think that's a question for you," Cooley returned.

"Right. Sorry." Webb flustered, fiddled with her blazer until she pulled a tiny notebook and pen from an inner pocket. I couldn't decide if the flash of gun from her shoulder holster was an accident. "How long had she been an addict? What was her drug of choice?"

"Maybe ten years off and on. Maybe longer. It took us a long time to cotton on to what was going on, that she had a heroin habit. You have to know we'd known her since we were both around eleven. It wasn't obvious at first."

"You said she'd stayed with both of you. Were you familiar with her dealers? Could you name them, or know their nicknames, or pick them out of mugshots or a lineup?"

"Do you have someone in custody? Was it DNA or something that finally linked the cases?"

Mr. Cooley nodded. "There are a lot of stories in the news about that. Innocence Project. DNA clearing some folks. Implicating others."

"Please let me ask the questions here," Webb asserted. "I want to put together the information without anything being tainted. We never want a defense attorney to suggest that we've influenced a witness."

"Let them do their jobs, honey," Mr. Cooley said in soothing tones.

Webb lined up her next question. "Did she ever prostitute herself? Was there a pimp who might have been jealous?"

From the way the Cooleys' eyes shuttered, I could tell they didn't want to think about, much less talk about that possibility.

Independently, they both shook their heads.

"Can I ask you how Sarah Pope died? The only official record says the death happened here."

"It's not related to Wayne. Hers was just an overdose. It came much later, *nineteen years later.*"

"We're covering every possible angle. Overdoses aren't rare."

An understanding dawned in the Cooleys' eyes. They were making a jump. Seeing a link. Even my heartless soul had to look away.

"But sometimes, they're not an accident, either," Webb added.

Detective Darlene Webb was a quick study. At that moment, I knew that she'd cinched it. That she was going to get everything we needed to prosecute Sarah Pope's killer.

17

"This is the greatest injustice known to man," the woman said. She slapped a stack of documents on my desk. Then she slipped off her black hooded raincoat and put it on the coatrack in the corner. "Sorry. I'm Tyisha Cooley, but you should know that already. You're Justin McPhee. Casey Cort referred me."

I took her offered hand and shook it. Sized her up. Couldn't quite put a finger on what kind of client Cooley would be. She took a seat before I offered. Crossed her legs. Leaned in.

"You will *not* believe this."

I didn't tell her at this point, I'd believe anything. I think law had more surprises than any other

profession outside of psychology and maybe policing. And those folks had to expect it. Their very training was talking people down from proverbial ledges.
There were no such lessons in my courses at Case.

"Do you mind if I have a look at this?" I picked
up and waved the papers she'd dropped.

"Go ahead. It's, like, a murder scene."

As I read, a shiver of déjà vu went up my spine,
even though it was a balmy spring day. It was nearly
a carbon copy of Saldana's indictment. Involuntary
manslaughter was first. Corrupting another with
drugs was next. Possession of heroin came third.
Tampering with evidence was last. Every practicing
lawyer knew that very few documents were written
from scratch. We had forms. We developed our own
templates. Sometimes filing a pleading was as easy
as filling in blanks. This was no fill-in-the-blank
form, though. This was deliberate. I wondered what
Lori Pope was playing at.

"Did you see who the victim was?"

I'd been so busy being shocked about the doppel-
ganger pleading that I'd skimmed right over that.
Slid my finger to page one. Sarah Rose Pope.

"Any relation?" She didn't have to ask who I was
talking about.

"Direct relation. It's Lorraine Pope's sister."

I sat back. I'd never heard anyone use *the* prosecutor's full name outside of completing an election
ballot. I could feel my eyebrows hit my hairline, and
given that it may have moved back a millimeter or
two in the last few years, that was no mean feat.

"And how do you know the prosecutor's sister?"

"Deceased sister. She was my childhood best friend."

"She's…or the office is prosecuting you for…causing her death."

"That's about the size of it."

"Did you?" I never, *never*, asked that question. But if any case ever called for it, this would be the singular exception.

"That's a categorical no."

"So what in the hell is going on here?" I put my question more plainly than I normally would, but Cooley seemed the type to understand.

"If anyone is responsible for Sarah's death, it would be Rainey."

"Rainey?"

"Oh, sorry. That's what Sarah's family called her back then. *Lorraine* Pope as good as killed her dead."

After more than a decade of practice, I thought I couldn't be more surprised. This little revelation made me want to go back to bed, wake up again, have a third cup of coffee so I was better prepared for the day. I didn't have a time machine, so I soldiered on.

"That's a big accusation." I waited for Tyisha Cooley to lose her cool. Her face didn't change, though. So I pushed forward, "Let's go back to the beginning."

"When? The beginning? Forty-two years? That's a long way back."

"You're right. How about the night Sarah died."

Cooley had the same look ninety percent of my clients did. They wanted more than anything to forget the day or night or incident that had landed them in my office. Unfortunately, it was my job to make them relive what was probably the worst time in their lives over and over again.

"Before I get too comfortable, how confidential is this? Do I need to pay you first?"

"A consultation is one hundred percent confidential. It's the law."

"What could you share with the prosecutor?" she asked.

"Only what's authorized by you. Your constitutional right to remain silent holds from beginning to end."

"Then I think we're going to have a problem."

"Why?" I could feel my face pull into a squint.

"I already told the police everything."

This Tyisha Cooley didn't seem that naïve. I was surprised for the second time in less than an hour. That rarely happened anymore. I had a feeling if I took this case, it was going to keep me on my toes.

"How did that happen?"

"When they came to my door, I made a bad assumption."

"Which was?"

"That they were investigating the murder of my brother. It's an open case. This year is the twentieth anniversary. They implied that they had a suspect in custody, thought Sarah's dealer or maybe some pimp was the person responsible for her overdose."

"Unfortunately, the police can lie," I explained. When I saw the doubt in her face, I expanded. "*Frazier versus Cupp*. From way back in 1969 when the court was liberal. Thurgood Marshall wrote that opinion."

I think she coughed "sell out" under her breath, but we both pretended to ignore it. I knew feisty was up there with sassy as a word you shouldn't use to describe women, but both may have applied here.

"How much time do you have?" I asked. Many of my clients could only call off for an hour at a time. I wanted to prioritize if that were the case or maybe even reschedule.

"I have all the time in the world." Tyisha shifted her body as if to make herself more comfortable. "I think this is the kind of thing that I should spend time dealing with now and not from a jail cell on appeal."

"I wish all clients thought that way." Prisons were filled with magical thinking defendants who expected a miracle and didn't take it seriously. Criminal defense wasn't a do-over kind of situation.

"I wish I wasn't a potential client," Cooley said more quietly.

"Touché," was my concession. Since there was nothing I could do to alter the path that had led her here, I just clicked my pen and got on with it. "Tell me about Wayne."

"*I'm* the one facing jail." She thumped her first and middle finger against her chest. A tiger eye ring I hadn't noticed before gleamed in the office light.

"Most of my…potential…clients don't have a personal relationship with the prosecutor. I'm thinking I need to know more, not less." I wasn't quite ready to point out that something was giving me a hinky feeling. I didn't like to talk about anything to clients for which I didn't have solid facts or experience.

"Have you seen anything like this before?" she asked. Clients always like to hear that you got somebody off who'd done the same thing as them. This time I could.

"One other time, actually. February of this year."

"Seriously. So maybe it's *not* personal."

"The charges were exactly the same." I wouldn't normally have revealed something like that. It seemed important here, though.

"What's going on, do you think? Feels like something's going on, right?"

"The prevailing theory? That Pope's legislating from her office. This is her way of trying to crack down on the burgeoning opiate crisis."

"That makes sense."

"How so? It's the legislature's job to make laws." Not for the first time, I worried about our public education system.

"Her mother was an addict."

"Pope's?" It took me a long moment to reconcile my perception of a perfectly presented prosecutor and what Cooley was saying.

"Benefit of having 'known her when,'" Cooley added when I hadn't said anything more.

"What happened?" I didn't know if my curiosity had to do with Cooley's case or my own prurient interest. Since I wasn't charging by the hour, I didn't reign in my curiosity.

Cooley leaned forward. Her face serious. "This isn't exactly public knowledge."

"This isn't exactly the public," I replied using her words. I found it made clients more comfortable—to speak like them. "I think we established that," I continued. "The confidentiality part."

"Rainey…Lorraine and Sarah were only half-sisters. Sarah's dad had been married before Sarah's mom."

"Tell me more."

"I only overheard this at Sarah's house once. I mean, they talked around it at other times. Even Sarah didn't talk about it, and she told me almost everything. No one exactly said anything to me directly. I was downstairs getting Chips Ahoy cookies because my parents rarely got treats like that. Remember those?" I nodded, remembering my own after school snacks. "They kept the goodies in the pantry. Her parents weren't really sit-down dinner type of people. So I was kind of curious when I heard them talking in the dining room. My mother would have killed me for ear hustling like that."

"Ear hustling?"

"I was eavesdropping." She shook her head at her use of slang. "My parents raised me better than to spy on people. But Sarah's house was…always kind of a mystery, I guess."

"Mystery?"

Cooley didn't elaborate. I let it go. We'd get to that later.

"I...so I went to get cookies. We did that kind of thing, you know? Sneak snacks at each other's houses. We both found out we got in way less trouble when company was over. So you could walk into their pantry from the mud room or the kitchen. I came down the stairs and went through the mud room. That way I wouldn't have to talk to anyone."

I nodded. I remembered how awkward conversation felt with adults before you joined their ranks. Actually, it was still awkward now. We adults just had better skills.

"So I'm in there trying to figure out if I should bring up the whole bag or if I can just get a few on a paper towel when I heard her parents talking."

"What did they say?"

The way Tyisha Cooley's eyes glazed over, I knew she was traveling back to that place and time in her head. She related the story like the adolescent she'd probably been when she'd heard it.

"Where is Anna now?" Dot Pope had asked her husband.

"Halfway house in Parma," Frank Pope had answered.

"Is she clean?" That was Dot again. Her voice got more hushed, but her concern—or maybe fear—was still evident.

"She's tested clean the last two weeks." Frank now sounded exasperated.

"That's it? Hardly any time at all."

"She's just out of rehab, Dorothy." Frank was using her Christian name.

"Again?"

"It's the nature of the beast." Frank huffed.

"She had a daughter. Why isn't that enough motivation?" Dot's voice was full of judgment.

"She's not like you."

"We both grew up on the westside. Our parents stayed together. I'm here every day. Day in and day out. Raising our daughter. Raising her daughter. It's the least any mom can do."

"I don't have any more answers than I gave you just now." Frank's voice was tight with something—anger, frustration.

"Are you going to tell Rainey?" Dot's voice was quieter now. "She has a right to know where her mom is."

"It's why I brought this up to you." Anger and exasperation had left his tone, replaced by concern. "I know she's older now, but she seems to wig out whenever this happens. Her mom gets clean. Rainey goes to see Anna, then gets her hopes up. Her mother relapses, and our daughter isn't quite right for a while."

"Do you think Anna's relapses have anything to do with Sarah's accidents?" That part was almost whispered.

Frank's response was not. A fist or palm slammed against wood. "No, Dot! I hate when you say that. Your daughter is clumsy. Kind of like you are."

"I'm not—"

"I love you, anyway," Frank cut off whatever Dot was going to say. "I love Sarah. Rainey has always tried to help Sarah anytime something happens. I'm not sure why you and Sarah are so hard on Rainey."

"Sorry. You're right. Rainey loves her like a sister. Let's keep the mom stuff to ourselves for now. If she can stay clean for more than a month or two, then let's talk about it again. Okay?"

"Fair enough. I wish I'd married you the first time around," Frank had said.

Back from the past, Cooley's eyes shifted, landed on mine. She said, "His voice had started to sound the way Daddy's did when he and Momma went to their room. I know I went back up to Sarah's room. I'm not even sure I got the cookies. I was just so surprised at what they were saying. I'm not sure I had known they'd had a different mother. I knew they were six years apart, but as a kid I wasn't really doing the math and figuring out marriage and babies. I asked Daddy about it as soon as I got home. He explained what addiction did to people. Not on the family around them, but the person who drank or took the drugs. Until then, I guess I'd never really thought about it. But it made me way more sympathetic to Rainey...Lori Pope, that is."

I paused for a long moment, trying to fit this whole other side of *the* county prosecutor into my vision of her. Sadly, I'd paid almost zero attention to her first election, so I wasn't even sure if her past was common knowledge or fodder she'd used to pander to voters.

"So it's just a chip on her shoulder?" I asked, boiling it down to the most basic of human behaviors.

"I think so." Cooley shrugged. "She never liked me. But I could see that if she thinks I had something to do with Sarah's death, her being mad, I guess. I never thought she liked Sarah much. Maybe blood is really thicker than water, or my enemy's enemy is my friend kind of thing."

"Maybe," I mused. Though prosecutors were supposed to be objective and fair in prosecutions, there was leeway for human behavior. And even if not, there were checks and balances built in where someone senior had to sign off and the added layer, though as holey as Swiss cheese, of the grand jury.

"What happened in that other case?" Cooley asked. "The one with charges like mine?"

"The judge read the prosecutor the riot act. Accused her of overcharging."

"And?" She'd shifted to the edge of her seat.

"My client only had to plead to a misdemeanor."

"Misdemeanor?"

"No jail time. No felony record. Community service. Probation."

Cooley sat hunched for a long moment, taking in what I'd shared. She shook her head.

"I'd rather walk away because I'm innocent. But I'm a black woman in Cleveland. I know that sometimes we have to make sacrifices. You think I'll get out from under this if I take a slap on the wrist like your other client?" For the first time since Cooley had walked in my door, her body visibly relaxed—if only a little.

I looked at the papers one more time. Judge Kate Marsh's name was stamped on there. She wasn't exactly defense friendly, but she wasn't a former prosecutor, either. Marsh was a neutral judge. That was a rare thing on the bench.

"I'm not a betting man"—my voice was conspiratorial—"but I think you have a really great chance to get out from under this with your dignity and freedom intact."

Relief from prosecution was a greater balm than a slap on the wrist. Knowing there was a way out, however narrow, showed me a version of Tyisha Cooley that everyone else got to see. A handsome woman whose life had moved mostly on an even keel. This time when she leaned toward me, I knew it was only for practicality sake.

"So where do I sign? And how much is this going to cost me?"

18

I'm not sure if I ever believed in God, but right now I was praying that Wayne Cooley would answer the door. It had already been a couple of minutes without any response. I pressed the buzzer a third time for good measure. Finally, I saw him running down the stairs in shorts and socks. He pulled open the glass door to the building. He stood on the inside, I on the outside when no immediate invitation was forthcoming.

"Sarah? Is that you?" He looked at his wrist, then realized it was bare. "What time *is* it?"

"It's late. I know. I'm sorry," I blurted. I didn't want to answer the time question because it wasn't a decent hour for company by any polite standard.

And if there was one thing I knew about the Cooleys, it was that they followed all the rules of etiquette spoken and unspoken. "I just didn't know where else to go."

Wayne's face was a squint of confusion. "Go?"

I hoisted my duffle so he could see it. "Dad kicked me out."

"What?" Realization dawned. He stepped back and motioned me inside. "Come on upstairs."

I followed him up the steps all the while looking around. It was a new brick apartment building in Brooklyn. I wondered if there were other Negroes here. Or why he was living on the westside. I didn't ask anything about any of that, just watched him fiddle with a key and the door. After I dropped my duffle, I walked into the living room. There was a woman sitting on the plaid couch. She had a glass in her hand. Probably had beer in it. She looked very comfortable. In an instant I understood why he'd taken so long to come down, why he had no shoes, why he had no watch. Oh, God. This was a very bad time to have come.

"You have company," I sputtered as I tried to back out of the apartment, but Wayne grabbed my arm. "I'm so sorry," I whispered for his ears only as he steered me back inside and closed the door behind us.

"Mary, this is Sarah. She's my sister's best friend."

"Hi. Um. You have the same name as his mom?" It was probably the stupidest question I could have asked.

This much younger Mary put her glass down on the table. "Wayne, I'll go. This doesn't appear to be a good time."

"You don't have to—" Wayne protested.

She waved a hand. Interrupted before he could say more. "Call me later. I'll get a bus. Don't worry."

Before I could object or Wayne could get words out convincing her otherwise, Mary put on a rain jacket and slipped rubber galoshes over her shoes. She picked up an umbrella I hadn't seen and let herself out. After his door closed a second time, I spun on my heel at a loss for what to do.

"I didn't mean—"

His wave was as nonchalant as Mary's had been.

"She's just a girl. We've been dating a couple of months. She's not as important to me as you are. Don't worry about Mary. She can take care of herself. Answer *my* question. What do you mean your dad kicked you out?"

All the hurt and humiliation I'd felt over the last hours landed on my shoulders like the kind of yoke you saw on those historic black-and-white pictures of oxen trying to tame the Midwest soil. I wanted to tell Wayne *everything*. Like no one else I could think of, he wouldn't judge me. He'd probably even make me feel better. But first, I needed just a little more space and time from the situation. Time to absorb what had actually happened.

Maybe even something to make me feel…less. I'd never told anyone, but over the last few months, I'd snuck a beer here and there from the fridge. I'm sure

Momma and Daddy suspected Rainey. Neither one of them would say anything to *her*, though. I think they were a little afraid of her, too.

"Can I have one of those beers?" I gestured to the leftovers on the coffee table.

Wayne eyed me. "You're not eighteen."

"I feel like I'm forty."

He looked me up and down again. Decided something. Then went and got me a beer and a second one for himself. Without saying a word, he went back to the kitchen for a bottle opener and pried the caps off. I picked up the small circle of gold colored metal, then ran the pads of my fingers along the grooved edges. Looking around, I really took in the apartment. There was the couch I was sitting on. A brown La-Z-Boy was near the living room window. It was dark, but I could see the street lights filtered through the trees.

"Are you going to put something up over the window?"

"You sound like Ma. It's the third floor. No one can see in."

His third floor apartment in this new brick building was located not more than a few miles from my parents' house. It was convenient considering what had happened with my father kicking me out and all, but it was kind of weird.

"I can't believe you live here," I said. It was really a question, but a rude one wrapped in a statement.

"In this apartment?"

"No, you know. On the westside. There aren't many...Negroes out here." With the Cooleys, it was mostly okay to say the quiet part out loud. Even when what I asked or what I said was...insensitive or impolite, they mostly answered matter-of-factly. Usually that was accompanied by a mini history lesson from Mr. Cooley. It was amazing what school teachers in Rocky River left out.

"Maybe I'm the trailblazer." My mind flashed on those news clips of those Negroes desegregating schools in the south with the National Guard preventing them from going in and the Army guys on the other side making sure they could. If everything was like that for them, I had to applaud him. I wasn't that brave. Maybe Wayne was.

"Seriously?" I probed. The westside didn't have the national guard. But I was starting to learn there were other ways to keep people from where they weren't wanted.

"No. Sarah. I was joking, really." I didn't want to feel relief, but I did. He continued, "I moved here because it's close to my new job."

"Do you like it? Engineering?"

Wayne shrugged. We both knew his choice of job was more his father's than his.

"It's no better or worse than any other job, I expect. Pays well."

I didn't want any old job, going to an office every day, being bored out of my mind typing and filing. I wanted to be a novelist, holed up in a dusty apartment writing out the stories in my head. I took a swallow of the bitter pale liquid. Looked like Daddy and Rainey had pulled the liberal arts rug out from under me and my path was no longer assured.

"That your girlfriend? Mary?" I asked. The more questions I asked of Wayne, the fewer he'd ask of me.

Wayne pointed the neck of his bottle at me then him. His smile was big. "Once I realized you and I were never going to be a couple, I had to look elsewhere."

Something about his words took all the fight out of me. I kicked off my sneakers, pulled my legs up on his couch and took a long drag from the green bottle.

I'd loved that he had a crush on me. For a few long weeks, I even thought about going out with him. It would have been so easy, choosing Wayne. Maybe we could have gotten married. Then I would have been safe in the bosom of the Cooley family. Free from Rainey. I couldn't imagine her trying to get at me there.

For the first time in a long time, I indulged in the fantasy again. Mary and Nelson would have been my parents. Tyisha would have been my sister. I could have read all the books I wanted without anyone making fun of me. I'd have learned how to make all of the good food they ate. The Cooleys would have been my children's grandparents.

For all those reasons, I'd almost done it. Pretended to be something I'm not just to get that promised future. But I'd been hiding and pretending and covering up for as long as I could remember and I just couldn't do it to Wayne. Lie to the Cooleys. So instead of a Sarah, there was a Mary.

Wayne put his beer on the glass-topped coffee table, then turned toward me. I took another long drink, emptying my bottle, then I put mine next to his. It was time to talk about why I'd barged in on his date.

"What's in the duffel?" He kicked his socked foot toward the front door where my bag had landed.

"Everything I could fit."

"What in the heck happened, Sarah Rose? Did you have some kind of fight with Rainey?"

For once I wished it had been as simple as one of Rainey's pranks.

"I had a friend over," I started. Wayne was no dummy. After seven years, he could read me almost as well as Tyisha could.

"Friend?" His left eyebrow rose just a little.

"Gwen Simpson." I said her name like a prayer. "She's my...I..." I couldn't begin to find the right words for Gwen. Wayne waved a hand at me letting me know I could skip that part of the story, at least for now.

"What happened?"

Skipping part of the story had gotten me where I was right now. I was done keeping secrets. I closed my eyes, reliving the scene. "It started out good," I said.

"Do your parents know about me?" Gwen Simpson had asked as we walked up the stairs to my room six hours ago. We'd been next to each other, shoulder to shoulder. I was holding tight to her hand, as if she could disappear at any moment. I sort of knew what she was getting at, but there was no way I wanted to talk about it then or any time ever, really.

"There's nothing to tell them." There would never be anything to tell them. I was trying to be as invisible as possible. It was only four and a half months before I was safely a first-year student at Bryn Mawr. Once I escaped to Pennsylvania, I wasn't planning on ever coming back.

"Then why are we hiding out in your room?" Gwen asked after I'd pushed my door nearly closed.

"We're not hiding out exactly," I lied. "My sister is a pain and I don't want to deal with her." That part was the absolute truth.

"You're seventeen." Gwen kicked off her shoes and scooted onto my bed, propping up my pillows against the wall. She looked comfortable. I liked the look of her against the orange and brown shams I'd crocheted. "How old is your sister?" she asked.

"Rainey? Twenty-three."

"Then why are you worried what she thinks? I haven't really fought with my brothers or sisters since I was twelve. Everyone outgrows that phase."

"Rainey's different." I didn't want to go into it. That's not the reason I'd asked her to come over. One hundred percent not the reason.

"Oh, you're just paranoid," she scoffed as she played with the yarn fringe.

I had to ignore that. Gwen had said what every-one said. They were always wrong. I didn't want to think about how misguided all the unhelpful advice was. Instead, I firmly shut my bedroom door. Gwen may have gotten along with her brothers and sisters, but there were far too many of them in her house. There wasn't any quiet or even anywhere private to spend time. I only had Rainey, and if she weren't around, then we had nothing but uninterrupted time together. I wanted to make the most of it.

I walked to the edge of my twin bed. Took her hand. Intertwined our fingers—the thing I always wanted to do outside but couldn't. Cleveland wasn't New York or Los Angeles. It wasn't one of those cities where girls could hold each other's hands. But in here, in my little corner of Rocky River, behind my own closed wood door, I could.

"I've been thinking about you, you know." I swallowed hard. Saying things like this to her was super hard for me.

"Thinking?" Gwen's blink was slow. "I'm right here."

"And we're here. All alone, for once." I squeezed her hands.

"That's why we're here all closed up in your bedroom? You want me alone?" Her smile was small, but was getting bigger by the moment as understanding finally dawned.

"I love your family. There are a lot of them, though."

"You didn't invite me here to talk about your sister or my family, did you?" Her smile was bigger, her eyes clouding over with the same desire that was rushing through my own body.

"No." I wanted so much more than kissing in dark movie theaters and holding hands in the shadows. I didn't have the guts to say any of that. But at least I had the guts to get her here alone.

I squeezed her hand again, pulled her where I wanted her—closer to me. I didn't have to say anything more, because before I knew it, she was kissing me. It was the most amazing sensation. Sometimes I never thought I'd get over my feelings for Tyisha, but when my brain went fuzzy a moment later, I was starting to think I could.

Gwen's plaid bell bottoms only had one button and a short zipper. My minidress was over my head in a matter of seconds. I kissed my way up from her belly button to her halter top. It took two hands to untie the yellow cotton knot. She wasn't wearing a bra. I couldn't keep my hands away from her breasts. My right one covered her flesh.

When I felt her nipple against my palm, I could scarcely breathe. I didn't think I'd ever get air in my lungs again. I didn't care if two girls weren't right, it was what I wanted. My desire overcame my usual caution because it was too late by the time I heard the door open. Wood banged against the doorstop so hard it nearly closed again. My father's palm slammed against it.

"Rainey said—"

"Daddy!"

I watched his eyes scan all four corners of my room, take in everything. There was nowhere to run. No way to hide.

"What in the hell are you doing? Who is this?"

I reached for the blanket at the end of my bed and threw it over my girlfriend.

"This is Gwen, Daddy. She's a…friend…from school." I wanted to kill myself for that hesitation, although I didn't think there was any right word that would have pleased my father.

"She looks like a lot more than a friend." His voice was whisper soft. In his full uniform, gun strapped to his side, it was just a little bit scary. I'd never before been afraid of him.

"Daddy, I can explain—"

"Gwen I-don't-know-your-last-name," he interrupted. "Can you make your way home? I need to speak with my daughter here—alone."

Under the blanket, Gwen had already pulled on most of her clothes by the time Daddy finished speaking.

"Yes, sir. Of course." She threw off the covering, picked up her shoes and ran down the stairs. I heard the front door open and slam closed. Again, I was alone.

"Daddy. I'm sorry," I started when I noticed he was looking at me with an odd expression. Oh God, I was still half dressed. I scrambled to get my dress back on. Daddy at least had the good manners to look away.

"What were you doing?" he asked after I turned back to him. I couldn't meet his eyes, but the way he looked at my legs made me pull the hem as far down as I could.

"Gwen is my friend," I offered.

"Looks like a lot more than your friend."

"I can explain."

"What's there to explain?" That question came from Rainey. I don't know when she'd appeared, but my older sister was standing in the doorway, her back against the jamb. Of course I knew she'd been the one to send Daddy in here. Lord knows what she'd said to him before he'd stormed through the door.

I looked from her to him, and got really scared. Daddy had always taken Rainey's side, but he still had a soft spot for me. I was his daughter from Mommy. The woman he claimed to love more than anyone else in the world. She wasn't a druggie. She cooked and cleaned and kept our lives on track. He had to love my momma more than he loved Rainey's mother. He had to love me at least as much as Rainey, even if he liked her better.

"Gwen. I…" I tried to think of a lie. An explanation that could work. My mouth opened and closed like a fish out of water.

"Spit it out!" he demanded, leaving me no time to think up something.

"I love her, Daddy," I blurted. "She's my girl-friend. Like if she were my boyfriend, only she's a girl."

"Rainey here had said as much, but I didn't think it could be true. Not from you, my little Sarah Rose. I've been more open-minded than most parents. After all, I let you spend time with that Negro family. But this…this is one step too far."

"Why, Daddy? I really like her. We're not hurting anybody."

"It's not right. This isn't what God had in mind."

"Since when do we believe in God?" I could count the number of times we'd been to church on one hand. Two weddings. One baptism. A funeral.

I didn't see the slap coming. But I felt the sting. My hand flew to my cheek. It would swell.

"God is everything!" Daddy yelled. "Who are you? I don't even know who you are."

"I'm sorry," I said, though I didn't have any idea what I was sorry for.

"So, then you'll have no problem." I turned toward the door. Rainey had put a bug in Daddy's ear.

"Doing what?"

"Giving her up. You're not to see that girl again. Or any girl in that way, for that matter."

"We're not hurting anyone." I was too old to whine, but I heard it in my voice anyway.

"Are you saying you're going to disobey me?" Daddy was getting very red in the face. It was the angriest I'd ever seen him.

"No, Daddy, I won't do it. I'm so tired of having to do what everyone wants. Tiptoeing around Rainey. I'm your daughter same as her. I have a right to be here and live my life. I don't hurt anybody. I

won't be in your hair much longer anyway. Graduation is next month. I'll be in school in Pennsylvania—
"

"What's it called again? That out of state school
you want to go to."

"Bryn Mawr, Daddy," Rainey drawled. "Bowling
Green or Ohio State weren't good enough for her, remember." That took me back to the discussion last
fall when I'd been filling out my applications and I'd
had to explain casting a wide net beyond Ohio. "It's
an all-*girls* school. She's been fooling you all along
with this liberal arts stuff and classical education
nonsense. She could have gone to Oberlin if any of
those was important. This is about being able to be
around nothing but women."

"Is that true?" Daddy's head whipped back to me.
He'd taken in every word Rainey had said like he was
mesmerized.

I wanted to deny it. I did. It hadn't been my first
reason for going. Tyisha had suggested the Seven Sisters. She was going to an all-Negro girls' school in
Atlanta. Obviously I couldn't go there, but after some
research, I'd decided Bryn Mawr was the next best
thing. I could even take creative writing classes. Tyisha didn't want to be a writer anymore. Her parents
had talked her into eventually doing something more
practical. But I still wanted to be a writer. I thought
I could move to New York. Live in a tiny apartment.
Write a novel. Fall in love. Be safe.

"IS THAT TRUE?" Daddy was yelling. His face
was turning a darker shade of red. I didn't know why

he was so angry. I hadn't really done anything that could hurt anyone, let alone our family.

"No…Daddy. It's a really good school."

"Bowling Green not good enough for you?" He'd never said it out loud like this. I knew he thought it was weird, me wanting to go farther away than my sister. But I'd convinced him and Momma it would be best. I had thought that me being far from Rainey had been part of the reason they'd gone for it. They wouldn't have to take sides in our fights any more.

"It's just a different kind of school," I tried. When he didn't look convinced, I went a different way. I'd probably already lost Gwen. I didn't want to lose my escape route as well. "Our school guidance counselor said that each person should choose the right school for them."

"Right school for them." He nodded. I waited. At least his face was returning to its regular color. "You've been around all these people too long. The Cooleys with their uppity nature. This Gwen. They're all making you into someone different."

"That's not—"

He swiped his hand at me. I'd clammed up.

"You need to give them all up." The wave of his hand had, just like that, swept away my future plans. "Let Rainey here guide you. She's doing life like it should be done. Not shooting too high for people like us."

"I'm seventeen years old. I don't need Rainey's help," I'd said, but by then it was obvious he wasn't listening.

Back in the apartment with Wayne, after that monologue, I looked at him. Tried not to cry at all the sympathy and kindness there.

"It's like my sister has him under some kind of spell sometimes. When he's like this, there's no reasoning with him. I tried for another, I don't know, ten or fifteen minutes. After all my begging and pleading and explaining, he gave me an ultimatum. Give up Gwen. Give up that school or get out. Maybe he'd have been better in the morning. I'm not sure. But I didn't want to stay. Not with Rainey there. Not anymore."

I got up and went to the kitchen. Took out another two beers. Found the opener and popped the tops. Added them to the collection on the table.

"You thought you were in danger?" He left out the word "again." "Can you ever be safe there, Sarah?"

"Maybe not tomorrow. But I was hoping I could stay here for a few days. I know Daddy will calm down. He's never angry for too long."

I took a big swig of the beer, trying not to spit out the bitter brew. The way it would make me feel in twenty minutes would be worth it.

"Like it?" He could tell that I didn't much.

"Bitter. I don't know why people like this."

"They like the effect. Give it a few minutes to hit you." I didn't tell him I already knew, which is why I'd asked for it. Staying at his place for a week was a lot. I backtracked. He hadn't exactly said yes. Maybe I needed more to convince him.

"Rainey came in. Daddy was right behind her. He said I was an abomination." I'd left out that part because it was embarrassing.

"I thought you said he was on your side. That you had someone there who could keep Rainey in check. That your mom was that person. Where was she today? How is it you think you can ever go back there, Sarah? I don't think it's safe."

"I just said that so you and Mr. Cooley wouldn't do anything. They always believed her over me. I'm not sure they even believed her. I think that they mostly felt sorry for her. Her mom is a junkie—"

"If you've said that once, you've said it one hundred times. That's no excuse for anything that she's done to you. If I learned anything living in Hough, it was that. People are quick to put blame on others, the welfare system, the cops, the 'man.' They're right. Those things aren't fair. An explanation is not an excuse. People are responsible for their actions. There's no one to blame for anything here but Rainey."

"Even if you're right, Wayne, what do I do now?"

"What exactly did he say?"

"That he wasn't paying for me to get a fancy degree at Bryn Mawr. Rainey was standing right there egging him on. Saying I wanted to go to an all-girls college because...not because it's a good school."

"It's not just good, it's a Seven Sisters school. It's a topflight education," Wayne argued, incensed on my behalf.

"If Bowling Green was good enough for Rainey—"

"You told me all that. Here's my question. Is this about the school or the other thing?"

I didn't have to think before answering. I wasn't blind to the truth of my father's biases.

"It's mostly about me liking girls. I think they all long suspected it because of how close I was with Tyisha. But we didn't talk about it, ever, because there was the plausible excuse of just being really close girlfriends. I was just planning to go to college and it wouldn't have ever come up. I only had to make it three or four more months. But I kissed Gwen at this party a few weeks ago and I couldn't stop thinking about her. She invited me to her house, and I thought that would be perfect, except she has a big family in a tiny bungalow in Parma."

"You wanted to be alone." He reached over, grabbed my hand. Patted it. "It's a natural impulse."

"I should have been able to control that, right? I feel like a pervert. It was only a few months more."

"Desire doesn't make you a pervert. It makes you human."

His compassion made me want to cry. I sniffed back the tears.

"I don't have anywhere to go."

"You can stay here."

I'd been hoping against hope he'd say that. The only other alternative I had was his parents' house. But they'd ask too many questions I didn't want to answer. Everything in me relaxed. I slouched against the couch, suddenly exhausted. All the fight gone from me.

"For real? It'll only be a couple of nights. I'm sure once Momma is back, Daddy won't be mad anymore and I can go back."

"Maybe you shouldn't go back."

"What? Why not? How?"

"Because your parents let Rainey get away with hurting you." I nearly dropped the beer. It was a miracle that I caught it. Wayne didn't even blink at my clumsiness. His stare at me remained unblinking. "There. I said it out loud."

"It's not—"

Wayne's hand made a swift violent motion in the air, cutting off my explanation.

"Don't you dare say it's not that bad. She burned you. She broke your arm *and* leg. She killed your dog. And now she may have pulled the college rug from up under your feet. I don't want you dead."

"She's not going to kill me."

"She already tried."

I'm pretty sure we were thinking the same thing. The night Rainey had left me in Hough. The night I'd met all the other Cooleys. The first time his family had saved me.

19

If I'd thought my earlier cases were an uphill battle, prosecuting Tyisha Cooley was going to be like climbing Mount Everest. Any prosecuting attorney worth their weight could indict a ham sandwich. Actually *convicting* America's favorite lunch, now that was a lot harder.

Darlene Webb was in my office sitting on the other side of my desk. After our last case where we'd charged the wrong defendant, I didn't think either one of us would be here gainfully employed, much less working on another case.

"Where does she work?" I asked.

"Key Bank."

I looked over to my window. It didn't face south, otherwise I'd have a view of Cleveland's tallest skyscraper, which Tyisha's employer owned. I sighed and sat more heavily in my chair. Tried not to roll my eyes into the back of my head. Something told me this was going to tell me a story of the impressive life history of a solid citizen. The kind of person we wanted in a jury box, not behind a defense table.

"How long has she been there? At the bank?"

"Seventeen years. She's some kind of compliance officer. Cleveland Clinic before that."

"Oh, gosh, law adjacent. Says she's a rule follower. Not great for a jury. Whoever represents her will use the word so much, we'll all have a case of semantic satiation."

"What word? What do you mean, sati—"

I cut her off. Explained. "Compliance is the word. The other is when you say a word so much it loses its meaning." Then I switched back. "Any history of arrest, conviction?"

Webb shook her head oh-so-slowly, emphasizing Cooley's lack of visible vices.

"Traffic violations?" I tried, desperate. I could work with a moving violation. Make Cooley running a red light look like she was ready to mow down moms and babies in strollers at an intersection.

"Clean as a whistle." Webb wasn't even looking at her papers. Probably because there wasn't anything to see.

"So her only crime was being friends with an addict?"

"And killing her," Webb reminded me. "According to your boss, and thanks to that, now mine as well."

So now we were getting squeezed from all sides. I'd wanted to be head of Major Crimes. Get ahead. Make up for the past. Make a name for myself. But for a singular moment, I really missed putting children in juvy lockup. That was as easy as pie. And because the court cases involving minors were sealed, politics or media were hardly ever a factor. If attacking Cooley's character wasn't going to work, I needed to come at this from a different angle.

"Okay. Did you look into that Wayne thing?"

"Had to. Of all the things, I didn't expect to walk into that situation. I mean, I know people make assumptions when we ask questions. But never one hundred eighty degrees off like that."

I didn't want to rehash or relive that little scene with Tyisha and her father, both of them practically in tears while we were there to figure out how to put the sister of a murder victim in jail for...murder. It was a clusterfuck.

"Is there a story?" I threw up my hands hoping Webb would toss me a bone for this dog of a case.

Webb opened her bag, pulled out a murder file. It was thinner than any I'd ever seen. Didn't bode well. She flipped open the blue cover.

"The people there at the time were...sketchy. We talked about that earlier. Sarah Pope had a pretty consistent group of...user friends. But they were all inside when Wayne got shot. Perfect alibis for all of them. The worst of the bunch was Daniels…Zachary. He was a dealer. Had a few thousand in cash on him when the police got there, but no drugs."

"Dumped them?" My question was rhetorical. Only stupid drug dealers were caught dirty. Most weren't that stupid.

"Probably. They were partying. Coke. Heroin. Pizza. Beer. No gun shot residue on any of them. No weapon found in the house. They were high, and maybe drunk, but not killers."

"Did someone follow the dealer…Daniels, did you say his name was? Some guy think the black guy outside with the fancy car was the dealer instead of the guy inside with…"

Webb scanned the file. "Daniels' car was a Toyota Corolla. That was the working theory in the beginning. Bullet was meant for him and someone shot Cooley instead. Wrong place, wrong time kind of thing."

"And then…what?" Murder cases were rarely abandoned at the first setback. "Who were the detectives on the case? Are they still with the department?"

"And then nothing. I'm not sure of the politics around this case then, but there wasn't much of an investigation. Both detectives—a Rocco Nicola and Thomas O'Callaghan—were senior, both a few months from retirement. Apparently, Wayne woke briefly at the hospital before he died, but he didn't know much."

"Did he say something? Anything?" A dying declaration was an exception to hearsay. If he'd named his killer, that person was as good as convicted.

"When the detectives got to the hospital, his sister was there. All he said was that she needed to watch out for Sarah because she was in danger."

"Was the bullet meant for her?"

"What I'm telling you is all I know," the detective answered. "The forty-five caliber didn't come with an invitation or introduction."

"Okay, that doesn't feel like it's related. I don't think whoever her lawyer ends up being will raise it during trial. I say we keep the Wayne Cooley file out of storage, but put it aside for now."

"Agreed."

I kicked off my shoes, but kept that fact hidden from Webb. Pulled a new yellow pad off a stack from the credenza behind me, clicked my pen, and got ready.

"Let's start with what *we* know. First, what was the date of Sarah's death?"

"July of last year. The twentieth to be exact. It was a Friday."

"Anything special about that day? It's after the holiday."

"Addicts don't need a special occasion to get high."

For a brief moment I thought she was talking to me, *about me*. But she didn't *know*. And if she did, Webb wouldn't dare. I leaned my elbows on the desk.

Summoned up my engaged face. This case was going to be a dog I couldn't shake.

"From looking at all the reports, what's your best guess as to what happened?" I asked Webb. She wasn't the most creative. But I had to start somewhere.

"She was probably partying...getting high with her regular band of cohorts and was either crashing at her friend's house or using it without her friend's permission. No one asked those questions, given there was no investigation opened."

"You don't have to keep making excuses. I get it. We had one policy in the county. Overdoses weren't suspicious deaths unless there was evidence. Now Pope has another—off the books—policy and you're feeling caught up short. Don't worry. We all are. Between you and me, no need to justify. If it comes to that later, we'll deal with it."

Webb, if not exactly agreeing, nodded.

"So she was partying. Pills, booze, and heroin, probably. They had *Call of Duty* up on the flatscreen TV. Tyisha came home and asked the friends to leave, or maybe they just did because it was clear she was straightlaced. The only one who stayed around was this guy Ja Roach, whose name you love, though I'm not sure why. According to him, Sarah was coming down pretty hard and the withdrawal symptoms were starting. The shaking. The sweating. That tweaker look addicts get when their last fix was too far away. Tyisha starts pleading with her to get help. Go into rehab. Sarah's crying, nose running, agrees that she'll do it this time. *Finally.* But she needs one last fix until they can find a bed. Mind you, it's Friday night. Not exactly prime rehab check-in time."

"Maybe it should be," I muttered under my breath. That's when it was needed. Rock bottom never happened on Tuesday at eleven a.m.

"So Sarah's too messed up to give herself an injection. Roach gets all squeamish."

"A squeamish user? You think he'd be an expert with needles."

Webb shrugged. Then continued, "So Tyisha gives some whole talk about morality or something, and then Ja Roach explains how to do it. He holds Sarah, and Tyisha does the one shot into some veins in her thigh."

"Oh God, she was that bad." The indignity of late stage intravenous drug use was pretty awful. Drinking looked as sophisticated the last day as it did the first. Smoking as well, at least as long as you weren't doing it through your neck after removing your oxygen. Heroin needed a better delivery device.

"We're talking a thirty-year habit off and on from what I gather," Webb interrupted my thoughts. "She was sober for stretches, but none too long."

"Why the overdose? Obviously her body could tolerate a fairly wide array of dosages if she's been doing it that long. Street drugs aren't known for their consistency."

"Ja Roach made some noises about this being special. How some new dealer looking to establish new turf or get customers or whatever found them and

offered this one up for free with something added—
a synthetic anesthetic. Hold on." Webb flicked
through some printed pages. "Fentanyl. That's what
it probably was. The word on the street is that as the
Mexicans have gotten in the game, the price is going
down and competition is going up, so dealers are trying to differentiate their product."

"Capitalism of the drug trade?"

"America." Webb shrugged.

"Crap. There was no autopsy, though. No way to
validate the fentanyl theory. I don't know this Ja
Roach, but my gut says he wouldn't make good witness material."

"Nope on Ja Roach and Cooley, obviously, and
nope on the autopsy."

"Cremated?" I asked. Not that the county nor my
office had the money for an exhumation. Those kinds
of things only happened on television where the cops
and prosecutors had offices with good interior design
and lighting on the government's dime and everyone
wore Burberry raincoats on civil servant salaries.

"At Lori's direction. She was the closest living relative. Their parents moved to Arizona years ago."

"Did anyone else turn up over that weekend OD'd
on the same cocktail?"

"No."

"Is that unusual?"

"Yes and no. Sometimes there's a rash of ODs
when something new comes on the market. Sometimes it only affects the most vulnerable."

"Is there anything showing that Tyisha Cooley knew what was in the shot?" I was tired of beating around the bush.

"Other than Roach's speculation? No."

"How are we going to get a jury on board? We have a long time best friend. Long time addict. Fully employed compliance officer. Addict. Homeowner. Addict. Who do you think the jury's going to root for?"

"If the jury's from the westside, then maybe they'll side with Sarah. Sad white girl who wandered to the wrong side of town and died because of it...at the hands of a black woman."

I couldn't tell if Webb was being factual or racist. One issue with finding out I was black in my twenties was that I didn't have the experience to gauge things people said like my otherwise enlightened brethren could.

"That's the way you'd play it?" I asked. It was as neutral a question as I could manage.

"I'm not the lawyer. Just throwing it out there."

I let that go and decided to follow the only thread we had. I'd just have to play this one straight. Keep to the letter of the law and dare the jury to nullify. Couldn't really see any other way.

"Poke your head farther into this fentanyl theory," I ordered Webb. "Check all across the eastside or the county to see if there were any autopsies from ODs that weekend or the days around it."

Webb closed her pad. Shoved everything into a pile and then into her bag.

"I'll do everything you asked. Report back to you in a day or so. Is that it?"

"For now."

20

"What are you doing?" I wasn't exactly a naïve teenager in a cliché high school movie, so I couldn't see how trashing my best friend's house would be acceptable.

"You said I could make myself at home," Ja Roach insisted as he kicked off a second boot that went flying toward the same bay windowed wall of the dining room, narrowly missing the tiny diamond-shaped panes a second time.

"That's leaded glass. You have to be careful."

Tyisha had bought an old house like her parents' was. Though it was in a better neighborhood well east of where she grew up in Hough. I'd heard her talk about how much she loved the dining room's windows with their tiny panes of warped glass you could hardly see through.

"That's leaded glass," Roach mocked. He was not my favorite person in the world by any means, but he had the money my dealer was sure to ask for. I owed our supplier, and the man was getting impatient.

"When's he coming?" That was Randee. This new girl I'd never seen before tonight, Jodi nodded in concert with Randee, then she turned toward me expectantly.

I lifted the cordless phone that was still in my hand to indicate I'd done all that I could.

"I paged Zach. He's on his own schedule. Anybody want a beer? I'm going to the kitchen."

"Do you have anything besides that fancy stuff in the green bottle?" Jodi asked. "Like *real* beer."

When I'd been on the phone, apparently this one had helped herself to a tour. I only hoped that's all she'd helped herself to.

"I'll be sure to get you a Budweiser or a Miller," I said like I was a waitress. Actually, I'd been a server for a few months at Yours Truly. It hadn't been a bad place to work. Free breakfasts and customers who'd tipped well. The all-day breakfast restaurant fired me after not showing for Sunday brunch. They hadn't believed a single one of my flimsy excuses.

Dutifully, I went to Tyisha's kitchen and came back with four Heinekens, two in each hand. Passed them out and then got comfortable on Tyisha's sofa.

"You won the lottery or something?" Roach asked.

"No, why?" I tried to stop my heart beating out of my chest and not panic. "Did you bring the money we talked about?"

"I'm not sure you need it." When I squinted in question, he waved his hands at my temporary digs.

"I need it," I insisted.

"How you stayin' in this house, then?"

"It's my friend's house."

"You got rich friends?"

"She's not rich." It was a regular house, not like one of the grand ones on Fairmount Boulevard that measured their yards in acres. I didn't think he was looking for a comparison, so I kept that to myself. Instead I said, "She works at Society bank."

"Oh, that definitely means she's rich. Banks don't do nothing but spend your money. It's why I would never keep my money in a bank. Not when a lockbox works just fine."

I hoped he'd put a key in his box, opened it, and brought some of that stash of cash. He'd never quite answered my question.

The doorbell sounded, and I dropped my beer on my way to open the door. When I looked back, I could see that it had seeped into the couch cushions. Damn. I'd have to clean that one up later.

"You all look like you're ready to party," Zach said as he walked in. He was wearing a leather bomber jacket, even though snow dusted his shoulders.

"Do you have—"

"You owe me a hundred fifty."

I looked over at Roach. He lifted his pant cuff and pulled a wad of bills from his sock. Counted out some twenties and handed them over. Zach did a second count. Stuffed the wad into an inside pocket of the leather jacket. From somewhere else in his jacket, he produced one plastic baggie and a foil envelope.

"Want to stay?" Jodi asked.

I tried not to grit my teeth because I knew that Zach would take her up on the offer and snort half the drugs we'd just paid him for. I tried to catch Jodi's eyes, but she was too busy trying to seduce Randee or Zach. In the few months I'd known her, I'd watched her pay for her drugs without any actual currency.

Not interested in waiting to see what everyone else was doing, lest I get the short end of the stick, I tipped white powder from the baggie and made a line on the glass coffee table. I squinted when a pleasant familiar feeling rolled through me. I didn't have many of those. This glass-topped coffee table had to be a hand-me-down from Wayne. I was sure that it was the one from his apartment back when my dad had kicked me out.

The beauty of glass is that it's easy to get up everything. I took a second sniff. Wiped my nose and waited for the high. Looked for my beer to take another swig and realized that it had spilled into the couch cushions. Right. Damn. How had I forgotten that? I needed a towel.

I went to the bathroom and came back with one of the big bath towels. The doorbell rang again. Who in the heck could it be this time? It wasn't like I'd put out formal invitations or something. I didn't want Tyisha's place to get too crowded. She'd trusted me to watch her house while she was in Atlanta. If it ended up trashed, I don't think she'd let me stay here again. Towel in hand, I pulled open the door without checking the peephole.

"Hey…Wayne." I tried not to act surprised, or worse, guilty. "I didn't expect to see you here. Tyisha's not here. But she let me stay here. It's okay that I'm here."

I knew that I was speaking too fast, but if I couldn't remain, I had nowhere else to go. It was hard to find a couch or bed when it was cold and snowing. Everything would be taken. My car had been repossessed a couple of weeks earlier, so my normal safety net had big holes in it.

"It's okay, Sarah," he soothed. "Tyisha just told our parents is all." Wayne's voice was full of reassurance. It was something I'd heard time and again over the years.

"Oh, okay." Even though my shoulders came down from around my ears, I didn't budge from the doorway. "Did you need something?"

"It's really cold out here." Wayne's broad shoulders had him standing sideways in the tiny vestibule, half in and half out. My back was firmly against the inner door. Which was a thing people did when they wanted to keep the heat in, not necessarily when they wanted to hide something. When I ignored the hint, he got right to it. "Can I come in?"

"Um..." I fidgeted, uncomfortable. "I have some friends over." I hoped he took the hint this time.

"I'd love to meet them." I couldn't tell if it was that his manners were perfect or if he didn't trust me, but he didn't take the hint. Because of how he said it, using his perfect diction, I didn't know how to protest.

"Oh, okay. Um. Come on in." I turned the knob and pivoted in the frame like I was a door on a hinge.

When I got to the living room, there were a few more lines on the table. Like I suspected, Zach was doing three of them. The way this was going there wouldn't be anything left when Wayne was finally gone. By the time Wayne had wiped his feet, unwound his scarf and come into the room, the table was clean. Coke disappeared faster than snow flurries on a warm day.

"Zach?" He wiped his nose and looked up at our visitor. Gave Wayne a two-finger salute. "These are my friends, Randee and Jodie." A minute later, Ja Roach came back into the room. I hoped he'd only left for a potty break. "This is Ja Roach."

"Nice to meet you." Wayne didn't reach for anyone's hand. Just waved at the group. "This here is my sister's house. Just stopping by to check on the roof. It leaks sometimes when the ice freezes and thaws on warm days," he said to the room. To me, he said, "Did the plow come through?"

I nodded. "Snowed four inches yesterday. They come when it's more than an inch or two. It's come down a little since then. If they don't come back, I'll do it myself. We can all help. Want us to do it now?"

"No. Not now. Maybe in the morning. It's still coming down out there. Cold, too."

"Sorry. I forgot that I have to clean the couch. Made a mess over there." I couldn't calculate how long it had been since I'd spilled the beer. Ran over to the couch and felt around for the wet spot. Liquid came out when I pushed down. Immediately, I covered it with the towel. Pushed down until it was soaked. Damn, I was going to need another. Turning back around, I looked Wayne in the eye. "I'll fix that, no problem. Don't tell Tyisha, please."

He motioned for me to come closer to the door away from everyone else. They were talking and laughing and ready to party. The doorbell rang again. This time, it was a guy with three pizzas in hand. Roach was at the door in a minute with a new wad of cash he pushed into the delivery guy's hand.

After the delivery guy left back through the doorway, we followed him to the front step where it was quieter. The delivery guy got into a hatchback and drove away slowly, hazard lights blinking. Wayne took the first step. I pulled both doors closed this time, but kept my feet on the doormat.

"What's up?" I tried not to shift from foot to foot in my socks, but I was itching to get back in there to get mine before all the drugs were gone. To fix the sofa, so Tyisha wouldn't be mad. I could maybe clean it up so she never knew what happened. Also, my stomach was growling. Couldn't remember the last time I'd eaten anything.

"Mom and Dad are worried about you." Wayne didn't hide the fact that he was looking me up and down. I looped a finger in a belt loop, hitching up the jeans that were falling around my ass. It was hard to keep any weight on when I was walking everywhere nowadays.

"Tell them I'm fine." What I really meant was, tell them nothing, but I knew at this point he wouldn't keep that promise even if he made it. I waved my hand back at the door. "This is it, I promise. No one else is coming over."

"Do you even know these people?" Wayne cast a skeptical glance over my left shoulder just as a burst of laughter came from Tyisha's living room, audible even through the closed door.

I tried to look insulted. I wasn't sure I was mastering it.

"Of course. They're friends. I...well...I've had a few jobs over the years. Pick someone up at every one of them probably. People say I'm friendly." That was a big ol' lie I trusted he wouldn't probe at for the truth.

"I'm going home," he said, satisfied, I guess, that I wasn't going to burn his sister's house down. "It's going to be a long drive through the eastside. Less snow on the westside, but I have to get over there first."

"Are you driving that fancy new car?" I knew I was bouncing on the balls of my feet, but I couldn't figure out a way to stay still.

"It's just an Audi." Wayne was trying for modest. He may be succeeding, but his parents and sister had made that hard. They'd talked up his success and how this new car symbolized that.

"You like it?" I paced a tight square.

"Has heated seats. I like that for sure. I'll give you a ride, if you want."

"Now?" I looked up at the white sky. The snow was still falling.

"You have guests," he reminded me. "Another time, okay?"

"Right. They got pizza. Better get back in there before it's all gone. I lifted myself up on my tiptoes to embrace him in a hug. It was kind of awkward for the long moment when he didn't quite hug me back. I guess were weren't as close as we once were.

"Be good, Sarah. See you soon, okay? Maybe next Sunday the three of us can have brunch when Tyisha is back."

"As long as we don't go to Yours Truly." I'd meant it to be a joke, but Wayne winced.

Maybe he remembered the day when I'd gone to the restaurant to get my last check. I'd been a tiny bit high, and the manager had threatened to call the police when I'd gotten loud. They'd asked me for my uniform, and I hadn't a clue as to where I'd left the damned thing. They'd wanted to hold my check, but I'd already mapped out my route to a check cashing place where my dealer would meet me and wasn't having it. Eventually, I'd called Wayne to rescue me and help me get my money. He'd come without question, but had tried to talk me into rehab while he was driving me home.

"I'm sure we can find somewhere else," he said, bringing me back to the cold snowy night. "Eggs are everywhere."

"Okay. That'll be great. I can't wait."

"Go back inside. You're in socks."

"Oh, Jesus. You're right." Sometimes I needed people to point out the obvious. Once he mentioned it, I realized that despite staying on the mat, my feet were wet and getting colder by the moment. I ran back inside. Before I got the door closed, I heard something strange. A popping sound. Damn, maybe I did need to shovel. Sounds like Wayne had skidded and hit a garbage can, or worse, the mailbox. Grateful something wasn't my fault for once, I jammed my feet into my shoes and ran back outside to check if it was someone else. I'd need their info for Tyisha.

There wasn't any car in the street or near the driveway. Wayne's car wasn't running, either. The windshield was still dusted with snow and the motor wasn't humming. I ran across the lawn and bracketed my hands around my eyes. Pressed them to the car window. The car was empty. What the heck? I knew that I had hearing like Superman when I was high; I didn't think the noise had come from that far away.

"Wayne!" I screamed into the night. He couldn't be that far. Maybe he'd been hit by a car swerving on ice. I ran down the lawn to the street and saw new car tracks that were quickly being filled in. With the mailbox still standing on its post, I couldn't make sense of what I'd thought I'd heard. My head snapped right and left on my neck. No Wayne, though. God, he must have been hit. How far would he have been dragged? Would he have bounced off? Would there be blood?

"Call 911," someone croaked. I whipped around, trying to figure out where the voice was coming from, all along dreading what I might see. Life with Rainey had made me super scared of cries for help.

"Wayne?" I whisper shouted. I hoped beyond hope it wasn't him who would answer.

"I...someone shot me." The voice was getting hoarse.

I ran to the other side of the car. Wayne was laying on the ground. Red flecks dotted the snow around him. My mind was going at a million miles an hour from the coke, from fear. Even with my brain working overtime, I still couldn't figure out what was happening. There was no one around.

Just me.

And Wayne.

I ran to him and knelt in the snow. I patted his head, his chest. But gunshots were tiny and he was big.

"Where are you hurt?"

"My stomach. Call an ambulance."

"Oh. Oh my God! Okay."

Back into the house I went, through the living room, and into the kitchen. Ignored the panicked look on everyone's faces. Picked up the yellow phone and dialed emergency services as fast as I could. I wish Tyisha had listened to me and gotten a pushbutton. Finally it connected and I yelled into the phone.

"Please send help. *Please.* Wayne…someone has been shot."

21

"But what *happened*?" Tyisha's voice was frantic, pleading as if I were hiding something. I wanted to reassure her that I was telling the full truth. Given how the last few years had gone between us, I wasn't sure there was any way I could get her to believe me. "Can you please try to explain it to me again?" she asked. "This makes no sense. No sense at all. No one hates Wayne. Everyone loves Wayne."

"I love him, too."

We were on the other side of a double room at Cuyahoga County Hospital, the second bed empty. Wayne was attached to a load of apparatus that were keeping him alive. Doing everything his body otherwise couldn't. Each machine beeped or hissed its own rhythm.

"Did one of your…friends…do this?"

My best friend's normally warm stare was growing colder by the moment. I'd let her down so often. I needed her to know that this wasn't one of those times.

"Why would they?" I pleaded with my eyes.

"Because he had money and they needed drugs, Sarah. That's how it works, doesn't it. Addicts do whatever they have to get their fix. Whether that's pawn their best friend's electronics or shoot a guy for the twenty dollars in his wallet."

I wanted to say they'd had all the drugs they wanted just inside her house. I wanted to apologize *again* for the time my friends had all but cleaned her out of her new VCR and CD player, stereo and boom box, leaving nothing but a tangle of wire in their wake. I wanted to point out *I'd* never crossed that line, taken anything from her. She'd said back then it was a distinction without a difference. I thought it was a huge difference. That it mattered I hadn't really betrayed her. Except for having people over. Her one condition to me staying at her house after all that was that I be alone.

Which would obviously be the wrong thing to say. I shrugged. I'd already answered these questions when the police had asked. When the Cooleys had asked. Tyisha would have been home sooner if not for flight delays due to weather. So now this was her first go at me.

I was saved, if saved was the right word, from Tyisha's relentless questions when two Cleveland Heights detectives came into the room. They hadn't been in uniform two nights ago and they weren't this time, either.

"Are you the sister?" one of the detectives asked. I took in his ruddy complexion. I think he'd been the Irish one. O'Something if I remembered correctly.

"Tyisha Cooley." She put out her hand. It stayed outstretched for a bit. She didn't take it back until each of them had shook it. After that, the Irish guy who I'd figured for the lead, spoke up.

"Detective O'Callaghan. This is my partner, Detective Rocco. We're investigating your brother's assault."

"Assault? Not attempted murder?"

"It's been deemed suspicious. We don't put a label on anything until we know more," O'Callaghan said. "Early assumptions can hamper the investigation."

"Suspicious? He was gunned down in front of my house. In *Cleveland Heights*," she said, as if he'd been shot at the police station itself, instead of in a part of the town a little too close to the ghetto for comfort. "If that's not suspicious, I don't know what is."

"Ma'am, no need to get upset. In eighty percent of homicides, the killer was known to the victim. Geography doesn't change that."

"No one had a grudge against my brother. He was the nicest guy anyone could have ever known. Knows…"

"That's what your friend here said and we haven't come across anyone with a bad thing to say about him. Why was he living on the westside? It's unusual."

"He worked over there," I answered. Though I knew the question wasn't for me. It was a different kind of question than what they'd asked me. I knew Tyisha was family while I wasn't. I didn't think that was the difference, though.

"Did your brother ever have a problem with drugs? Maybe he was over on the other side of the river trying to avoid a dealer? Someone he owed?"

"For the last time," Tyisha huffed. I'd already told her blow by blow everything they'd asked me. "My brother wasn't involved with drugs. He was an engineer. I asked him to come over to the house."

"He wanted to check on the snow plow contract," I added, repeating the story I'd told a bunch of times already. "We talked about ice on the roof. Heaving or something…" I trailed off because I needed to contain my desire to scream, to tell them that they needed to leave Wayne alone. That he wasn't some criminal. That, in fact, *I* was the one with the druggie friends and a criminal record. And I might have done if I thought it would make Wayne wake up from his medically induced coma or if it would make them find his killer. They hadn't run me yet, though. Didn't come up yesterday. I'd been fidgety the whole time because I was pretty sure there was a warrant out for me and I wasn't in the mood to spend the night in lockup. I wanted to be exactly where I was, by Wayne's side.

"Did he have a girlfriend?" It was only the second time I'd heard Rocco speak.

Tyisha shook her head emphatically. "No. He told me about all of them. Met about half of them."

When Tyisha's eyes tried to seek out mine, I looked everywhere but at her. I was starting to feel a little bit of a craving. When I needed a hit, I had a hard time lying. Rather than speak, I just nodded in confirmation. Looked toward the door as if the Cooleys were on their way in, though I knew they were getting much needed fuel in the cafeteria.

Wayne *did* have a girlfriend. Maybe they were six months in. But it was looking like I'd been the only one he'd told about it. He'd kept this one secret, even from Tyisha because he wasn't sure his family would accept her. He wanted to make sure it was serious before introducing her. She was white *and* from Parma, a double whammy. I had to assume her family was in the dark as well, so to speak. I would have bet all the money I didn't have that she didn't have anything to do with this, so I made the decision to keep her name out of it.

Ready to escape for as long as it would take me to get a fix, I took a couple of steps away from the three toward the door. I would have made it out if the machines attached to Wayne hadn't started beeping at just that moment.

"What does that mean?" I asked, as if Wayne's sister or cops could answer that question. It didn't matter because in moments, someone in blue scrubs sped into the room, sneakers squeaking on the shiny floor. She pressed a button, quieting the noise, and immediately attended to Wayne.

"What's happening?" Tyisha asked as she practically ran to the bedside opposite the hospital worker.

"What's happening is that he's awake. I'm paging the doctor on call right now." A scratchy intercom came on just that moment, summoning someone to the room we were all in.

The detectives and I stood back as the woman in scrubs shone a pen light in his eyes and squeezed his hand, all the while maintaining a stream of chatter at the patient.

"Sarah?" Wayne croaked.

I made like Tyisha had and scooted to the bedside as well. I took his free hand in mine. It was warmer and dryer than I'd expected.

"I'm here. I'm okay. You're okay."

"Did I get shot?"

"Yes—" Detective O'Callaghan cut me short with a motion of his hand.

"Wayne Cooley. I'm the detective on your case. Can you tell me what happened?"

A white man in a whiter coat rushed in, stethoscope swinging.

"Excuse me," he said, cutting the detective short. "I need everyone out. I'll have the nurse let you know when you can come back in."

Ignoring the detectives, who looked like they had more questions, Tyisha pulled me into a small hallway nook.

"What aren't you telling me?" She pushed up the sleeves of her bulky sweater. I mimicked her movements with my own big sleeves.

"What. Nothing. Why—"

"I've known you for twenty-two years. I can tell when you're lying. It's usually about drugs, but I don't think so this time."

Tyisha reached out and grabbed at my shoulders. Shook me—hard.

"You have to tell me if you know who hurt Wayne. That's not a secret you get to keep, Sarah. Even if it's someone you know or have some kind relationship with or whatever. Wayne trumps any of that."

"I didn't lie," I lied.

"Sarah." My name from her mouth was two long drawn out syllables.

"I'm just...I need a fix, okay?"

"I thought you were getting into a program."

"Look, I am. Just need to find a bed is all. You know how it is. More users than free beds. It has to be, like, literally free too because I don't have any money. My parents certainly aren't going to help. I can't ask yours...not again."

"Sorry," she said, her chin dropping to her chest.

I relaxed because the talk about drugs and beds and money did exactly what I wanted it to do, discourage her from asking more questions.

"It's just that I maybe thought you knew more about Wayne's shooting than you were saying."

"I don't. Really I don't." *That* was the truth. "The police, they already talked to everybody who was there."

"Why was there an everybody? I thought we'd talked about this. Your so-called friends being at my house." Tyisha air quoted friends. "My couch smells like beer, by the way. Someone made a huge mess there."

A quick calculation in my head revealed I didn't have the money to replace an entire sofa.

"I'm sorry. I just didn't want to be alone. I was the one who made the mess, *by the way*." I'd long ago found that if I fessed up to the little things, the big things could fly under the radar a little bit longer.

"Let's talk about this later," Tyisha said as she looked over my shoulder. "That nurse is waving us in."

We both ran-walked to the room.

"Is he—"

"Can he—"

She cut off our questions. "Go in. I'm going to page your parents, so you can go in now until they come. Then you should switch. Only fifteen minutes, though. He has to rest."

"Can we talk to him?" That was from Detective O'Callaghan. Rocco obviously didn't have permission to talk.

"Later." Tyisha batted them away.

"We need to get his side of the story," O'Callaghan bellowed. "He's key to the investigation."

"He's key to my *life*." Tyisha's tone brooked no argument "Later. *Please*."

We walked in. The detectives didn't follow. We took up positions on either side of the narrow hospital bed.

"Wayne. It's me, Tyisha. And Sarah. Momma and Daddy are coming up any minute. Who hurt you?"

"I'm so glad you're awake." Looking at him. Seeing his eyes open. I could breathe, finally. I knew that this was somehow my fault. Everything always was. Maybe this one wouldn't end badly. That everyone I loved and everything I did wouldn't turn to shit—for once.

"Tyisha, I don't think I'm gonna make it," Wayne croaked.

"Don't say that." Her head shake was emphatic. "You're awake. Did the doctor say that to you—that you're going to die?"

"Doctors never tell you anything," Wayne whispered. "I need you to listen to me. Can you do that?"

"Sure. Okay." Tyisha leaned in closer. I did the same from my side.

"You're going to be fine." Wayne squeezed the hand his sister held. "I'm so glad about that." My best friend's brother turned to me. "Sarah, my dear girl. Tyisha, you need to promise me something."

"What?"

"That you'll take care of her. No matter what. She's going to need it. Even for a white girl, her life's gonna be hard."

"Okay, Wayne, but what about what happened?"

"Promise me first."

"I promise."

Then the machines went all alarm again. Only this time it was louder than the last. I didn't think that was good news. When a team of medical people rushed in with a cart full of equipment and implements wrapped in plastic, then ordered us out, I knew it was bad. The Cooleys were running down the hall, but an orderly stopped them from entering.

Five minutes later, at 11:03 a.m., a doctor pronounced Wayne Cooley—dead.

22

"Tyisha Cooley?"

"This is me. What can I do for you, officers?"

The Cleveland police officers had left the window open a small crack. Not so I could hear, but probably so I wouldn't suffocate. It was one of those cold, rainy, one hundred percent humidity days where it was impossible to get warm or comfortable. I was in a squad car on Brunswick Road in front of my best friend's house. The police had walked to her door and knocked loud and long enough to get her to come out. All three looked at each other warily. I imagine none of them were what the other had expected: her—police, them—a black woman.

I wasn't going to choke on my own breath, and I could see and hear what was going on as well as anyone could from fifteen feet away. I'd convinced the patrol officers not to issue a citation when they'd found me prowling the East Cleveland border looking for a fix. They agreed on the condition that they leave me somewhere with a responsible adult. While I wasn't a truant fifteen-year-old, I didn't protest because while a night with Tyisha might come with a lecture, a night in jail could come with any number of unknown dangers I wasn't much in the mood for.

"Do you know that woman in the car?" One of the uniformed officers lifted a small pad myopically close to his nose. "Sarah Rose Pope?"

"What's the issue?" Tyisha was being cagey—on purpose. Her dad always told these stories of how unsuspecting black folks could end up in a lineup and march themselves right into jail for something they didn't do if they answered too many questions. Mr. Cooley had always said the best approach for cops was to be quietly cooperative while never giving any information.

While I appreciated the reason for the whole song and dance, I wanted to get out of this car where the rain was starting to blow in through the window crack, and into my friend's house that I knew would be cozy and warm and maybe even have something good on the stove. Tyisha wasn't as good a cook as Mary Cooley, but sometimes she came pretty damned close.

"Do you know her?" the officer asked again, gesturing toward me in the car. I turned my face to the window.

Everyone was quiet for a moment, then the screen door opened again. I almost groaned out loud. Or maybe I did, but not loud enough for anyone to hear me from my position at the curb. It was Tyisha's boyfriend, Patrick Bailey.

He was as straight as an arrow and not my biggest fan. I had to wonder what he was doing at my friend's house on a Wednesday. Bailey was the kind of man who adhered to a very strict schedule. Tyisha was Friday and Saturday. His mother was Sunday. Weekdays were dedicated to reading the *Financial Times* or *Wall Street Journal* or whatever he did to make himself more money to buy more furniture to put in his big Glengary Road house he lived in alone

"Pat Bailey." He put most of his body in front of my friend's. "How can I help you, officers?"

"We don't want trouble, sir." I couldn't see the officers' faces. But their backs stiffened. The one without the pad in hand rested his on the butt of his weapon, his elbow jutting back.

If I could have gotten out of the police car, I would have. But there were no handles on the inside of the back door. And the cage over the front bench seat meant I couldn't escape the other way. Instead, I lifted my cuffed hands and banged on the window.

They both turned toward me with matching glares.

"Pipe down."

I banged again. If I knew anything, I knew they wouldn't hurt me. My father may have pulled a college education and even a safe place to rest my head out from up under me, but I could still exercise the friend of the family card. He'd left me that.

"Then what *do* you want if it isn't trouble?" Bailey's voice had gone from conciliatory to antagonistic.

"To know if you'll take responsibility for Sarah Pope. The woman there in the car."

Tyisha shouldered her way to the front again, stepping down one step. I couldn't see much of her with three men towering over her, but I could still hear.

"Yes, you can drop her here. Thank you for taking care of her. I'm sure her father, First District Deputy Commander Francis Pope, will be grateful for your care and discretion." Now *she* was using the friend of the family card.

"Yes, of course." The one with the hand on the gun dropped his arm. "We'll go get her."

They turned on their heels and came down the walk. Pulling open the passenger door, they lifted me out a lot more gently than they'd put me in. One of them took the small key from his belt and undid the cuffs that held my hands to my front. I shook out my stiff arms, not minding the rain coming down on my head and shoulders now that I was free. They walked me up to the door and handed me off to my friend and her boyfriend without a word. We were all in the house, door firmly shut, before the squad car drove away.

Before I could explain what had brought me to their doorstep on a Wednesday, my eyes snapped to the muted television. On top of the CNN banner was a grainy video. It took me a good thirty seconds to figure out what I was looking at.

"Oh my God, is that video of police beating someone?"

"Some guy named Rodney King," Bailey said. "Tried to run from the police."

"Where? Here?" I couldn't make out any familiar landmarks in the colorless video.

"Los Angeles."

My shoulders dropped. "At least it's not Cleveland."

"Could be here or anywhere in America," Tyisha said. She lifted the remote as if to turn it off or change the channel, but her hand dropped to her side. It was hard to look away.

"I guess it's a good thing my father's a cop. Saved my bacon a time or ten."

"Including tonight," Bailey concluded.

"They thought I was soliciting."

"You weren't?"

"I don't…that's not." I tried not to be hurt that my friend's boyfriend thought of me that way. More emphatically than necessary, I said, "No. I was just looking for someone on Euclid, near Shaw High school."

"There was something in the paper the other day about an active police sting over there arresting johns," Tyisha said, eyeing Bailey.

"Didn't know that," I said. It's not like I had the time to drink morning coffee and read a paper. Most of the last days, I was just trying to hustle up enough money for rent. "Cops just said it was best if I wasn't over there. Asked me if I had somewhere to go."

Tyisha looked me up and down. I took my hands from the pockets of my hoodie. I didn't have much with me. Some money hidden in my shoe. My ID was in my jeans pocket. A set of keys to a place I'd been evicted from were in another. There was a chance the landlord was too cheap to change the locks and I could squat there with him none the wiser.

"You didn't drive. Where's your car?"

I thought about lying, but we were far beyond that. My shame had left my body years ago.

"Impound right now. I'll get it out as soon as I get the money together."

"You're wet. Why don't you go back into my room and dry off. Shower if you want. Some of your clothes are in that pink box under the bed, okay?"

"Thanks. I…uh…appreciate it."

"You hungry?"

"A little," I said, though it was untrue. I was craving something altogether different, but would have to grit my teeth and hopefully make it through the night. Or at least make it until they went to sleep and I could slip back out. Without another word or looking either of them in the eye, I skulked back to my friend's room. Kneeling on the carpet, I slipped the pink box out. There were sweats, jeans, and even pajamas. Some of the items were new. It made me want to cry. She had been a great friend all these years and I had never returned the favor. Filled with emotion, I started toward the living room ready to tell her how grateful I was to have her in my life, but the raised voices stopped me in my tracks in the hallway.

"I thought you said you were practicing tough love." That question had come from Bailey.

When I could hear him talking, I realized I'd forgotten to close the door. But I didn't think he was doing anything to try to keep his voice down.

"What would you have me do? Turn the cops away at the porch?"

"That's an idea," rumbled from Bailey's chest.

"How can you say that? You're watching the news the same as me. Leaving her with the cops is bad news."

"For us." When he said that, I knew he meant black people. He wasn't wrong. I knew that as surely as anyone watching that video would, but—

"For her, too," Tyisha interjected on my behalf.

"Her father's a cop, for Christ's sake. How can you say that?"

"She's an addict. The police treat them like garbage. If they think a woman's a prostitute, that's worse. Most of these cops expect free favors. And when they don't get what they think they're due, they sometimes take it. The women have no recourse. I'd rather have her here than go through any of that."

"Why can't she go home to her people?"

"Where is that? Her parents chose her sister over her. I told you that. There's always been something wrong in her house. I'm not sure if Rainey is clinically crazy or what, but once they kicked Sarah out, she could never go back. I *am* her people."

"Let's not talk about her," Bailey huffed. Surprised that he was moving on from me so quickly, I froze in place as if being still would make my hearing keener.

"You were just getting to why you wanted to come over tonight," Tyisha prompted.

"You know how I bought the house on Glengary..."

"It's nice."

"It's a house for a wife and a family," Bailey started. "We've been seeing each other for three and a half years, Tyisha, I think it's time we made it official."

"Official?" Her question ended in a high-pitched squeak.

There was a long moment when I couldn't hear anything. Towel fisted in my hands, I stood frozen like a statute. I also really wanted to know what he meant by official.

"I know you think the house is too big, but the truth is that I bought the house for us. I want you to move in. I want us to get married. Start a family. All the things we both have talked about. All the things that we've both wanted."

"Oh…I didn't…"

"I love you, Tyisha Adea Cooley. I have loved you since practically the day I met you. But that wasn't too soon after your brother. I knew your grief was a hard thing and wanted to respect you. Give you time."

"I really appreciate that."

"But you get to move on with your life. You don't have to sacrifice your future because your brother didn't get to have one."

"I know that. I haven't been doing it…on purpose."

"No one said you have. But neither of us is getting any younger. If we want to build the kind of future we've talked about, then the time is now."

While I wasn't Pat Bailey's biggest fan, his dressing like Mr. Rogers and not drinking alcohol or caffeine weren't indictments of character. I tiptoed to the shower. I didn't need to hear anymore. I half hoped my friend would take him up on it. If anyone deserved the kind of marriage her parents still had, it was Tyisha.

Clean and warm in my favorite sweats that I was grateful she'd kept plus fresh underwear, I moseyed out to the living room ready to congratulate a newly engaged couple. That's not what I found. Instead, they were standing in the dining room, oblivious to my presence. The TV was still muted. Rodney King was still being beaten on repeat. Talking heads still looked shocked.

"So you want me to move in, but you want to put rules and restrictions on my life?"

"It's for your own good."

"I'm a grown ass woman, Patrick Kelvin Bailey."

"Do you think it's a good idea for our kids to be exposed to addicts?"

"Kids? Our theoretical but still nonexistent offspring? You're worried about with whom they'd associate?"

"Yes, we're not *those* black people."

"Those?"

Pat Bailey was on thin ice. If there was one thing that the Cooleys hated, it was class divisions. They'd talked more than once about their belief in living in the heart of the black community. Mrs. Cooley talked about how they could live anywhere, but it was important for educated, middle-class blacks to stay in the neighborhood. That's what she'd said when me and even Wayne and Tyisha had asked why they wouldn't move out of Hough, which was going in the exact opposite direction of some other neighborhoods.

"The kind that live east of one sixteen," he tried to explain. "Cycles of poverty and welfare."

"Like my parents."

"Obviously not, they're different."

"Different. Like I'm different because I went to Spelman? Like you're different because you went to Middlebury up there in Vermont, huh? Are you blaming them? These people caught in the poverty cycle who didn't have the advantages we did."

"I'm not blaming anyone. If they choose not to get out of where they are, there's no one who can really do anything about it. That said, I wouldn't want our kids exposed to people like that before they have the wherewithal to figure out the right people to associate with."

"So what? Hathaway Brown or University school until they shuffle off into the Ivy League?"

"I'd be willing to look at Shaker public schools. The real estate taxes are certainly high enough that the schools should be somewhat good."

"Somewhat good?"

Part of me wanted to save Bailey from the hole he was digging for himself. Tyisha didn't have many buttons, but he was pushing all of them. Poverty. Crime. Education. Fairness. She wasn't one of those non-profiteers trying to save the world, but she very much believed in equality and justice. It's who her parents raised her to be.

"We're getting off track, Tyisha. I don't want to argue with you. I was looking for you to promise me that nights like tonight wouldn't happen. That Sarah's not just going to pop into our house."

"Sometimes she needs help. I wouldn't just abandon her."

"It's not help that you can provide. That you're qualified to give."

"Who says?"

"Any book or article on the subject. I love you. I know you have this long and complicated history with your friend. So I gave it the benefit of the doubt. I went to the downtown library and took out a lot of books on the subject. They all say that she won't give up the heroin or won't get any better until she's motivated to do it. In the meantime, all she's going to do is wreak havoc in the lives of the people around her like she's doing tonight."

"Nothing's happened. She got dropped off. Took a shower. I'll make dinner and then she'll be back to—"

"Her old habits. She looked like she's jonesing now. I don't think she was over at Shaw High looking to take some nighttime adult education classes."

"I'm not saying that she's clean or sober. I'm saying that I can't imagine giving up on Sarah. She's my best friend. She got dealt a bad hand. I got a good one. It's only fair that I do what I can to even it out."

"And what if one of our kids dies or even I die as a result?" Bailey's voice was getting higher and louder. The Cooleys were a quiet family.

"What do you mean?" My friend's voice stayed calm in the face of Bailey's verbal onslaught. "She's not sticking a needle into anyone's vein but her own."

"What do I mean?" His huff was one of exasperation. "Wouldn't your brother be alive today if she hadn't been at your house?"

"I can't believe you...that's a low—"

That was the moment I chose to show myself. I'd quietly tied on my damp sneakers and pulled my jacket back around my shoulders. I loved Tyisha, and would have really liked a warm bed, but the cost was looking like it was too high.

"I think I need to go. Thanks for the shower and change of clothes. I don't want to be the thing that gets between you and a life of happiness. Ciao," I said.

I marched to the front door. I didn't want to, but I did take one thing on the way out that I knew I would never return—a large black golf umbrella— probably proving Bailey's point. I took it to stay dry. To remind me of the best friend I knew at that exact moment was probably lost to me forever. She'd marry him and ride off into the sunset. I walked the mile back to the high school. This time there weren't any police around and my dealer was there. I leaned against a brick wall and got my last dollars from my shoe.

23

The moment I literally smacked into Judge Kate Marsh, I started to worry that luck wasn't going to be on my side.

"I'm so sorry," I said as I stepped back from full-body contact with the jurist.

"It's always crowded." A brief smile flickered over her face. "No harm, no foul."

"Justin McPhee." I put out my right hand for the appropriate amount of contact. "I have a pretrial hearing upstairs with you in half an hour."

"Kate Marsh." She shook. "But I guess you already know that. So see you in a few. Nice to meet you."

Once the judge moved past me, I craned my neck, looking for a woman with messy dirty-blond hair. I was sure I'd seen Casey behind something that looked like a moon rover, but had to be the modern interpretation of the classic stroller. The jolt of recognition had been so strong, I'd lost all sense of direction, then had stopped moving with the crowd and had hit the judge. Now that the path was clear again, I tried to spy my ex-lover.

More than anything, I wanted to see that baby. I'd heard through the grapevine that she'd given birth to a little boy two months ago. It made sense that she'd be out of the house even if it didn't make sense for her to be at the justice center. I couldn't imagine what case would be so important as to bring a mother of a newborn down to the bowels of the justice system.

"Justin?"

My head snapped around at the sound of my name in a woman's voice.

"Casey?" I asked before I looked. When I did see clearly, it was obvious I wasn't looking at the attorney. My client's frown was curious.

"Tyisha Cooley," she said coolly. "I thought I was early enough." She eyed the large crowd in front of the small elevators. "How long will it take to get upstairs? It's the twenty-fifth floor. No chance of using the stairs, right?"

The people were ten deep. If I hadn't been distracted, I'd have made it upstairs well before the after lunch crowd had formed.

"The judge made it up ahead of us," was my non sequitur.

"You okay?"

"Thought I saw a ghost is all," I demurred. "Let's get to Marsh's courtroom."

Ten minutes later, we were on the twenty-fifth floor in the courtroom waiting area, a duplicate of some five floors above and below. Only the tiny placards for courtrooms A through D signaled location.

"What happens this afternoon?" Cooley asked.

"What happens is hopefully your first and last visit to this part of the building."

"What's the plan?"

"I'm going to lay out for Judge Marsh the prosecutor's overreach and the dismissal of my other client's case by Judge Cox in April."

"Then what? I walk away?"

"That's the hope. The prosecutor probably doesn't want to go to trial on this. They only want to go to trial on sure winners most days. But even if they don't dismiss entirely, I'd work on getting them down to a misdemeanor like we discussed."

"No jail time?"

"Not on a majority of them. No promises, of course. It hardly ever happens outside of DWI cases." At her curious expression, I clarified. "Driving while intoxicated."

"Right. Of course. This system loves to put users in jail rather than treat the addiction."

I didn't do political debates about the criminal justice system with clients. Everyone thought it was broken even if we couldn't agree on how. No matter, it wasn't going to be fixed in time for whatever case I was handling.

"Let's go in. You can sit in the courtroom gallery. I'll go back to chambers and see what the plan is for the day."

Once Cooley got as comfortable as anyone could on a hard wooden bench, I walked behind the witness chair and high bench until I was in the area where the real work of court was done. Told the bailiff I was on the *State of Ohio versus Cooley* matter, then turned to find an empty seat in the narrow hall. Before my butt could hit the chair, I heard my name from a different woman's lips this time.

"Justin McPhee. You're representing Cooley?" It was Nicole Long.

"How's Major Crimes?" I asked, both surprised and not to see her here. I looked around wondering if there was some newsworthy rape or murder going on here that I'd missed. Department heads only came out for the big cases. Cooley's certainly wasn't one.

"Yes. What are you here on?"

"Cooley."

"Oh, I thought…" I trailed off, sure what I'd thought shouldn't be repeated. I shifted in my tasseled loafers, starting to feel a tiny bit discomfited, like I'd missed something.

"Special request from the big boss," Long explained.

"Are you aware of a Libby Saldana?" I didn't need to talk politics. I'd come here ready to make a deal. "Same charges about two or three months back?"

"Dismissed those. Judge Cox was not on board. Pope agreed and pled it to a misdemeanor," Long rattled off.

I nearly sighed in relief. This wasn't going to be that hard. I could give my client what I'd promised.

"So what are we doing here? Is this some kind of vendetta? Did Pope mention the victim was her sister?"

"Cooley," the bailiff called. "Judge is ready for you."

"Sorry. Elevator got stuck," an out of breath Valerie Dodds huffed as she ran down the back hallway toward us and the judge's chambers.

"Marsh just called us in," Long said to her colleague. "Take a deep breath. Let's go."

I'd thought I'd have more time to hash out something. Didn't have any choice but to walk into chambers blind.

"Justin McPhee, long time no see," Judge Marsh said, then laughed heartily. She stood and shook my hand again. A bracelet heavy with charms jingled below the cuff of her powder blue suit jacket, which looked like a dead ringer for the outfit Hillary Clinton had danced her way through Puerto Rico in.

"Nice to meet you formally," I replied.

"No one's on the pleadings." She turned to the women. "Please introduce yourselves."

"Nicole Long, deputy prosecutor and head of Major Crimes. This is Valerie Dodds. She'll be on the case as well. She's an assistant prosecutor in the office."

Judge Marsh shook both of their right hands in turn. She sat back down and scooted her office chair forward. Flipped open the file. I could tell that she was just glancing at the indictment and other pleadings. Something in my gut told me she'd already familiarized herself with the case.

"So what are we doing here?" Judge Marsh started. "Your client's not in jail. Low bail, too. Her time runs out on the first of February of next year. I believe strongly swift adjudication is fairer to everyone. So how about a trial date sixty days out? That puts us at August twenty-fifth. That's a Monday. Work for everyone?"

I hadn't been addressed, so I kept mute and pulled my trial calendar from my briefcase.

"Yes, your honor, that works for me."

Long nodded, her agreement going for Dodds as well, I imagined.

"Pretrial motions and jury instructions are due August eleven. Any arguments will be scheduled for the fifteenth."

I scribbled furiously in my calendar.

"Great. That was easy." Marsh flipped the court's file closed. "I look forward to working with all of you to have a speedy and orderly trial. Should you need anything resolved before August, my door is open." Judge Marsh stood again. Shook all our hands. Dismissed, Marsh's bailiff came in to usher us out of chambers. Marsh wasn't a "knock attorneys' heads together until they reach a deal" type of jurist. For once I was disappointed by something I found down-right annoying from most other judges.

"Can I talk to you?" I asked the prosecutors. They were walking away as if a plea wasn't on the table. In all my years of practice, a plea was *always* on the table.

"What do you need, Justin?" Long asked. At least she wasn't pretending not to know me. Especially after Long'd really had her ass handed to her when we'd gotten murder charges dismissed against our wrongly accused client. Sometimes when you beat a prosecutor on a case, they actively forgot about you.

While I'd have preferred to have this discussion in an attorney room or even the jury room if it were empty, they weren't budging. This talking in the hall in front of all our peers and colleagues lacked the discretion I was looking for. When I stepped forward, though, neither Long nor Dodds moved. Semi-public it was, then.

"I was hoping to plea Cooley down, like Saldana. Same charges, same overreach. Cooley is a solid citizen. No drugs. No convictions. Not even any arrests."

I wasn't exactly throwing Saldana under the bus, but not all defendants were created equal. In the back here, behind the courtroom, we didn't need to pretend they were.

"Not going to happen," Long responded.

"What? Why not? Cooley isn't any more guilty than Saldana was."

"This was Pope's sister." Long's voice was lower now. "You didn't think it was somehow going to be the same, right?"

"Equal justice under the law and all that."

"You want to make that argument, you can take it up with our boss. I have no room to negotiate. I'll see you at trial."

Long pivoted on her heel. Dodds quickly followed behind, and in less than the time it took to lift my jaw off the floor, they were gone.

"Tough going counselor," the bailiff said in sympathy. He shook his head, then went back to typing whatever he'd been working on. I looked at everyone else, but no one made eye contact. There was no sympathy to be had. I took a very deep breath because I was about to disappoint my client. My entire job was managing expectations, and I'd done a piss-poor job of it.

"That was quick," Cooley said when I walked through the courtroom door. "Do we need to go outside or will the judge be okay with us being in here? Do we need to sit at one of the tables?"

Clearly my client had been watching late-night re-runs of *Law and Order* over the last few weeks.

"There's no hearing today. I talked to the judge and the prosecutors on the case while I was in back, in the judge's chambers."

"So what did they agree to? The misdemeanor? Are they insisting on something more?"

"The judge set the case for trial." I sighed. "In the last week of August."

"What does that mean? Set it for trial. Like a judge and a jury?"

"Yes, a judge and a jury."

"What...what about a plea?" For the first time, Cooley looked uncertain.

"The prosecutor's office is unwilling to make a deal."

"Any deal?"

"Any deal."

"Why? Why a deal for that other client and not me?"

"Best I can figure, either it's because of who the victim is or because of who you are."

"Can she do that...Rainey...Lori...Lorraine Pope? Can she prosecute me, put me in jail, out of revenge? Out of spite?"

"She can, and it looks like she will try."

"How is that legal? How is that just? Rainey was always a monster." Cooley lowered her head, shook it. "I just thought I'd stayed far enough out of her grasp."

"It's not over until it's over. Between now and the moment a jury deliberates, we need to fight like hell." I only wished I knew exactly what that meant.

24

It wasn't working. I'd tried to be friendly and casual in jeans at the Friday meeting. In previous weeks, I'd worn a pencil skirt and stilettos, and tried authoritarian. Neither one was earning me the respect my title and office deserved. Every one of the prosecutors under me was acting as if I'd be gone any day and their true boss would emerge.

I wanted to yell and announce "acting" had been removed from my title. Tell them that I, Nicole Long, *was* Major Crimes whether they liked it or not. I knew that wouldn't work for sure. I wasn't stupid. My reputation was tainted. Whether it was my years of child support enforcement in juvy, the crap assignment in the grand jury, my probationary periods, or

Tom Brody throwing my win record under the bus, I knew my trajectory wasn't *exactly* straightforward. That didn't mean, however, I wasn't up to the job. That I couldn't handle supervision of plea negotiations or give advice on which judge was likely to be prosecutor-friendly. But they all treated me like I was the red-headed stepchild they could ignore.

I shifted the files I'd taken from the meeting so I could push the call button. I tried not to fume as I waited for the slow as molasses elevator. Even if *they* didn't think I could do this job, I still had to actually do it. All my direct reports would be long at the Side Bar on their third drink while I was here reviewing cases. The assistant prosecutors certainly hadn't invited me, nor tried to hide the fact they were making plans while I was still standing there able to hear them.

When the door dinged, I hefted the files and stepped in. When I heard a throat clear, I looked around and saw what appeared to be a skinny black guy, hoodie up, slouching in the corner.

For too long a moment, my heart pounded and my hands sweat, making me almost lose hold of my files. I took a deep breath, telling myself that nothing bad could happen here in my own office building. Our part was closed to the public and subject to some pretty heavy security. When I couldn't feel my heart any longer, guilt flooded through me. I was behaving like some scared southern white woman.

If I was no longer anything, I was no longer that.

He moved from the back corner to stand near the buttons. Only the light from the ninth floor was lit. We had the eighth and the ninth floors to ourselves—admin, civil, and conference rooms on eight, and the bulk of attorney offices on nine. The police had the nine floors below. The rest of building was shared with Cleveland municipal court.

"Can I help you?" I asked. Maybe he was in the wrong place. This elevator only covered the floors from the police and prosecutor's office. Everyone else used the two even slower public elevators. For a brief moment, I wondered if he was an undercover or in plain clothes. But the telltale bulge of a holster was missing. I'd rarely seen any sworn officer without his gun. Usually they covered it with a big flannel shirt, but I could see a change of wardrobe maybe with younger cops.

"You're Nicole, right. Nicole Long?" the man asked.

Hairs rose on the back of my neck. I wasn't a hobbit, but I wasn't exactly Kiera Knightly, either. Given my job, I tried to be as anonymous as I could, though.

"Can I help you?" I asked again.

The elevator jolted to a stop. I looked around and finally saw his hand near the red emergency stop button.

I went from raised hackles to a near full panic attack in moments. I'd read somewhere that rape victims were more likely to be victimized a second time, more likely to be victimized than the average woman. Probably something biological about us being the weak ones in the herd. I could live with disrespect from my colleagues and a boss who was constantly breathing down my neck. But I couldn't ever, *ever* be a victim again. I stepped forward, ready to fight to the death, if that's what it took. For once, I was glad I was sober.

The man pulled back his hood—he looked vaguely familiar. I couldn't quite place him, but I was one hundred percent sure I knew him. I'd probably put him in jail at some point. I was guessing he was out on probation or parole. Or maybe clear of the criminal justice system entirely. It didn't matter which—I was in trouble.

This was every prosecutor's worst nightmare. It was why our addresses, and those of judges and cops for that matter, were carefully stripped from public records.

But I wasn't the president or even a governor, so my job didn't exactly come with a security detail.

The man laughed at my fear. It wasn't menacing, but it wasn't nice, either. I hated the fact that my phone didn't work in these old elevators or most of the building. There was no way to fix the cell phone issue other than demolish everything and start over. In this economy, it wasn't a priority. The county didn't have money for that.

"I'm not going to touch a hair on your head, Ms. Long. Don't you worry about that."

I wanted to believe him.

"Then what do you want?" I asked because I didn't.

"I want to make sure that you do your level best to put Tyisha Cooley in jail."

"Who?" The name wasn't familiar in this context. Plus panic was slowing down my brain. I knew from personal experience, and my job, that fear and logic did not work hand in hand.

"The woman you're prosecuting for Sarah Rose's death."

The pieces fell into place right then. Was this the opposite of witness intimidation, jury tampering? Except for victims, fanatical victim advocates, or pundits with too much time on their hands, no one ever really pushed for conviction. My job was mostly anonymous. People trusted that I was zealous enough for everyone else.

"What do you care? Was she somebody to you?" I deliberately tried to make my tone glib so he didn't know the hold he had over my emotions. Once you let them see you sweat, you were beat.

"We was friends for twenty years. That's someone to me. I just want to hear that you're doing every-thing you can to make sure that the person who killed my friend is—how is it you white people say it?—brought to justice."

My mind went in a few directions. I resisted the urge to correct him about my heritage. He hadn't locked me in this elevator to discuss genetic expres-sion or the history of miscegenation in America.

"What do you really want?"

"Exactly what I said, Cooley in jail."

"And what happens if...say the jury doesn't see things your way?"

For the second time in minutes, I was afraid. His face changed from surly to menacing. Even if he wasn't someone I'd personally convicted, he no doubt had a rap sheet as long as my arm. No way he'd skulked around the county like this and come out unscathed.

He didn't answer. Instead punched at the emergency button again. The elevator creaked back to life. When the doors finally opened on my floor, I nearly fell in relief. Stiffening my spine, I took one small step, then another, and when he didn't do anything, I stalked from the car which now reeked of nervous sweat.

I didn't turn my back, though I was relieved to hear the doors closing.

"You wouldn't want that to happen, Ms. Long," was the man's answer through the open slit in the beefy metal. When I finally had the guts to turn around, the door was closed.

For a long second, I stood in the lobby. The clock above the empty reception desk read 4:45 p.m. The likelihood anyone else occupied these two floors was nearly zero, so there was no one to cry to for help. I'd get to safety in my office, have a shot—maybe two—then I'd call Darlene Webb. Calmed, I strode as fast as I could, but I never got that far in my plan.

I dropped all the files I'd been holding after I'd opened my office door. County prosecutor Lori Pope was sitting on my desk. Her legs were crossed, spike heels swinging. Next to her hip were two of my mini Maker's Mark bottles, wax peeled, screw tops gone, and two glasses. The laser etched tumblers were law school souvenirs I kept on a shelf.

"Want a drink?" Pope inquired, a single brow raised. "After your discussions with Mr. Roach in the elevator, I have a feeling you might need it."

25

Was today the day I was going to die?

I looked outside of my car window at the snow swirling by. It wasn't the blizzard of 1978, but it was looking like it was darn close.

Twisting the key in the ignition, I started the car again. Turned the heater on full blast and waited for warm air to push out the cold in the cabin. I'd have kept it on, but the gas gauge was getting pretty close to the E.

I crawled through the seats and to the bench in the back. Scooted into my sleeping bag and hoped I'd make it until morning because I was out of alternatives. None of the Cooleys were speaking to me. My friends from high school were getting married and having kids and no longer seemed to appreciate me showing up to crash on their couches.

Despite the cold, I must have dozed off because someone knocking on the window startled the hell out of me. I couldn't see through the fogged-up glass on the inside or the snow on the outside, but I knew my time was up. I was in the little parking lot by Madison Park in Lakewood. No one would have bothered me if I'd tucked my Ford Fairlane into a spot in Lakewood Park, the bigger one by the water. But the arctic breeze off Lake Erie made it feel at least ten degrees colder over there.

I rolled down one of the back windows a crack. "I'm leaving, okay," I said to whatever police/security guard was tasked with keeping the park free from people like me.

Before I could roll the window back up, the knock came again. That woke me all the way up. Being a woman out here alone was the worst. Either some messed up guy would want to hole up with me in here—I wasn't desperate or cold enough for that—or they'd somehow try to trick me to get me outside to steal the car or whatever I had. I'd hoped the weather would keep all those sketchy people inside. Maybe I'd been wrong.

I rolled down about an inch farther.

"Gimme a second, please. I'll move for sure."

The person, a man about my age, brushed some snow from my window. "Do you have anywhere to go?"

His brown eyes were filled with nothing but compassion. Chilled, I was both curious and wary. I shivered now, half out of my sleeping bag and with cold air replacing the warm.

"I was just going to go to Edgewater Park, probably," I answered truthfully, figuring because he was black that he was the kind of guy who would understand my plight. "The rangers usually forget to close the gate by Whiskey Island."

After the truth came out, I tried to size him up. Lots of curly hair poked out from under a ski cap. The why of him being here was the missing element.

"You want to stay at my place?" He jerked a thumb somewhere behind him. "It's a blizzard, yo. No one needs to be out here."

"Umm…" I debated hard in my head. If I weren't half frozen to death, I wouldn't have ever considered his offer. I may not have made it to Bryn Mawr, but I wasn't stupid.

"Look, I know it's not exactly kosher on most days, for me to ask this, okay? But it's getting bad out here. It doesn't seem like it happens in America, but every year someone freezes to death in Cleveland. It's always in the back of the paper in tiny print." When I didn't say anything, he sighed, breath a ball of mist in the air. "I'm not some rapist or murderer, I promise."

If I'd learned anything in the last seven years since Dad had kicked me out, it was how to judge other people's character. A wrong move out here on the streets of Cleveland could get me hurt or killed.

There were a lot of things I hated about my life. Missing my high school graduation. Not going away to college in Pennsylvania. The fact that neither Tyisha nor Wayne were speaking to me right now. That I didn't have any real friends anymore. But I didn't have a death wish, either.

"C'mon," he said. "I know you want to." Of course, right then, a gust blew snow everywhere, including into the car the moment the words left his mouth.

"Where do you stay?" I asked.

"Across the street, actually. That big brick building. Used to be a screw factory or something. Now it's apartments, upstairs at least."

"Let me see," I said. I waved him away from my car, then pushed open the Ford's big door. I pulled my Salvation Army wool coat from the wheel well and buttoned it up against the wind. I got my backpack, twisted the keys in the car's lock, then looked at the guy.

"What's your name?"

"Ja Roach."

"Ja?"

"African. Means magnetic. My mom was an activist back in the sixties. You?"

"Sarah."

"No last name?"

"Pope. Nothing fancy."

Without saying anything, he took off. I followed him to the parking lot exit. Roach looked both ways, even though there was no traffic to speak of. No one with a head on their shoulders ever came out in this weather. I lifted my boots high as I walked behind him. I didn't want to trip and fall in case some dare-devil did come careening around the corner.

The building was legit. I followed him through one of two side-by-side doors that looked wide enough for a horse carriage or a car. Carefully, I picked my way across polished concrete floors, try-ing not to skid in my boots, caked as they were with fast melting snow.

There wasn't anyone on the bottom floor, but I could see that the doors were decorated like visual artists spent time here on days when the weather was better. For a brief moment, I felt a sharp stab of envy. Were there writers in here, too? Tucked away in small rooms with nothing but a typewriter and their imaginations? I'd wanted that for myself, but I had to tear my eyes way before they pricked with tears.

That dream was long dead.

Roach opened a gate to a huge industrial elevator.

"What floor are you on?" I asked, looking up at the huge ceiling above us, crisscrossed with indus-trial pipes.

"The top. They have some kind of meeting rooms or something on the second."

"Okay," I said, following him in. If this situation was going to go sideways, now was the time for that to happen. I braced myself while Roach pulled the gate closed, fiddled with a big door, then finally pushed a button. The elevator car heaved itself up, creaking in slow motion. In a minute, Roach repeated the whole thing backwards, and we were on another floor with bigger doors farther apart.

He walked to one, twisted a key in a lock, and walked inside. I waited a beat, then followed him in. Left the door open. It was what he said it would be— a loft. Not much in the way of furniture beyond a bed in one corner and a futon in another. He had a TV, of course, because guys never seemed to go without.

"You could have the futon. I have an extra blanket here somewhere. The bathroom is over there in the corner. With the door."

I didn't point out that the door seemed kind of pointless where the new walls didn't meet the tall ceilings. Privacy was an illusion, I guessed. Didn't say that. I was starting to think this guy was a legit sent from heaven guardian angel. That I should be grateful instead of suspicious.

"Why'd you come outside?"

"I saw you pull up. Wondered what someone in such a nice car was doing in the park during a blizzard. For a minute, I thought you had a dog or maybe you were some kind of photographer. Those are two kinds of people who come out in all weather. You never got out, though. The car went on and off. Took pity on you after the weather report went on."

"So."

"Let me get that blanket for you."

Only when Roach moved to the far side of the loft did I relax the tiniest bit.

"Staying?" he asked when he came back with a blue wool blanket, its edges covered in satin. My heart squeezed in recognition. It was an exact duplicate of the one I'd had on my bed for my entire childhood. When I took it and held it up to my nose, it even smelled like my room. Sense memory, I think I'd once heard someone call it. This weird déjà vu feeling after encountering something similar to one's past. Of course this couldn't be *my* blanket. Probably used the same soap powder as my mother or fabric softener or something.

I'd nodded in agreement before my brain had caught up. His shoulders hitched down a little and I realized this situation must be weird for him, too. Maybe he was honestly just trying to do the right thing.

"You hungry?" he asked next. I put the blanket down next to me. Thought long and hard about when I'd had my last meal. Probably yesterday afternoon at The Coffee Pot which had big portions and low prices. Over the years, I'd learned how to ignore an empty stomach. Worrying about food was the death of a life on the road. As if my belly had ears, it growled loudly on cue.

"Actually, I am," I had to admit. "But I don't want to be any trouble."

"I was going to eat anyway. No trouble."

He walked over to the area of the loft with kitchen counters and started pulling stuff out. I wanted to offer to help, but I wasn't much good in a kitchen. I'd seen Mary Cooley work wonders. I'd seen my own mom open cans and packages and mix stuff together for casseroles. The hows of food prep were still a big mystery for me. I hadn't ever had my own kitchen long enough to figure it all out.

In a couple of minutes, the little space smelled wonderful. I'd never really seen a man cook before. Probably had a girlfriend who made all of this for him. I shifted in my seat, then stood and walked over to the area where Ja Roach was moving around.

"Is it going to be okay that I'm here? You don't have a girl who's going to be mad that I'm here, do you?" Men were the first to put you in the middle of drama, then throw up their hands to avoid responsibility for the conflict they caused.

"Got no girl. You a picky eater?"

I wanted to point out that if I wasn't picky about where I was sleeping, I certainly wasn't going to be picky about a hot meal anyone put in front of me. Instead, I just shook my head and took a seat at the small two-person table.

Potholders along the sides of the dish, he brought a big plate to the table. I recognized collard greens, black-eyed peas, and pork chops.

"Thanks for this. Looks good."

He eyed me for a second, then went to get plates, forks, and knives. I lifted the salt shaker to pull out two paper napkins. I let him fill up his paper plate first. Then took what was left for me, grateful to have anything to eat. The food was good. Not Mary Cooley good, but not bad, either.

"You make this?" I asked before putting another forkful in my mouth.

"Nah, my sister dropped it off. I just reheat in the oven."

"What do you do?"

He cocked his head like a dog hearing a far-off noise.

"Trying to get on at one of the factories. I got in trouble a while back, and putting that on an application gets it thrown in the basket right quick. So next time I'll leave it off. It's not like they're going looking."

"Good idea. I don't put that stuff on applications."

"You have a record?" Roach asked. "For what?"

"Just drug possession. Not anything like prostitution," I blurted. When you were out on the streets past a certain hour, I'd found out that men had certain ideas about you.

"Don't we all," he said.

I fully relaxed then. He wasn't going to be a secret proselytizer, trying to beat drugs out of me with a bible in exchange for a hot meal and a warm bed.

"What was your vice?" I asked. From the looks of this place, he was clean. One of those guys who did their time, then turned it around. The ones everyone points to as examples of setting your life straight and doing it right.

"Nothing but dope," he said.

I didn't want to talk about myself, so I changed the subject to how old he was. He had a year and change on me. And where he'd grown up, which was all over. I didn't ask how he could afford such a nice place. It was small, but anything with the word "loft" in it went at a premium. Industrial to residential building conversion had started in New York City and was creeping slowly west as all trends eventually did. Even if the rent wasn't high, he'd have to have enough money for first and last or a generous relative. Having neither, I tried not to envy his fortune.

When our plates were clean, I asked him where to dispose of mine. I took myself into the bathroom and tried to do the best job I could cleaning myself up without using too much soap or having to ask for his shower. Once I'd brushed my teeth and changed from jeans to sweats, I was comfortable. I fished in my backpack for the book the Rocky River librarian had recommended for me, then left the bathroom. I made my way to the couch and opened my book, ready to lose myself in a life different from mine.

In what felt like a few minutes later, there was a tap on my shoulder. My heart sped up because I knew that tap, it meant I had to go. I must have been sitting longer than I thought because at some point I'd stretched out my legs and had pulled the blanket up over them. I closed the latest Arthur C. Clarke offering and turned toward my impromptu roommate.

"Sorry, do I need to go?" I asked, ready to haul myself back out into the cold.

"Nah. I'm not fickle like that."

"What's up?" I realized maybe he wasn't looking for sex, but did expect me to entertain him somehow.

"I don't usually share, but it's snowing."

He opened his hand. Where I'd expected an Oreo, there was a baggie with a sticky brown substance. I'd only seen it a few times when partying with friends.

It was heroin.

My desire to get high warred with my fear of the drug.

"I've…uh…never done anything like that. Usually me and my friends party. You know. Beer. Coke. Maybe a little weed. I can't afford anything like this."

"It's my treat," he said. I'd heard him the first time. What Ja Roach hadn't understood was my true meaning, that I was afraid to be like one of those dope fiends I'd seen wandering up and down streets like zombies from the late night movies that came before the test pattern.

"I don't want to be addicted to anything," I said. Being an occasional partier was one thing. An addict was something else entirely.

"Do I look like an addict?" Ja Roach asked. I took him in. He was tall, skinny but muscular. He had a full fridge and a full belly. There weren't any fiends nodding off in the corner. He was a lot like me.

"No."

"So?"

"What the hell? It's a snow day." My whole body filled with the pleasure of anticipation. He went to a cabinet and came back with a brown-and-orange metal disco-themed lunchbox that looked like he'd picked it up at a flea market. He flipped the latch open and it was like a small first aid kit inside.

"You'll have to go first," he said as he started mixing the gooey tar-like substance on a piece of foil.

"This isn't a trade. I don't owe you anything. I don't like guys," I spit out. Once I got high, I wouldn't be this articulate. I needed him to know this wasn't a tit for tat.

"Then we're even, because I do."

"Like guys? As in gay? Oh." I don't know why that shocked me, but it did. Any last hesitancy I had fell away. I leaned forward toward his beckoning hand. Then extended my right arm, sleeve pushed all the way up.

"How will it make me feel?" He was snapping rubber around my arm and tapping at the pale underside.

"Like you never want to come down," he said. There was a tiny pinch when the needle poked my arm, then after that nothing but euphoria.

26

"You brought the baby." My voice echoed from the four walls of my office.

"Shhh."

Casey Cort was pushing the stroller into my space with one hand, and patting at the baby in some kind of kangaroo-type thing strapped to her chest with the other.

"Yes, I brought the baby. Let me just get him situated and then we can talk. Okay?"

She took the tiny person out of the stroller and bounced him on her knee for a second. He looked annoyed. In a second, his face screwed up. I knew very little about babies, but even I could see that a shrieking cry was next on the horizon unless she did something to stop it. I had no idea what tools she'd pull out of her maternal bag of tricks. The diaper tote clipped to her stroller's handles looked like it could hold an entire baby management arsenal.

"Damn." She glanced at a watch on her left wrist. "I'm gonna have to nurse him. That alright?"

I didn't really think she was asking my permission, so I treated the question as rhetorical and said nothing.

Without fanfare, Casey did something with her shirt. Lifted one part. Lowered another. Unhooked something, and then her breast was out. If I hadn't seen it before, looking away probably would have been polite. I didn't turn my head.

After all that, she tilted the baby, then he latched on to her nipple like he was in a desert and she was the only source of liquid. For a long second, baby and mom looked at each other, then his eyes fluttered closed as if he'd found manna from heaven. Casey smoothed back light brown wisps of hair. Then her eyes flicked to mine.

"What's the case you wanted to talk to me about?"

"What's his name again?" I needed to ask that to give me some distance from the feelings bubbling up inside of me. I'd studied her email announcement hundreds of times—looking for clues. The first line had read: *Announcing the birth of our son.* Though the email had come from Casey's personal account, the use of the word "our" had caught me up short. The next line had been his name in a newspaper head-line-sized font. *Simon de Viera Pinheiro*.

I'd paused at the mixture of an English name with Ron's Portuguese heritage. Somehow I was partially insulted that the baby's German, and more importantly his Polish roots, somehow felt like they'd been eliminated. Below that had been a huge picture of a newborn swaddled in a blanket and hat. Then in smaller type were the statistics I never understood why people shared. The date and time he was born. His length and weight. That mom and baby were doing well. It was signed by Casey and Ron. The whole thing had been a punch in the gut. I hadn't been sure before, but I knew now that Simon was mine. But I'd forsaken any right to the baby or that conversation. Pretending ignorance seemed like the better approach.

Casey gave me a look, then answered.

"Simon."

"His full name?"

"Simon de Viera Pinheiro." I could see her work hard to keep her exasperation at bay. I was being an ass, not caring to use the manners my parents and Catholic school had drilled into me.

"Nice," I answered.

It was the exact opposite of what I meant. If I'd chosen her, the baby in her arms would be Simon McPhee. He would have my middle name as his instead of Ron's. Mentally I rolled the name Simon Patrick McPhee around in my head. Or maybe my mother's maiden name, Symanski, instead. Would

Casey have gone for that? Would her father have been proud to see his origins represented?

"What are you working on?" Casey asked, interrupting my thoughts. I knew I'd been quiet far too long. I was happy to answer with something other than what had been on my mind.

"Lorraine Pope is kicking my ass," I offered.

"She's working on a case? I haven't been reading the papers, I guess." Casey's hunch was right, of course. *The* prosecuting attorney rarely made courtroom appearances unless the defendant was on the *Plain Dealer*'s front page.

"Not directly," I clarified.

"What's with the cryptic talk, Justin? Just fill me in. I've asked you for help enough times. If I can assist in any way, I'd love to do it."

I could see that she was genuine. Meant what she said. Casey had always been like that. Earnest. Honest. It's what made me trust her implicitly.

"Pope is throwing the book at my client. Or more like a whole law library."

"What? Pope's always been a straight shooter as far as I know," Casey started. "Overzealous. Overcharges. But that's par for the course for anyone in the job. Certainly was for Liam Brody before her. I mean, maybe sometimes her office is unwilling to plea where it's warranted. But she did support diversion for low-level, nonviolent drug offenses. And even got behind those domestic violence and sex crimes initiatives, keeping those out of Common

Pleas. What's your best guess at her thought process on this particular case?"

"I can see no reason other than revenge."

"You're thinking retribution." Her eyebrows shot up. "Why?"

"The vic."

"Is who?"

"Was Pope's sister."

"*Was*?"

"Died of an overdose."

"Wait, what's the charge?" Casey shot forward, her attention on me. Baby Simon popped off the nipple. His protest was vocal. She got him resituated, then I gave her the details. In the middle of the telling, little Simon popped off Casey's boob and fell back. No protest this time. His little face didn't look that dissimilar from that of a drug addict taking a hit. I'd trailed off. Stopped speaking. Couldn't look away.

"We call it Simon's milk coma." Her smile, when she was finally able to tear her eyes from the baby to meet mine, was positively beatific. Suddenly all the museums full of Madonna paintings made sense.

Casey put herself back together. Wiped the baby's face with a big cloth that appeared out of nowhere. She did some folding thing, wrapped him in the same cloth, then stood and oh so carefully put him back in the stroller's flat part. She put a hand on him, made shooshing noises for a few minutes. Then lifted her hand slowly.

"Can we talk?" I asked in a whisper.

"Oh, it's fine," Casey answered in her full voice. "He can sleep through anything. We walked past some jackhammers the other day and that didn't wake him one bit. Neighbors' dog neither. So he'll be alright with a little law talk."

The baby settled, Casey lifted herself from half stoop to her full height, adjusted her clothes again, then made herself comfortable on my black leather couch. I pushed the memory of the two of us tangled up on it from my mind. That hadn't been the night this little one had been conceived.

"So you were saying that not only did Pope over-charge, she's not willing to plea, and you have a client who if she isn't quite innocent, isn't really guilty, either. Did I get the gist of it?" Casey asked.

"That's it in a nutshell, I guess."

"So what's the question?"

"How do I get Pope or Long or even Dodds to plea out? I don't have any leverage that I can think of."

"Dodds, as in Valerie Dodds?"

"You know her?"

"Went up against her in juvy on the Grant case. My first big client. I thought Dodds left. Moved to DC or something."

"She's back and in Major Crimes. With Nicole Long. Odd bedfellows. How do you think Long got there?"

"Payback for not outing Tom, I'd guess."

"Outing Tom?" I had no idea what Casey was referring to about her former fiancé.

"I think I can't say anything." Something shuttered in her hazel eyes. She uncrossed then recrossed her legs the other way. "So between the three of them, they're not willing to plea? At all?"

"I wouldn't be as bothered by it, if they hadn't charged another client of mine with exactly the same offenses, then pled her out to a misdemeanor."

"What's the same in both cases?"

"The circumstances...the hot shot."

"Then the difference is relationship. I'm going to guess the first victim wasn't anyone most people would care about. Maybe that was a test balloon. Now the second is her sister. Did you ask around? Is anyone else being charged like this?"

"I went down to the basement." The county files weren't quite electronic yet. When case folders weren't in the clerk's office or chambers, they were down in the basement on large rolling metal shelves. "Went through all the recent indictments. Couldn't find any beyond these two."

"What's your objective?" Casey asked.

It was a fair question. The answer wasn't always dismissal or acquittal. That was certainly preferred, but not always practical.

"My client is willing to plea to a misdemeanor. It's what happened before."

"Wait. Was that the time I saw you outside of Cox's courtroom? That woman?"

I nodded. "I made the classic mistake of mentioning that outcome to this client. Mismanaged her expectations."

Casey sucked in a breath, which told me she'd made the same misstep herself. Probably more than once and wasn't judging me for it.

"So now what?"

"I go to trial and hope for a nullification? She doesn't exactly have a defense. She did it in plain sight of a witness." It was the best I'd been able to come up with.

"Or?"

"That's what I want to ask you. I need a plan B or even a much better plan A."

"Obviously, you'll go for reasonable doubt with your cross examination. Don't give up on that one so quickly," she advised. "When the prosecution thinks they can win the case, they mostly don't try hard. Sloppy forensics, if at all. A few ill-informed or badly prepped witnesses. Use that laziness against them."

"Anything else?"

"Nicole Long is a toss-up. When she's sober, she's a force. When she's not...well...she's beatable."

"What else?" I was no longer worried she'd think less of me for all my questions. My client's well-being trumped my pride and ego.

"The big play? Try the case in the court of public opinion," she answered without a moment of deliberation or hesitation. "You know Lori Pope is up for reelection? I mean, she sailed through the primary unchallenged, but now Ted Strohmeyer is making noises about November. His family name is on a stadium, he's a strong contender."

I could feel my eyes growing wide at the name. Casey's lifted brows were the only acknowledgement. That was another conversation for another time. Priorities.

"How would you frame it? Overcharging? Revenge? Neither? Both?" I got back to the matter right in front of me.

"I think you'd have to work that out with your client. But before you talk to her, I'd put out some feelers to the American Civil Liberties Union. They've criticized Lori Pope's stance on the death penalty, so this may be up their alley.

"Also I'd dangle some bait in front of Nellie Gregory at the Plain Dealer. She's a shark, so you'll need to know what would make her salivate. And also Emery Wilkerson. But...do it all without the specific charges or your client's name. I mean, it's public record, so obviously they could go digging. But I know them all to be busy enough not to. Then circle back with your client and make a decision. Let her know it's irreversible, though. Sunshine may be the best disinfectant, but once something is exposed, you can't hide it again."

It was risky.

It was brilliant.

"Thanks, I'll consider it." And I would, very seriously.

Casey stood and looked at Simon. Satisfied with what she saw, she started checking to make sure she hadn't left anything behind.

"He sleeps in ninety-minute increments. If I leave now, he'll be waking up when I get home and I can change him, nurse him, and hand him over to Ron." She lifted the neckline of her shirt, sniffed herself. "I need a shower. I smell like milk and sweat." Her face when she looked at me was full of embarrassment and contrition. "Sorry, that was probably TMI."

I shook my head. It wasn't too much. It was actually too little. We'd shared nearly every intimacy a man and woman could. I pushed my office chair back slowly, quietly, and stood. Walked over to little Simon. The few hairs he had were light brown. A couple of unruly curls poked up. I wondered if he were going to have a mop of untamable hair like Casey's.

"What color are his eyes?" I asked.

Casey's hazel eyes flicked to mine, then flicked away almost as quickly

"Brown," she said *sotto voce*, then blurted out, "but they can change. Happens all the time."

My mind did a quick spin through ninth grade Mendelian genetics, and it was then I knew for sure.

"Are you going to send him to Catholic school?" I asked instead of any of the questions I really wanted an answer to.

"Justin, he's two months old. I think I have a few years to figure it out."

"Don't do it," I whispered. "It's not a good place for a boy."

"What?" She stopped folding, tucking, zipping, and packing for a second. Gave me a strange look. "We're both products of a good Catholic education.

They're way more liberal nowadays. You didn't even know about the nuns, they were so stealthily dressed. Ron said that the diocese has even allowed the schools to teach sex ed. I know women can't be priests, but sex ed? C'mon! That's progress."

"Pope Benedict has walked back a lot, though," I argued, though he was not my problem with the church. "He's a bit of a fundamentalist."

"He was in Hitler Youth. I think his biggest problem is not his papacy, but his belief system. He hasn't been there long enough to really affect things. I'd be surprised if he isn't asked to resign," Casey said. Her hands were fully on the stroller handles. She looked down and flicked at a foot brake with her high-top canvas sneakered foot.

"Thanks a lot for coming downtown."

"No worries. It was a good excuse to check in with Letty and go through my mail. Gotta get going, though. Time is moving."

I opened the door, and she maneuvered the buggy then herself out. I followed her through reception. Pressed the elevator call button for her. The ding sounded and the metal doors separated with a hiss. Casey did the backwards thing again and got situated in the car.

Before the doors closed, I caught her eyes with mine.

"Casey?"

"Yeah, Justin?"

I tamped down the buoyant feeling her use of my given name brought up.

"Don't marry him."

With another hiss, the doors closed, cutting off whatever response she would have made.

27

"You like to come here on a Saturday." Webb's voice was deadpan. I couldn't tell if she were joking or annoyed. I looked around the nearly empty Cleveland Heights police squad room and decided it didn't matter. "Long drive from Lakewood."

"We need to talk," I said, cutting to the chase. Even though she wasn't exactly behind me, it felt like Lori Pope was breathing down my neck. I needed some way to push back against my boss. Some way to get back some of the power this job was supposed to have given me.

"Private?" Webb asked vaguely gesturing to the uninterested cops lazily spinning in various office chairs.

"It's urgent," I said. "You'll have to trust that I'd rather not be here on a weekend."

Decision made, Webb took me back to the same unoccupied office we'd been in weeks ago. I didn't wait for her to shut the door. Kicked it with the sole of my shoe. Once closed, I took a seat in front of the desk and hefted my bag onto my lap. I didn't have time for power games today. Webb didn't sit.

"What's up?" She crossed her arms across her less than ample chest.

"I was threatened." I scratched the front of my neck where it was getting hot.

"By who? Where? Did you call in the Cleveland police? Nothing with your name came up over here."

The fact that she was keeping tabs on me didn't go unnoticed, but I'd get back to that some other time.

"Do you have the Cooley file?" I asked instead. "I need to see it."

When she saw I wasn't going to answer her questions, she left the office and came back through with the now two-inch thick file in hand. After she closed the door, I practically snatched the file from her hand without apologies. I laid it down on the desk and flipped through until I found what I was looking for.

"This is the guy." I jabbed at the paper. "Ja Roach. I thought I recognized him."

"This druggie friend of Sarah's. He's the person who threatened you? Why would he do that? He's got a bit of a record. He was her friend. Was he trying

to convince you to throw the case? Not convict Cooley? Someone from her side hire him? We need to go
to the judge. Tampering with witnesses, much less
prosecution—"

"No, nothing like that. The opposite, actually."

"He threatened you if you *didn't* get a conviction?
That makes no sense."

I didn't say anything. Just pushed my finger along
the documents until I came to what I was looking for.
Pushed the paper toward Webb.

"Look at this. *This* is what doesn't make any sense.
Roach was arrested for possession of a controlled
substance, and possession with intent to distribute.
Both should have been a felony and kicked to Common Pleas. If he had enough on him for the distribution charge, the possession alone would have been a
felony. But the distribution charge was dropped, and
the possession reduced to a misdemeanor. He got
probation. Was he ever arrested after this?"

"If it's not in the file, no."

"Double check."

Webb sank into her boss' office chair and woke
the computer. I pushed the file across to give her access to Ja Roach's date of birth. In less than a minute,
she was typing into a database. She pressed Enter
with force and we waited.

"He was never arrested after 1979, the first
charge was busted down to a misdemeanor. Maybe
after that massive stroke of luck, he saw God or the
light or something and he went straight." Webb

shrugged. I wanted to jump across the desk and shake some sense into her. She wasn't getting it.

"If he was straight, then what was he doing at Cooley's house on the night Sarah Pope OD'd? Most straight people don't hang out with drug addicts."

"What are you suggesting?"

"That my boss, Lori Pope, was behind the threat."

Despite how rash Webb made my mad drive through the city sound, I'd thought long and hard before driving across the Cuyahoga River. But I couldn't think of any other person who'd have access to Roach and me. Any other person, besides Pope, who had a stake in the Cooley case.

"What?" Webb scared was more animated than she'd been any other time. "Keep your voice down. That's a serious allegation."

I described the scene in the elevator, leaving no detail out.

"She was in my office right after that. Offered me a drink."

"She being Lori Pope...Lorraine Pope, the county prosecutor?" Webb was squinting as if trying to wrap her head around all of it. I could only nod. "Aren't you sober?"

I let that question go unanswered. Instead, I said, "She didn't say she sent Roach, but he was in a restricted access area."

"What did she say to you...besides offering you...the drink?"

"That I needed to make sure the charges stuck on Cooley. The same thing he'd said."

"Coincidence?" Webb was grasping at straws. I wasn't going to let her.

"No chance."

"What do you want from me?"

"I need you to do a shadow investigation."

"Because two people need to be on the verge of losing their jobs. Sorry, no, you can keep that to yourself."

"I was just promoted." I wanted to sound sure but could hear the quaver in my voice. It was a result of the beat my heart had just skipped.

"That's not what I heard."

"That I wasn't promoted?" When her face screwed up, I leaned forward and used a little bit of the intimidation factor I'd held back when I'd first come through the door ready to ask for a favor. "Tell me more about these rumors."

"I don't like to gossip."

"If my job's on the line, I'd like to know. Probably need to know so I can start stocking up on cat food."

"Some prosecutors talked to come cops. Said your days are numbered. Supposedly Valerie Dodds is slated to get your job after the election."

I wanted to be shocked. I wanted to be surprised. I was neither. The other shoe had finally dropped. I should have known. Probation to deputy wasn't the usual path. But I'd wanted to believe that someone saw who I could be, saw my talents, wanted to finally give me a chance to be the lawyer I always should have been.

"She's using me," I concluded.

"What? Who?" Webb had the perplexed look I was coming to despise. I wanted her to be onboard team Long. "You're full of conspiracy theories to-day."

"Not theories. Look, I'm going to tell you something in confidence." Webb's assent was contained in a curt nod. "Pope got the county to pay for my rehab. It was my ticket to the promotion. I completed Journeys and came back. She put two cases on my desk. Off the books cases."

"Saldana and Cooley."

"If I don't convict Cooley, I think she'll push me out. That Ja Roach visit was just a bit of...encouragement."

"How could she do this? I mean, it's a civil service job. You're not unionized like cops. But can she just fire you?"

"If she's willing to get this Roach guy to threaten me, then anything goes. Only one or two prosecutors have been fired for pretty massive misconduct. I wouldn't put it past her to frame me for something. Not turning over evidence in discovery would do it." It wouldn't be hard. And with prosecutors having a bad rap for honesty, and me having a reputation for drinking, no one would come to bat for me.

"If *the* prosecutor is corrupt, then all our cases are in jeopardy," Webb admitted.

"Exactly."

After that, I waited. I needed Webb to come to her own conclusion. Come to the idea that she had to pick sides and team Long was her best bet. She dropped her head, so that her face was parallel to the floor. Massaged the hair at the back of her neck. When she lifted her head finally and met my eyes, it was with a hefty sigh of agreement.

"What do you want me to do?"

"Get the skinny on Roach." Then a thought struck me. "And Libby Saldana. What's up with that as well? I don't know why I didn't link it before. Something's fishy here. The same charges for both of them in pretty different situations. Saldana's were dropped. Pope refuses on Cooley. I'm missing something. I need to know what's missing. I may not be perfect, or even the best lawyer out there, but I want to keep this job because bringing the bad guys to justice is still the most important mission I could have."

28

"How do you call a press conference? How do I get the actual press to show up?" was the question I'd put to Casey frantically last Friday. I'd done all she'd suggested, put a bug in the ear of an ACLU attorney, thrown bait before a reporter and Reverend Wilkerson. But I had no idea how to do the second part, and Cooley's freedom was too important to fuck up.

"Are you ready?" Casey's voice was deadly serious.

"It's now or never."

"Let me draft a press release. If you think it works, I'll use it and set up the conference for you."

"Seriously?"

"It's the least I can do, Justin." I tried not to think what she was making up for. "Can you get access to the banquet room behind the Tipsy Jurist? You're going to need that kind of space.

"When?"

"Monday morning. In time for the noon and evening news. At the beginning of the week to carry over. Unless we get a hurricane, you'll stay in the news. Are you sure this is what you want? Life has one-way doors and two-way doors. Most decisions are not final. This one will be."

"I understand," I had said. Then I had to wonder if my decision to turn down her proposal of a life together was a two-way door. I didn't ask that question. Instead, I took the help she offered, and here I was three days later standing next to my client behind a podium ready to play all my best cards.

"Before we get to the important subjects we need to discuss with you all here today, let us bow our heads and pray. Dear God, we come to you today asking you to give us strength. Asking you to look down upon the Cooley family with grace. Asking you to give this family the strength to stand here today and stand up to injustice. Dear God, we've been here before after the death of Marcellus Blount. After the death of Troy Duncan. While this isn't the police shooting at an unarmed man, this is the prosecutor's office using all the weapons at their disposal to take aim at an upstanding citizen whose only crime was compassion. Thank you, Lord, for hearing our prayers and giving your blessings to those of us in need. Amen."

With that, Reverend Emery Wilkinson stepped aside and turned the podium over to me. It had been a low-key speech for the civil rights firebrand. I had almost nixed his involvement in the press conference, but Casey had convinced me that the knowledge that he'd be here would double the number of press folks that came. And from looking out at the crowd of reporters that may top forty, she hadn't been wrong. Wilkinson was a card that once played, couldn't be put back in the deck. With him, I was going balls to the wall against Pope. I hoped the fallout wasn't too toxic. I took a deep breath and stepped fully in front of the microphone.

"My name is Justin McPhee. I'm here to share a huge injustice with you. Tyisha Cooley, my client here, is being prosecuted because Lori Pope is out for revenge, not justice."

All movement stopped in the room. I knew the boldness of my statement was going to knock everything else off the front page of the *Plain Dealer*.

"Before I take questions, I'd like my client to read from her prepared statement. Copies are being distributed now." I looked to the side where Casey's assistant, Letty, and some other hired helper were walking down the aisle between the chairs, passing out the sheets we'd photocopied only this morning.

"My name is Tyisha Cooley. I'm a compliance officer with Key Bank here in Cleveland. I was born and raised in Hough and now reside, as a homeowner, in Cleveland Heights. Before this case, I'd never been arrested or involved on the wrong side of the law. I cannot, however, say the same for the woman, who for forty-two years, was my best friend. I met Sarah Pope during the Hough riots in 1966. Her sister Lorraine Pope had dropped her off there as a prank.

"After hiding in an alley behind a dumpster all night, my dad and I found Sarah shivering, so we took her home. Despite us coming from very different parts of the county, we became best friends. Even though we had a lot in common like books and music and other stuff teenage girls share, there was one thing that was always different.

"She became an addict after her family disowned her for being gay. She was what they call a polysubstance user. For years, whatever made her high was her drug of choice—until she discovered heroin. On the last night of her life, I'd found a bed for her in a rehabilitation facility. She'd agreed to go but wasn't willing to go through withdrawal. I'm so very sorry that she's dead, that there was something in the drugs that she took that pushed her past her limits.

"I'll never fully recover from this loss, but I refuse to take the blame for having killed her. Years of drug use and a bad batch of heroine is what killed her. I will mourn for the rest of my life. I will always regret not driving her to Journeys immediately, but we can't change the past. I don't believe I'm truly responsible for what happened to her. A family that abandoned her, a system that failed her, that's what to blame here. Thank you."

My client stepped back with her mother and father, poster children for an intact black family. Reverend Wilkinson held their hands. If the clicking of cameras was any indication, we'd created a picture-perfect moment.

It was my turn. I'd thrown down the gauntlet, and now I needed to run with it. Somewhere a Jesuit priest was shaking his head at the mixed metaphor.

"In February of this year, the Cuyahoga County prosecutor's office made a pivot in policy. It decided to legislate without the legislature. I had another client who was overcharged. Manslaughter. Possession, et cetera, et cetera. But the judge saw through it. Forced the prosecutor's hand. We reduced it to something reasonable.

"We've worked hard as a society to decriminalize addiction. Fewer arrests. Fewer sentences. Diversionary options. 'Just say no' and high mandatory minimum sentences for non-violent crimes haven't worked over the last twenty years. Yet Lori Pope is trying to bring them back. Not for everyone accused, but very specific defendants. In our case, against Tyisha Cooley.

"Pope's using the office to grind out her personal vendetta, and that's an abuse of the office. Don't get me wrong. Sarah Pope's death was a tragedy. For her family. For the Cooleys who were her second family. But one tragedy shouldn't beget another. Instead, we call upon the prosecutor's office to use its considerable resources to find the man or woman responsible for the murder of Wayne Cooley. Tyisha's brother was gunned down in cold blood, and that case remains open and unsolved."

Like Casey had prepped me, I stopped there. I'd laid enough groundwork for my client to be the victim and Pope to be the bad guy. It was fertile ground I didn't expect reporters to leave alone. Nearly every hand in the audience went up. I looked at Casey's carefully cribbed notes. Start at the top, then to the most defense friendly. I zeroed in on the local television reporter first. She didn't hesitate.

"Victoria Greenlee. Why didn't Lori Pope offer to kick this case to the attorney general to avoid the appearance of any conflict of interest?"

"You'd have to ask her. I have no control over her office's decisions."

"Did the judge make that offer?"

"It's an attorney's job, or that of their office, to recognize a conflict and take the appropriate action."

"*Sun News,*" I chose next.

"Blake Hardin Tatum of the *Sun Post Herald.* Are you saying that there's an open murder case involving this family?"

I looked over my shoulder and raised my eyebrows, the cue for the Cooleys to step forward and tell their story.

And the three of them did it, quite eloquently.

"Are you saying that Sarah Pope was there the night your son and brother was murdered?"

I walked back to the podium. The Cooleys moved to the side, smoothly letting me take center stage again. I had to wonder if Casey was some kind of savant because this whole thing was going as if according to some script even with all the wildcards of the press.

"On the twentieth of December 1988, Sarah Pope was in Tyisha Cooley's home, supposedly house-sitting. But she was getting high. Wayne Cooley stopped by at his parents' behest to check up on her. While he was leaving, someone drove up and shot him dead in cold blood. This night, as some of you may recall, was the blizzard of '88, not a night when most were cruising the streets.

"It had all the markers of a deliberate hit. Wayne Cooley had never been in trouble, had no gang affiliations, was an engineer, lived on the westside. Yet the Cleveland Heights police pursued the case as if he were somehow responsible. The killer got away clean, and the theory that Pope was the target was never pursued. So here we are, some nineteen years later, and Sarah Pope gets a hot shot. No one else overdosed that weekend whose drugs were laced with fentanyl. Lori Pope somehow managed an immediate cremation."

"There was no autopsy?" a reporter asked as Casey said they would. "I thought there were autopsies in all suspicious deaths."

"The death was ruled an accident and Pope, Lori Pope, that is, rushed the process. She signed on for the cremation. So if there was something suspicious, none of that evidence was ever gathered. Yet, now Pope is pointing the finger at Tyisha Cooley when she has conveniently destroyed the evidence that could exonerate my client."

"Which goes to the history of prosecutors not only in Cuyahoga County, but in this great country tilting the scales in their direction and not in the direction of justice," Wilkinson interjected.

After that, the crowd of reporters were mostly on board with our argument. The Cooleys were innocent victims and the prosecutor's office was full of thoughtless zealots. It wasn't a touchdown by any means, but this got us past the first down and toward a not guilty verdict.

29

Nicole
July 20, 2008

"You want the bad news or the worse news." Webb asked her non-question from her uncomfortable perch on my couch. I'd have invited her to make herself at home, but I didn't want her to take the common courtesy to heart.

"Well, at least you're giving me options." No smile cracked detective Darlene Webb's lips. One day I hoped she got a sense of humor. Had to wonder if she sat straight-faced and tight-lipped through a stand-up comedy special or a rerun of *Friends*. I looked at today's drab olive suit. Nope, probably never watched either. "Start wherever you are," I offered.

"Libby Saldana was the wrong defendant."

"That's a theme around here." I tried to keep my sigh just this side of dramatic. It still stung that in my last case before rehab, I'd gone after an innocent woman when the killer had been right in front of me. For once, Webb looked empathetic.

"Seriously. This is not a murky crime scene where we charge bad guy one instead of bad guy two, though they're both guilty of something. Libby Saldana was *literally* the wrong person."

"How so?" I leaned forward, elbows on knees, intrigued.

"I called in a favor. Cross-referenced cases from Cleveland and Lakewood with Saldana. No hits. Then I started changing things up. There's a Libby Saldano in the system. Her name isn't Elizabeth, though. It's Liberdad."

"Liberty, in English."

Darlene Webb was still talking, but my mind was flashing back to the directive from Pope, to throw the book at her if a Libby Saldano came through the system.

"Sorry. Can you go back?" I hadn't heard a word she'd said after the woman's name.

"Liberdad Saldano has crossed paths with Pope."

"When? How?"

"She was a witness in Pope's first murder trial."

"What year?"

"1997. November and December, actually. Why?"

"I'll tell you in a minute. Just go on."

"So Lori Pope's trying a murder case. The story is that two guys got into it over Saldano at a bar on the near westside. Her boyfriend shoots and kills this guy who wouldn't leave her alone. The bartender was in the basement getting a keg, so there were no other witnesses and this was before security cameras were everywhere. There was no one else in the bar. Saldano, who's the only witness at this point, didn't show up for trial."

"Even with a subpoena?" There had to have been one. No prosecutor, no attorney worth their salt for that matter, would have let a key witness go without pulling out all the stops to get them on the stand.

"Bench warrant and everything," Webb said. It meant not only had Pope used all the power she had to get Soldano on the stand, the judge had put out a warrant to arrest the witness if she came into contact with any peace or court officer. Webb continued, "Liberdad left the state. Went to her aunt's house in the Poconos. Obviously the jury only had the cops' words to go on. You can guess how that went. Supposedly took them less than half an hour to acquit. A few months later, Soldano and her boyfriend, they move back here as bold as day. Got married. Had a couple of kids. Both stayed on the straight and narrow more or less, though."

"That sounds like a mostly good ending." After being in this job for this many years, even I no longer thought prison was the right answer for everything, though it was really the *only* answer the justice system provided.

"Except for Pope losing." Webb shrugged.

"Yeah, except for that."

"After the trial, the cops said Pope was on the warpath. Screaming at them in the bull pen about how they let a witness skip town. Didn't make an effort to keep eyes on her. How they ruined her win record. I mean, every so often a prosecutor gets mad at one of us, I guess. But they usually keep it private, in the hall or in an empty holding cell. Some of those officers are still mad over what Pope did. She kind of had a Jekyll and Hyde thing going on."

"Do you really think that was revenge? This is revenge? That she'd use her office like that?"

Webb refused to speculate. Instead, she shuffled papers and got on with it.

"Ja Roach has crossed paths with her as well," she said. "There's more than what we dug up the other day."

"Speak to me."

"Here's Lori Pope's CV."

I took the paper, surprised to see such a thing. It wasn't the kind of document elected officials needed. Mostly I'd read glossed-up versions of her professional career that she used on the official website. The three-page, single-spaced document, in addition to the jobs she held, listed her most well-known wins.

"If you look on page two, you'll see that she held a couple of positions while at the Lakewood law department. First, as a lower level, then head after Liam Brody was elected as county prosecutor."

Elected positions in Ohio were like a game of musical chairs. Politicians moved from one position to another through every election cycle. Only the convicted and dead lost their positions.

"So she was in Lakewood for ten years from '78 to '88." I shrugged. It wasn't much different than the CV of half the judges in Common Pleas.

"Ja Roach got popped for possession in November 1979. Case doesn't get referred to Common Pleas. No jail time. Looks like some kind of fine and probation. Gets popped again in January 1980. Possession again. Bigger amount. No transfer. No jail time. Then it stops in its tracks."

"What do you mean?"

"This guy has no record from that last day in 1980 until now. Despite that we know for a fact he is still using."

"Is that unusual? I mean, maybe he wised up and got more careful."

"I've never seen that even among the rich. Users, addicts, they always get popped for something. It's the nature of engaging in illegal behavior many times a week. I even asked around and no one has seen this clean a rap sheet unless they died, left town, or got clean, and even then not always."

"What do you think happened?"

"The guys in the squad room say this is possible only if he's a CI—confidential informant—because those guys can skate provided they do something for the cops or prosecutors."

"Or?"

"He worked for her in exchange for amnesty."

"Is that something that's done?"

"Rarely, and always off the books. There's a certain kind of law enforcement person who thinks they can do stuff for the greater good if they...bend the rules a little or a lot."

"So you're thinking she paid Ja Roach, to do what? Keep an eye on Sarah? Is that how Sarah made it so long where the life expectancy is so short?"

"No, Nicole." Webb made a rare show of exasperation. "I think she paid Ja Roach to get her addicted, keep her addicted, or kill her."

Her frankness threw me right to the back couch cushions. When I'd gone to the detective's office with my nascent conspiracy theories, that had been one thing. Her coming back confirming my worst nightmare, and turning it into a night terror, was something different completely.

"Do you think Tyisha Cooley is guilty of Sarah Pope's death?" I asked Webb.

"Did Cooley put the needle in her veins and inject the drugs that caused an overdose? Yes. Was she responsible? I don't think so. But there's really no way to prove it unless Ja Roach talks or turns."

"Why would he? He's got a sweet deal. If what you suggest is trust, he can do whatever he wants and not go to jail. Plus the only thing he gets is self-incrimination and not for manslaughter, but murder or felony murder." I shook my head. "Jesus fucking Christ."

While I raked my fingers through my hair, Webb sat still and mute. If she felt any of the outrage that

I did, she kept it to herself. Finally, into the silence, she said, "So what are you going to do?"

"Try the case I was assigned. Justin McPhee seems like he's capable of keeping the pot stirred in his bid to defend his client. If the justice system was designed to work, then I guess we have to let it."

30

Justin
August 8, 2008

"Justin Patrick McPhee, I don't think we've met formally." Lori Pope stretched out her hand.

Working hard to keep the surprise from lifting my eyebrows toward my admittedly receding hairline, I switched Morro's leash from my right hand to left and without thinking took the county prosecutor's hand in a firm shake. Hers was unusually cold for August.

"You...uh...live around here?" The words came out of my mouth in a jumble. I had no idea why I was nervous, but I was.

"Tremont? God, no. I'd never live this close to hipsters and wannabes. Rocky River born and bred." Her take on Tremont wasn't wrong in one respect—

it was slowly being gentrified. But there was still quite a bit of diversity in the neighborhood.

Morro pulled at my left hand, undoubtedly upset that I'd stopped his information gathering mission along the diagonal path that bisected Lincoln Park.

"Good seeing you," I said. Lifted my right hand to my forehead in a mock salute. Then switched the leash back. Morro, though generally well behaved, couldn't contain himself around the swish of a bushy-tailed squirrel. I needed my stronger arm in control for when he lost his.

"Let me walk with you," Pope said. She was in step with me and the dog, not giving me much in the way of choice of human companionship.

"Can we reach a plea agreement on Cooley?" I asked. I wasn't sure why Pope was here, but I may as well argue my client's case while I had the chance. Talking to *the* prosecutor was a rare opportunity for someone like me for whom criminal defense nor campaign donations weren't my bread and butter.

"You haven't donated to my campaign," was Pope's non-answer, as if she'd read my mind. Surely she wasn't shaking me down. That had to violate at least a dozen laws. My nerves ratcheted up a notch. It was like having a parent or a teacher lurking about ready to punish you for something you've done when you weren't sure what the infraction was.

"Just a Common Pleas lawyer." I hated the hesitation in my voice. Somehow, I thought, a better man would be more confident. I hated that about myself. "Not much of a budget for political donations."

"I heard you came into some cash recently. I think that should allow for a more generous financial plan."

Was that the reason she'd held a hard line on Cooley? It couldn't be that diabolically simple. I'd been thinking some kind of personal vendetta the whole time and maybe it only came down to something as simple as throwing a couple of hundred in the campaign coffers. I'd poo-pooed Casey when she'd asked about my donation strategy. Since I wasn't waiting for judges to hand out cases to me, I didn't see the need to keep up with who was running for office and who could grant favors.

"I'll see what I can do." I made a mental note to put a check in the mail this week, though it wasn't something I could write off as an expense.

"I didn't come here hat in hand, counselor. Nor did I come here ready to plea."

The fuck? I couldn't keep my annoyance at bay.

"Then why have you deigned to come down to our little hipster area of the westside?" I asked before I could filter. Nerves and anxiety were turning to aggravation. Working to keep my feelings in check meant that I couldn't use my brain to figure out her motives, so I did the only thing I could do. Keep the dog at heel and wait.

"I'm actually working on a case and I thought that you could help."

"I'm a criminal defense attorney. I think I'm not on your list of likely helpers." I had to wonder if other lawyers sold out so quickly that she thought I might as well. I was all for justice, but her office was all about putting people in jail. Despite the overuse of the phrase "brought to justice," those weren't the same thing.

My dog chose that exact moment to squat and do his thing. The odor rose up quickly. Pope's nose wrinkled in disgust. She waved a hand in front of her face.

"But you *are*."

I pulled a plastic bag from the dispenser on the leash and bent down to pick up Morro's poo.

"We think we're smarter than them," Pope observed while kicking dirt around my dog's legs. "But clearly the pets are running the world. How is it they went from hunting and killing for us, to you picking up dog shit from the ground?"

"I usually find my evening walk to be a relaxing time. You're harshing my mellow, so if you could get on with it. Otherwise, I need to get home and finalize my motions in the Cooley case. They're due Monday."

I found a trash can and pitched the excrement in there, while my usually friendly dog looked up at some kind of animal in a tree, but showed little interest in our walking companion. Morro was a good judge of character. He loved Casey almost as much as I did but wasn't taken with Pope. I nearly gasped when I realized where my train of thought had taken me.

"You were saying...about this *help* you need," I prompted, turning toward Pope. I realized now that she was wearing pretty tight short shorts and a matching top. All with that symbol from the store with lemon in the name. She was an objectively attractive woman but inspired nothing but the willies. I wanted to get out of her orbit, run away. But it seemed like it would be best to hear her out.

"I think you'll remember Monsignor Gregory Cobb. He was in charge of service outreach at Saint Ignatius."

I stumbled over something in the grass, probably a tree branch. Morro let out a small woof of protest at the awkward jerk of his leash. Cobb's was a name I hadn't heard in a long time. One I'd tried not to think about for an even longer time.

"Of course," I started when the silence had gone on too long. "The monsignor led our service trip to Guatemala."

"Along with, Jerry…Geraldo Morales who was a native from there. Did I get that right?"

"That's what I remember," I said. I pulled Morro's leash hard and turned on my heel. Forget the regular route. It was time to get back to my apartment now. Right myself. Get back to those motions which wouldn't write themselves. I was doing this case all on my own. I didn't have Casey to rely on.

"Not so fast, Justin." It was as if Pope were walking behind me in one moment, then materialized in front of me in the next, halting my progress. My normally friendly dog let out a very quiet growl of protest. "Don't you want to know why we're investigating?"

I didn't want to know. At all. If there was one name I'd never wanted to think about or hear again, it was Cobb's.

"I assume you're going to tell me," I said through gritted teeth, "so please share."

"They somehow slipped through the crack of the Catholic church abuse investigation, Cobb and Morales, that is."

I sped up my walk home, not taking any care to see if Pope was following. Morro, for once, heeled like he'd been trained, as if he could sense I would be unable to manage if he moved away. I wanted to point out to Lori Pope that his animal smarts extended to having a second sense, knowing when the people in their pack needed comfort and solace, then gave it willingly without any expectation of something in return.

"Some new evidence has come to light that they abused students at the school. Specifically on service trips to Guatemala."

I stumbled again. This time on flat pavement. My pace quickened because I wanted to be anywhere but here. My curiosity got the better of me for a split second, and I spat out the question I'd been wondering.

"Are you going to prosecute?"

"That very much depends on what witnesses are willing to come forward. I was thinking you could help me with that."

"How?" I choked out. A dark corner of my memory, one with a very closed door, shut very tight, locked with the key thrown away, was starting to show light through cracks.

"I'd love to know what other students you remember from the trip or trips you took."

"Has someone come forward? Is that why you're looking into this?"

"Unfortunately, I can't discuss an ongoing investigation with you. What I *can* tell you is that it's very important for my office to have this win. If you can help in any way, then we'll do what we can to work with you on future matters."

I sped away, and this time Pope let me go.

31

"What are you going to do?" Detective Darlene Webb whispered to me from a corner of the gallery in Judge Marsh's wood paneled courtroom. I was in front of the bar, and she behind it. Valerie Dodds was at the prosecution table, next to the empty jury box laying out yellow legal pads and sharpened pencils

"Try the case." I shrugged in my fitted dark blue suit, then self-consciously tugged at the hem, making sure everything was in place. I'd already had one drink to smooth out my nerves. I couldn't afford another right now. I was walking the knife's edge between nerves, calm, and a little bit tipsy. It was a very delicate balance, and I was already feeling wobbly. Pope had caught on during my last trial. I couldn't afford to fuck up like that again. Precarious didn't even begin to describe my position.

"Can you do that? Ethically? Don't you need to disclose the information you have on Ja Roach?" Webb asked. I turned and looked toward the defense table. Cooley was sitting, unmoving, her face and body facing toward the empty bench in what my mother would call a "secretary dress." Black with a flower pattern. McPhee was doing his own pad and pencil arranging.

"What do we have?" I hissed, my voice a whisper. "A guess? A suspicion? That's nothing concrete. Not even enough to add up to circumstantial evidence. What remains one hundred percent true is that Ty-isha Cooley pushed drugs into the veins of her long-time friend. Did she have intent? No. But that's not what she's charged with here. She's well represented. She's not in jail. Cooley is guilty of a statutory crime and that's exactly how I'm going to handle it."

"Are you comfortable with that?" Webb asked. I wanted to know when the sober-faced detective had started caring about nuance, or morality for that matter.

"Unless you can bring me something in the next week that changes my mind, then yes. All we're doing here today are pretrial motions. So there's a solid ten days to change tack, if that's what we're going to do. This here, however"—I gestured at the whole courtroom and now the judge who was coming to the bench—"is not how I want to go down."

The compromise wasn't exactly sitting well with me, but as between the defendant and myself, I was going to pick me every single time. Basic survival instinct. Lori Pope was the enemy of us both. Cooley and Justin McPhee seemed to be battling her their way. I had to find my own path.

"All rise," the bailiff cried.

Judge Kate Marsh's walk to the bench was brisk and without fanfare. She waved us all to our seats then looked between the prosecutor and defense tables before lasering in on Justin McPhee.

"Well, it seems like a lot has happened since I last saw all of you. Mr. McPhee, it appears, you threw a big party and invited every reporter in town. Emory Wilkinson was even a guest. And when the right reverend is behind a dais, there's always a spectacle.

"I see we have a stack of motions here, and I'll dispense with those in a minute. But first let me put on the record that I'm taking judicial notice *sua sponte* of the allegations of impropriety and conflict of interest raised during that little press conference."

The case hadn't exactly gone viral, but news of the press conference was on page one of the suburban papers, page three of the *Plain Dealer*, and teased on the local news for two nights in a row. This morning an AM talk radio host had taken issue with an editorial suggesting Lori Pope may not be the right person for her job. In a county as small ours with its declining population, news like this was a hot commodity and hard to ignore.

"Mr. McPhee, you seem to have a problem with the fact that the victim here is the sister of the county prosecutor." Judge Marsh didn't so much as ask a question but leave a big hole for Justin McPhee to fill with a defense-friendly request. I turned toward him and waited.

"I don't want to impugn the integrity of the process, your honor," McPhee started. "The grand jury, of course, was free to hear the prosecutor's evidence and decide whether or not to indict. Because it's a secret tribunal, it's impossible to know if they were informed of the relationship. And if they had been thusly informed, whether they'd have chosen to indict."

I felt my mouth drop open. Quickly shut it. He wasn't asking for assignment to the attorney general or a change of venue. If he hadn't wanted either, then I was at a loss to the point of the press conference.

"I don't have anything related to this raised in your pretrial motions." Judge Marsh was giving him a second bite at the apple.

"As your honor is aware, an indictment is not subject to appeal except in limited circumstances, none of which apply here. Furthermore, a conflict of interest by the prosecutor can only be decided by the prosecutor or by your honor." He paused, took a deep breath. "I'm more than willing to try the case with the attorneys, Ms. Long and Ms. Dodds, as it stands. My understanding is that if the attorney general takes over, the charges will still stand. We're

past the investigative stage, your honor. The indictment has already come down."

"That's a fair decision, Mr. McPhee," Marsh said,
looking relieved not to have to pull in a new prosecutor at the last minute.

But was it? I had to wonder what McPhee had up
his sleeve. No defense attorney worth their weight
walked their client into jail. But that's what it
seemed like he was doing here. I glanced at Dodds.
Her almost imperceptible shrug told me she didn't
know any more than I did.

"Ms. Long, Ms. Dodds, do you have anything to
say on behalf of the state?" Marsh asked with a subtle reminder that we had a duty that was bigger than
our county office, to the citizens of the state of Ohio.

"Your honor, I assure the court that my office will
be as impartial on this case as any other."

"Ms. Cooley. Are you in agreement with this? Do
you wish to have this case's prosecution transferred
to the attorney general?"

"No, your honor."

"Then let's dispense with the motions actually before the court today."

"Your honor," McPhee argued, "I've filed a motion to dismiss with the court. I maintain that the
charges in this case are an overreach. The victim
here, the prosecutor's half-sister, was a lifelong drug
user and addict. There is no dispute that my client
administered the drugs that ultimately resulted in
Sarah Pope's overdose, but it was at the behest of
Pope herself.

"Involuntary manslaughter requires the commission of a felony. In this case, the underlying felony is corrupting another with drugs. That's not what was going on here. Pope was already addicted. Cooley had no intent to harm her. The latter two my client isn't guilty of. She did not possess the heroin. Those charges would be better suited for the dealer or Sarah Pope's friend, Ja Roach, who supplied the drugs. And getting medical aid should not be confused with evidence tampering. Should the last stand, it could, your honor, have a chilling effect on good Samaritans."

"Who's going on record for the state today? Ms. Long? Ms. Dodds?"

"I will, your honor," I said as I stood and walked from behind the table. With no jury to impress, McPhee had stayed back. Even though my college major had been religious studies and not theater, I knew the importance of making an impression.

"Nicole Long, assistant prosecuting attorney and deputy chief of Major Crimes. Assistant prosecuting attorney Dodds will be assisting me today. While I appreciate my opposing counsel's argument, this death and this crime cannot go unanswered.

"The Book of Exodus states that if there is harm, then the perpetrator shall pay, a life for a life, an eye for an eye, a hand for a hand, a tooth for a tooth. Obviously we've moved beyond biblical justice, but that doesn't mean people can just do what they like. We have crime and we have punishment. In the middle, your honor, is the jury. That sacrosanct body is the only one who should decide between guilt and innocence. Not my boss, not me, and excuse me, but not the third branch, either."

With a curt nod, I turned and strode to my seat, stiffening my body against the craving to top up my confidence with a little bourbon.

The judge looked between McPhee's table and ours. "Give me a moment," Judge Marsh said before giving the bailiff the signal to cut her mike. A young woman in a suit came through the doors from behind the bench. Likely a law clerk, Judge Marsh had summoned to clarify some point of law. Dodds took that moment to nudge me. She leaned in, her voice a quiet murmur.

"What were you talking about with Webb, Darlene is it?"

"Nothing."

"It looked like something," Dodds said, her tone full of suspicion that I was cutting her out.

"Just making sure all our ducks are in a row."

"So the witness lineup is still the officer on scene, the medical examiner, and Ja Roach. You think he's gonna show?"

"Subpoenaed everyone," I answered. I hadn't shared Roach's direct threat nor Pope's implied one. But if he really was on the payroll, so to speak, then his presence was guaranteed.

The bailiff's shuffling feet and Judge Marsh's bang of the gavel brought everyone's attention back to the bench.

"We're back on the record in Ohio versus Cooley. I've had an opportunity in chambers before and now after counsel's arguments to consider the defendant's motion to dismiss. That motion is denied. While I appreciate the defendant's conundrum here, the prosecutor's charges are not an overreach. We will proceed to trial on the charges as indicted. Mr. McPhee, your jury instructions appear sound, so I will use those as I instruct the jury when we get to deliberation. I think that dispenses with everything. I'll see you back here on the twenty-fifth of August. Until then, we're adjourned."

32

As I wheeled a dolly into the twenty-fifth floor court-room, bankers box strapped unceremoniously by a blue-and-red bungee cord, I tried not to miss my one-time co-counsel. As if I'd willed her there, I turned my head to the right only to see Casey Cort seated in the gallery. In a moment of weakness, I'd asked her to sit in when and if she could.

I nodded in greeting on my way past the bar. In a moment, a court officer escorted my client, Tyisha, into the gallery. She was dressed in an outfit that would be at home at Antioch Baptist. It was perhaps a bit much for me, but a jury would probably love it. Piousness was writ large across the double-breasted, gold-buttoned maroon dress.

"Are you ready?" Cooley asked me as I arranged my pad, pen, and papers across the table.

"As ready as I'm ever going to be, Ms. Cooley."

"Has anything changed?"

"Not since we've talked. Jury nullification, while not exactly encouraged, is solidly part of our constitutional law. The plan remains to convince the jury that someone such as yourself is undeserving of punishment, all the while sowing the seeds of unreasonable doubt. Fortunately, our justice system allows us to make two different plays at the same time."

"What are my chances?" Her tone so neutral and she so even-keeled, I had to worry she was one of those quiet ones who becomes explosive.

"Fifty-fifty, I'd say."

"Well, that's not zero." Cooley made as if to sit but bumped her chair. The heavy wood went tumbling to the ground. It was an unexpected display of clumsiness from a woman who was otherwise nearly always composed. I looked at the industrial carpet to see if there was a rip or tear that could have tripped her up. As I lifted the chair, however, my gaze roamed to the gallery. I nearly tripped when I saw who was idling behind the bar.

"Long time no see, Tyisha," Lori Pope said to my client. "What's it been—thirty something years? Even though we can't live more than ten miles apart. I used to see you so much more often when we were kids. You were at our house every other month, it felt like."

"You know the rules, Lori." I held up my hand to her. "My client can't talk to opposing counsel."

"Oh, I know. But given how we go back, I thought I'd make this single exception to reminisce with an old family friend. That's what you said at the press conference, right, that our history is the reason we're here. I just wanted to pay my respects based on that history." Pope turned around when Cooley's parents came down the aisle. "Mr. and Mrs. Cooley, it's good to see you as well," Pope said. "I remember you coming to pick up Tyisha on more than one occasion. I'm glad that you're doing well."

"I wouldn't exactly say well, given the circumstances that have brought us here," Mr. Cooley said. "Rainey. When did you lose that name, Lorraine?"

"Too cute for politics, wouldn't you agree, Mr. Cooley? You were always an expert in that arena. I'm sure you understand."

"Ms. Pope, please." There was a pleading note in my voice. The prosecutor was on the edge of impropriety.

"Of course." Pope stepped back far enough to look like an observer. "I do not wish to cross any boundaries. A mistrial would be most unfortunate."

"I'm glad to see that education improved your vocabulary, if not your morals," Mrs. Cooley said. While I waited for Pope's comeback, the courtroom door opened again. Seeking out reporters meant a full gallery. This place was busier than the Tower City train station. Upon seeing the visitor, though, I nearly tripped over the same empty patch of carpet my client had. Pope turned her head over her shoulder. Her smile was cold as she waved the woman forward.

"Mr. McPhee, it's good to see you again. Counselor, I think you'll remember Sister Angela."

"Sister." The honorific barely came out, and only out of very strict altar boy training.

"Little Justin Patrick McPhee," said the woman of my nightmares. "You've grown so very big. No longer a gangly young man. I'd have hardly recognized you. Not with these old eyes."

"What brings you to a county courtroom?" I was so surprised, I sounded completely normal.

"The prosecutor thought I should see what a Saint Ignatius education could do. She's suggested starting a mentor program at the school. That would be such a good idea for our young men to get an idea of what they could accomplish should they dedicate themselves to their studies."

"Speaking of, I must get back to my work. If you don't mind." I didn't want to be dismissed before I turned my back and nearly fell into my chair. The bailiff came and handed me the foot and a half wide printout of the potential jurors that would be subjected to today's *voir dire*.

I hunched over the list, red pencil in hand, and pretended to focus on what was to come. My mind was anywhere but in Judge Marsh's courtroom. It was in Guatemala on a mission. When I was only fourteen and impressionable. Easily persuaded by the pious. Led like a lamb to slaughter.

I shook my head to clear the cobwebs of memory. The judge came to the bench. It was time to get to work.

Long, Dodds, and I made very quick work of jury selection. With nothing controversial in the case, it was only a matter of getting the potential jurors' assurance, however specious, that they hadn't read news reports of the case.

Of course, I hoped they had. Long likely wished they were telling the truth.

Before long, we were back from our lunch break and again waiting for not only the judge, but the jury. Once everyone was situated in their rightful places, the judge looked pointedly at Long.

"Call your first witness."

"The State of Ohio calls Geoffrey Cummings to the stand."

Long had obviously prepped the officer to come in his uniform. Black pants, black button-down shirt, black tie. Shiny badge on his left breast and peaked cap under his arm as he made his way to the stand. Despite him looking like a nearly exact duplicate of his brethren, something about him was achingly familiar. I glanced back to the gallery and locked eyes with Casey. She nodded slightly, confirming what I thought. Cummings had been a witness in our previous murder case together. Kendrick Walker's death had come later. Cummings had been quite a rookie to death in Sarah Pope's case then.

At the podium, I watched Long's back, straight and stiff, as she asked all of the necessary preliminary questions qualifying the witness.

"Officer Cummings, can you tell the jury what brought you to the Cooley residence on Brunswick Road in Cleveland Heights on the twentieth of July of last year?"

"Dispatch received a call that a woman at the house was nonresponsive, possibly due to a drug overdose."

"Was that what you found when you arrived?"

"Yes, there was a woman, mid-fifties, white, lying on the floor of the living room."

"What did you do?"

"I called an ambulance and attempted to administer CPR. First, I had to clean away the vomit."

"Did she respond to your attempts at resuscitation?"

Cummings' nod was half-hearted. "Her breathing was shallow, but she wasn't conscious."

"What did you do next?"

"I opened the door for the paramedics, then followed the ambulance to the hospital. Unfortunately, she was DOA." The officer's voice cracked at the admission of his failure to revive her.

"Dead on arrival to the emergency room?" Long emphasized.

"Yes, dead on arrival."

With that dramatic end to his testimony, Nicole Long gave me only a glance before turning the witness over to me.

"Who did you arrest on July twentieth?"

"Arrest?

"Tyisha Cooley is here on trial for a crime. I want to know about the arrest."

"I...I didn't arrest...anyone?" Cummings' answer came out like a question.

"And why not?"

Cummings tried to look around me toward the prosecution table. I stepped in his line of sight.

"They can't help you to answer. Please tell the jury why you didn't arrest anyone that night."

"Our watch command had a standing order not to arrest drug addicts unless they were dealing or harming others."

"Did you arrest Ja Roach?"

"The other guy who was there that night? No."

"Why not?"

"Because it wasn't a crime scene, just a tragic overdose of a long-time user."

"No further questions, your honor."

"Redirect?"

"No, your honor," Long said. "We're ready to call our next witness."

Judge Marsh's gesture said, get on with it. "We call Jaleesa Chaney to the stand."

A youngish black woman made her way to the witness chair. Nicole asked Chaney about her title and tenure at the Medical Examiner's office. Deputy and six years were her answers.

"Can you tell us a little bit about the drug overdose landscape in the county?" Long asked Chaney.

I wanted to object for relevance. It was looking like Long was going to take us all around the barn to try to prove Pope's policy was sound. I almost glanced back to see what Casey thought, but remembered Sister Angela and thought better of it.

"Every year for the last eight years the number of overdose cases we see in our office has increased," Chaney testified.

"What kind of numbers are we talking?"

"From one hundred per year to one thousand." No one in the press or jury raised an eyebrow. It was an unfortunate fact that we were all used to hearing these kinds of statistics for Ohio.

"What causes an overdose?" Long pivoted. "Every drug user who shoots up doesn't die every time."

"Objection, your honor." I jumped to my feet before they went too far afield and made it seem like my client was single-handedly responsible for an opiate epidemic. "This is the province of an expert witness, not the coroner's office."

"Ms. Chaney, as part of your job, do you receive information on drug usage and overdoses?" Judge Marsh asked of the witness.

"Yes, your honor. We're the recipient of city of Cleveland, Cleveland suburb, and state statistics from the government agencies in charge of various municipalities or jurisdictions. Additionally, we contribute to the statistics for the county as well as the various levels of government."

"Your objection is overruled, Mr. McPhee. I think Chaney has sufficient expertise to testify to the rate and type of overdoses. Please continue, Ms. Long."

"I was asking you, what causes an overdose?" I wanted to object again, explain to Judge Marsh that cause was not effect, but I resisted. The jury may not understand the nuance and think I was trying to hide something. I practically sat on my hands and listened to Chaney's answer.

"There are two main factors. The relative health of the user, and what they've ingested."

"What's fentanyl?" Long asked.

"Fentanyl is a synthetic opioid that's sometimes added to heroin to enhance the effect and to make the already diluted drug go farther."

"Have you seen an increase of overdoses where fentanyl was a factor?"

"About twofold." Chaney's face was suitably somber.

"What happens to the human body when ingesting a fatal dose of fentanyl?"

"It massively depresses the organs. In most cases, breathing ceases."

"When you autopsy a heroin addict who overdoses, what do you typically find?"

"Collapsed veins. Sometimes they are also friable, meaning the flesh barely holds together. Also often malnourishment."

"Does the likelihood of overdose increase with age?"

"Yes. Many human bodies can withstand less as they get older."

"Does the likelihood of overdose increase as addicts have a longer period of addiction?"

"Yes, active drug use can weaken the body. Different substances have different effects."

"And fentanyl increases likelihood of overdose as well?"

"Yes, additives of almost all types change how the drug interacts. Most of those changes are more harmful than helpful."

"Thank you, Ms. Chaney."

I was starting to wonder if I was in some kind of dream. Nicole didn't really have evidence. She had facts of a death and the fact that my client gave the fateful shot. I was scrambling in my brain as to how to convey these evidentiary inadequacies to the jury.

"Ms. Chaney, what is the main duty of your job?"

"Performing autopsies on victims of death that are generally not by natural causes."

"How many autopsies would you say you perform in a month?"

"I'd say about one hundred fifteen."

"What percentage of those are overdoses?"

"In 2008 so far?" I nodded. "Maybe five percent."

"That has to be more than previous years."

"Yes, it's starting to appear there's an opioid epidemic."

"Did you perform an autopsy on Sarah Rose Pope?"

"No, I didn't."

"How do you know she died of a drug overdose?"

"I've read the reports from the emergency room physicians."

"But you personally, nor did anyone in your office, examine her body after death."

"No, we couldn't."

"Why not?"

"She was cremated two days after her death."

"Is that unusual?"

"Yes, she'd have been taken to the hospital morgue, then depending on manner of death, transported to my office or transferred to a funeral home."

"And in Sarah's case, to the best of your knowledge?"

"Funeral home."

"Is that unusual?"

"For a death that's not labeled suspicious, no."

"Thank you, Ms. Chaney, no further questions." I walked back to the table. The medical examiner had said what I'd needed—that Sarah Pope's death wasn't suspicious.

"It's four o'clock," Judge Marsh announced with a pointed look at the clock on the courtroom's far wall. "We're adjourned for the day. Be here tomorrow morning at nine-thirty. We'll start promptly at ten a.m."

33

"I call Ja Roach to the stand." Nicole Long was standing, self-assured.

Her witness strode to the witness chair with all the confidence of someone not facing a prison sentence. Long asked his name and address in Lakewood, then came her first substantive question.

"How did you come to be acquainted with Sarah Pope?"

"There was a huge blizzard in February 1980. I lived across from Madison Park in Lakewood. I was looking out my window at the falling snow and what I thought was a woman or child huddled in a car. I'd just turned off the news, which had all those warnings about people not turning on their oven to keep warm, and realized that the person in the car could, like, die. So I went out there and invited her in for the night. We became friends after that."

"How often would you say that you saw her in the last twenty-seven years?"

"Maybe three or four times a year. Sometimes more. Sometimes less." He shook his head at the memories. "Yeah, we've been friends a long time. You know how it can go."

"What would you say that you two have in common?" Long asked. I had to credit her with getting Roach's biggest flaw out there front and center. With...complicated witnesses, it was best to diffuse the shock.

"I'm a heroin addict." His admission was matter-of-fact. "I wish I were in recovery, but I'm not. I manage it."

"Are you high today?"

"No. I'd probably be asleep if I was." Several of the jurors laughed. He was disarming them with brutal honesty. It was going to take a little more work to paint him as the bad guy. I'd get my turn, soon, though.

"Can you tell us what you remember from the night of July twenty of last year."

We were getting to the meat of it. The one witness, besides my client, who was there the moment Sarah Pope took her last breath. Roach had not made himself available to me for questioning, so it was the first time I was hearing his side of the story. I needed to see where the stories diverged because I was sure

AIME AUSTIN

his version was going to be different. Addicts were nothing if not self-serving, especially when trying to avoid jail. It was no accident that he was free and Tyisha Cooley was not. The why of that was what I was hoping to hear.

"Sarah called me," Roach answered.

"Why?"

"She'd broken up with her boyfriend and she was temporarily turned out."

I leaned toward Cooley. "I thought you told me she was gay," I whispered.

Cooley nodded. "She was. It's easier to get men to support you, though." I nodded in understanding before turning my attention back to Roach and Long.

"Did she come stay with you?" Long was asking.

"I offered," Roach said, "but she said she'd rather go to Tyisha's house." I scribbled a note about the slippery answer. It was conveniently unverifiable and lowered his culpability.

"Tyisha Cooley, the defendant." Long pointed a single accusatory finger in my client's direction. I hated when prosecutors pointed the finger of the damned at the defense table. It hearkened back to every black-and-white movie where the defendant was as guilty as sin.

"Yes, Ms. Cooley, I'm sorry." Speaking of acting, Roach was overdoing it on the contrition.

"Why did you drive from the westside to Cooley's house?" Long asked.

"Sarah said later in the call that she was going to have to go into rehab. That she wanted one last party." I wanted to object to the hearsay because none of us would ever hear Sarah's version. But Roach's testimony didn't violate any evidentiary rules.

"So what did you do?"

"I drove over to Cleveland Heights. Called the dealer to meet us there."

"Then what happened after the dealer made the delivery and you had the drugs in hand?"

"Sarah was kind of shaky. It probably had been a day or more since her last hit. Tyisha offered to inject her."

Cooley shifted in her seat. Roach wasn't quite telling the truth, but there wasn't anything I could do while Long had the floor.

"Then what happened?"

"Cooley tied a rubber tube around Sarah's thigh. She tapped at a vein, then pushed in the needle and stabbed the plunger."

Damn, he'd done a good job of making my mild-mannered compliance officer sound like a world class phlebotomist.

"Then?"

"Sarah said she wasn't feeling well. She threw up the pie I'd brought over. Then she got real quiet and sleepy. Kind of like she was going to nod off, but different like. She looked tired. Her words were slow. Slurred. Then she stopped speaking at all. An ambulance was called then. The police came later. After I answered their questions, they sent me home," he finished, painting himself as a Good Samaritan. It was a minor miracle a gleaming, glowing halo didn't appear above his head.

"Thank you. Your witness, Mr. McPhee."

I strode straight to the podium ready to hammer away at the beatific portrait he and Long had burnished.

"You indicated that you met Sarah Pope in 1980, is that correct?"

"Yes."

"Have you ever been arrested?"

"Objection, your honor. Sidebar." Dodds took the lead on this one.

The judge motioned us forward. Both Dodds and Long came forward to the other side of the bench far from the jurors and witness. I joined them at the corner. Though the bailiff was charged with silencing the amplification system, the judge put her hand over the microphone anyway for good measure. A hot mike had taken down more than one elected official.

"As I'm sure Mr. McPhee well knows," Dodds argued, "admission of prior bad acts is impermissible under the Ohio Rules of Evidence."

"Miss Dodds' objection is misplaced," I cut in. "While Rule four-oh-four prohibits admission of any prior criminal record, that's as against a defendant. Mr. Roach is not a defendant." Though he probably should be, I thought.

"So, Mr. McPhee," Judge Marsh said, "then the admission of arrests would surely be discretionary. Why may I ask are we going down this path as the witness is neither a convicted felon, as that would have likely been your question instead, nor in county or state custody as he came in without an escort. So I can assume no charges are pending, either."

The judge looked toward the prosecutors for confirmation of Roach's freedom from prosecution. They nodded in agreement.

"It's to show, your honor," I said, "that Mr. Roach's motives are not what he says they are."

The judge looked between us as she considered. Her hand still covering the microphone, she said, "Go ahead, Mr. McPhee, but I'll rein it in if we walk too far down a path of irrelevance. Step back."

Long and Dodd went back to their seats. I went back to the podium.

"I'll repeat the question. Mr. Roach, have you ever been arrested?"

Roach looked around, clearly confused not only by the question, but by what had taken place between us attorneys and the judge, which even from his seat five feet away, he may have heard snippets of. I spoke swiftly, not wanting him to get ahead of me, mentally.

"I'd asked if you'd ever been arrested," I repeated, not for Roach this time, but for the jury. I needed to emphasize that he wasn't just a bumbling drug user, but had more nefarious motives, even if I didn't yet know if I could prove those.

"Um. Yes." He rose and dropped his shoulders. "It's hard not to be when you've been involved with drugs."

"Do you remember what you were arrested for?"

"Drug possession, probably." Another shrug. "I wasn't convicted," he said, as if it was a get out of jail free card.

"We're getting to that." That bit had been for the jury. The rest was for reasonable doubt.

Continuing, I took a stack of papers, gave a stapled portion to Long, and another to Judge Marsh. The remaining two, I kept on the podium. I said, "I have here what we sometimes call a rap sheet and several underlying police reports from the Lakewood police department. It says here that you were arrested on three different occasions. The first was drug possession for heroin. The second was drug possession for marijuana. The third was another controlled substance possession charge. This time there was the added bonus of an arrest for possession with intent to distribute. Do you remember them now, or do you need me to hand you these documents to help you refresh your memory?"

Roached briefly closed his eyes. Opened them. "I remember."

"Did you ever get convicted of any of these crimes?"

"No."

"What exactly happened?"

Shrug. "The charges were dropped, I guess."

"Dropped?"

"Police arrest people all the time. Not everyone goes to jail."

What Roach said was technically true. It wasn't, however, my experience in criminal defense nor probably that of most of the poor and marginalized people in Cuyahoga County.

"Why didn't *you*?"

"Objection. Roach isn't a police officer or prosecutor, nor subject to the basis of their discretionary decisions."

"Your honor, we don't know what Roach knows unless he can answer the question."

"Mr. McPhee is correct. Objection overruled. You can answer the question, Mr. Roach."

"I can't say." Roach made eye contact with no one. In fact, he was looking everywhere but at me, or the judge, or the jury, or Dodds and Long.

"Yes, you can, Mr. Roach." I moved from behind the podium and a few steps closer to the witness. "In fact, I compel you to answer."

I could have heard a pin drop. For a long, silent moment, no one moved. Judge Marsh's voice was jarring when it came through the low-quality speakers that dotted the courtroom.

"Mr. Roach, this is not your decision to make. It's mine. You are required to answer Mr. McPhee's question, if you know, why didn't you go to jail for your alleged crimes?"

Roach started shaking. Whether it was nerves or withdrawal, I couldn't tell. Finally, he stopped moving as if he'd decided something.

"Can I do that thing where I plead the Fifth?" Roach asked "You know, not answer because I could go to jail if I do."

"That is certainly your right, Mr. Roach. Please understand that you can only make this request if your answer could lead to arrest and conviction, or if your answer would lead to the discovery of facts that could lead to your arrest and conviction."

I tried not to smile as Judge Marsh did the heavy lifting of reasonable doubt.

"I plead the Fifth, then." Roach pursed his lips tight.

"Do you have any further questions, Mr. McPhee?"

I had more questions on my pad and a thousand more questions in my mind, but I didn't want to confuse the jury who had just been given a great excuse to acquit Tyisha Cooley.

"No, your honor." I took my papers, walked back to defense table, and took a seat.

34

My slam dunk case was quickly turning into a loose ball. Judge Marsh had mercifully called a fifteen-minute recess after Roach left the stand. The moment the jury was out of the courtroom, I turned toward Dodds. Her face was as perplexed as I tried to make mine out to be.

"Should we offer him immunity?" was her first question, whispered. I scooted my chair closer. The gallery wasn't empty and McPhee and his client were still too close for comfort.

"No, that's an awful idea. Justin was right about one thing—it's sketchy that Roach was arrested and not prosecuted." I lifted my phone toward Dodds, sharing the tiny screen and acting as if the information was new. "I just took a look at our own website. Have you ever done a closeup look at Pope's resume?

"She was in Lakewood for ten years. First as an assistant in the Law Department, then as the head when Liam Brody moved over to the county. That's not a coincidence. If Roach wasn't prosecuted, there was a reason. Maybe he was a confidential inform-ant. Maybe something else, but that's opening a can of worms we may not be able to close and would not be helpful to our case either way."

While Dodds chewed on that, I dipped out of the room, pleading a bathroom break. Once alone in a stall, I let the little fifty milliliter bottle of Kentucky bourbon take the edge off. A strong mint from a red metal tin soon covered my indiscretion. In ten minutes I was back at the table.

"Should we call Pope?" Dodds asked again. I tried not to roll my eyes. I'd have thought she would have been more confident after her years away.

"How would that change anything?" I asked. I wanted to tell her that we did not need *more* input, too many cooks and all that.

"She can pull the immunity trigger."

"We don't need her to tell us what to do. I have the authority to make those decisions."

"Maybe not." Dodds' neck nearly made a one-eighty. "Pope is here."

I didn't glance my boss' way because the judge was back at exactly fourteen minutes. The jury came in immediately after.

"Ms. Long, Ms. Dodds, do you have any further witnesses?"

"No, your honor. The prosecution rests."

"Mr. McPhee, do you have a motion?"

The defense attorney made the usual motion for a judgment of acquittal, arguing the prosecution didn't present sufficient evidence for conviction. It was *pro forma* and Judge Marsh denied it as swiftly.

"Are you ready to give your closing argument?" Judge Marsh looked between Dodds and me. In Ohio, the prosecutor had the right to go first *and* last. I could give an argument, then rebut anything McPhee had to say on behalf of his client. I thought long and hard for a moment.

"We waive, your honor." I stood to announce, then sat. It was the best strategy to rebut everything McPhee said and get the last word. Juries tended to go on the last things they heard.

"Mr. McPhee, the floor is yours," Judge Marsh said, nodding toward the defense table.

After flipping to a clean page, I made several bullet points, ready to design my closing argument around whatever defense counsel laid out. It was my best tactic to sway the jury.

"We waive as well, your honor. We're ready to submit the matter."

My pen skidded right across my pad and landed square in front of the jury box. Embarrassed that I wasn't able to hide my surprise, I left the ballpoint where it was and turned my eyes toward the judge.

Judge Marsh remained silent for a long moment. Then she turned toward the jury and started giving instruction. In a few short minutes, they were excused to the jury room for deliberation.

"What did you do?" Dodds turned to me when judge and jury were gone and McPhee and his client had exited the other way out of the courtroom's main doors.

"Bluffed and he called." I'd never expected that of McPhee. He'd been full of surprises, from the press conference to his willingness to push Ja Roach to plead the Fifth. He was a craftier attorney than I'd given him credit for. Now I was going to have to live with the consequences of my poor decision. The law didn't come with do-overs.

Dodds' eyes widened. "Pope—"

"Is right here." Lori Pope had made her way to our table. My heart skipped a beat as I waited to be chastised.

"Plea the case," Lori ordered.

"What?" Dodds blurted. "You said—"

"Ms. Dodds, I'm well aware of what I said. I need a conviction here. The jury is liable to let her walk. She cannot leave this courtroom a free woman. I can't allow that to be the legacy of my poor sister's death."

"What's the lowest?"

"She'd have to plea to tampering with evidence, the third degree felony. For that, we'll take manslaughter and the rest off the table."

"Tampering..." Dodds trailed off. I could practically see the gears turning in her head, but I already knew the play.

"She'll lose her job. FDIC insured banks can't have employees who are guilty of felonies involving fraud or dishonesty."

"Bingo." Pope pointed twin gun index fingers at us both.

"I'll go find them," Dodds said before scurrying out of the courtroom to do Pope's bidding.

Then there were only two of us in front of the bar. A lone reporter sat in the back of the courtroom. No doubt he'd picked the short straw and was the verdict lookout.

"Got a big case coming up, I want you to lead," Pope announced, as if we were in her office and she was handing out a run-of-the-mill assignment.

I wanted to ask what the catch was, but I just nodded my head like a good little soldier.

"How can I help?" I forced a smile.

"We're going after the diocese."

"For what?"

"Sex abuse. Some new evidence has turned up. Three priests and a nun ran spring and summer missions to Guatemala. The priests used that opportunity to groom more victims."

"Were they all children? Were they abused here or there?"

This time, the file Pope handed over was hefty.

"You'll need to review this, interview victims, decide on the charges. Other than routine supervision of your reports, this is the only case you'll be working on."

"Thanks." The sentiment was almost genuine. "I won't disappoint."

"No, Nicole, you won't. In the meantime, I'm going to be poking my nose into the Tia Wetzel case."

"Who? Are you asking me to work on that in addition to this? I just want to be clear what my priorities are."

"No, you do what I said. *I'll* be looking into Wetzel."

"Should I know that name?" My question was only partially in earnest. There was something familiar that was just outside of my memory.

"Wetzel was one of your first felony prosecutions. Defendant went to Marysville on a probation violation."

"Okay..."

"She's threatening to sue the department. Says that you put her away on a gun charge, assault, and resisting arrest. Girl got pulled over by the cops. They claim she didn't signal. Detained her while they ran her. Came back that she was on probation, so they did a search of her house. Claimed to have found crack and a gun. You got the case, won the trial, got your first stat. Surprised you don't remember."

It was coming back to me in bits and pieces. It was the first trial where I'd been...less than sober.

"It was some years ago. Gotta be well past the statute of limitation." Knowing former defendants were barred from suit let me sleep some nights when their cases haunted me. There were no do-overs for them either after some point.

"Some kind of technicality is tolling the limitation," Pope said, which meant someone somewhere made a mistake that left the city and county open to liability all these years later. "Turns out Wetzel had made a complaint. Said the cops had been harassing her, pulled her over, assaulted her, and came up with the bogus charges to keep her quiet."

"That's awful." And it was. It had been. Memories long buried came rushing back.

Wetzel's attorney had come to me. Showed me pictures of his client's bruised body. Claimed probation had done a sweep of her rented house half hour before and found no drugs. No one had been home until the officers had brought Wetzel home. So, the drugs had to have been planted.

I'd gone right to Pope with the information, begged to dismiss the case. She'd told me that I needed to get a win on my record to keep my job. When the probation officer waffled on corroboration of the earlier search, the jury convicted. I got a pat on the back and the right to stay. It had taken me a lot of blacked-out nights to move past that one.

"If what she says is true, then you're on the hook for more than a little prosecutorial conduct. I could see criminal or federal civil rights charges coming from this."

There it was, one of my worst fears realized. I never wanted the press going after me the way it went after Pope on the Cooley case.

"What are we going to do?" My use of the collective pronoun was deliberate.

"I'm going to protect you, Nicole, like I've more or less done for quite some time. As long as you keep doing your job, the office will be behind you."

And if I stepped off her designated path, then I was going to go down in flames, while she tossed wood on the pyre. I took a deep breath and hefted the new file. As long as I could do some good, get rapists and abusers off the street, then the other compromises had to be worth it for the greater good.

"She'll plea to the felony," Dodds said as she hustled back into the courtroom and up to prosecution's table.

"Then let's talk to the judge." I stood and made my way back to chambers with Dodds and McPhee. The trade-off was starting now.

35

Judge Kate Marsh cleared her throat.

"Tyisha Cooley," she intoned, "you are here today to plead guilty to a violation of Ohio Revised Code Section twenty-nine twenty-one point twelve, tampering with evidence. Is that correct?"

"Yes, your honor." My client's voice was loud, clear, proud. I'd tried to convince Cooley that all of this was a bad idea, when Dodds had been in the hallway making the offer to plea sound like a lifeline.

"Are you making this plea knowingly and voluntarily?" Judge Marsh locked eyes with Cooley.

"Yes."

"The maximum sentence for a third degree felony is definite prison term of thirty-six months, though you may be eligible for probation or other community control sanctions. Did your attorney explain this to you...the possibility of incarceration?"

"Yes, your honor." Cooley didn't hesitate, though many clients did when they'd agreed to probation. I always had to warn them that the prosecution's promise wasn't really that, but a recommendation, and a rogue judge could go their own way.

"By pleading guilty," Judge Marsh continued, "you are waiving your right to a jury trial, your right to confront witnesses against you, and your constitutional right to require the state to prove your guilt beyond a reasonable doubt."

"I understand."

"Tyisha Adea Cooley, I find you guilty of tampering with evidence in violation of the revised code. I'm ready to move on to sentencing."

My client sucked in a breath, then squared her shoulders. The judge continued.

"I've had the opportunity to review your presentencing report. You're an upstanding citizen with no record. Not so much as a parking ticket. I hereby sentence you to probation for eighteen months. Should you successfully complete this term, you will no longer be under the supervision and control of the department of corrections or Cuyahoga County. Do you understand?"

"Yes."

"Mr. McPhee, Ms. Cooley, we're adjourned."

"Thank you."

After getting the paperwork from the probation officer, Cooley and I walked down the aisle between the gallery seats, through the large double doors, and out of the courtroom where her fate had been decided.

"You could have taken your chances with the jury," I said, though I knew I shouldn't have because there was no going back on what had just happened in there. "I think there was a better than good chance at acquittal."

"Maybe." Cooley's shrug held little confidence. "But maybe this means it will be over. Rainey got the revenge she wanted. If I'd gotten acquitted, I'd have been looking over my own shoulder, and worried about my parents. Rainey Pope is like the Count of Monte Cristo. She would have waited for the opportunity to get us. I couldn't live with that stress."

"Are you going to be okay?" I asked. I wasn't one hundred percent on the side of believing Pope had some vendetta, but I wasn't ready to discount it completely, either. If what Cooley had said was true, then hopefully this would take Pope's focus off the Cooley family, and maybe put it where it needed to be, like on the Saint Ignatius case. I hadn't slept a full night since Pope's impromptu visit to my park.

"I have my life," Cooley answered. "I have about eighty percent of my freedom. I can't say the same for Sarah, or Wayne for that matter." My soon to be former client paused and stared at me with intensity. "If we ever get a prosecutor who isn't corrupt, you have to promise me to try to get those cases investigated. I'd bet everything I own that Rainey has something to do with Wayne's death, if not her half-sister as well."

"I'll do that," I promised. "Now, let's go. I'll walk you out." I made as if to move toward the elevators.

"I'm okay," Cooley said moving away, our tenuous attorney-client bond unraveling. "I'd rather be alone. I need to clear my head." And get away from her second guessing attorney went unsaid. I gave her a nod of good-bye, then took myself to a far corner of the hallway, empty save for a few lawyers whispering into their phones. I stared out the plate glass window at the clouds clinging to the tops of buildings. I couldn't decide how to feel: victorious, defeated, ineffectual.

"I missed it, huh?" Casey was a little out of breath when she came to a sudden stop next to me. "Sorry."

"Missed what?" I asked before I turned my gaze back to the window. I had to look away. Casey Cort here, in a fitted orange shirt, her chest heaving, all in support of me, even though I'd treated her shabbily. No matter how I behaved with her, she always bounced back and came to me with kindness.

"I wanted to see this case through since we talked about it so much. How are you feeling?" Her earnest tone broke me. It suddenly felt too hard to pretend not to care. I turned back toward her, even though facing her head-on made me monumentally uncomfortable.

"I honestly don't know. I think the result is okay. My client stayed out of jail." I tried to focus on the profes-sional with my answer. "But she's got a felony conviction for something that was no more than a tragedy."

"Everyone made the best choices they could given the situation," Casey said with compassion. "That's what we do…the best we can. This job rarely comes with a happy ending. If you want that, you'd have to be a Hollywood movie director."

"Do you have a minute?" I needed to get everything off my chest. I didn't think I could go a second longer keeping everything so bottled up.

"Sure a few, Simon's with Letty. What's up? Another case you want to talk about?"

The last thing I wanted to talk about was another case.

"I want to ask you about your two-way door theory."

Frown lines appeared, only for a moment, between Casey's brows.

"What about it, Justin?"

"Are you and me"—I gestured between us for emphasis—"are we a two-way door?"

There was nothing but silence between us for a long time. Eventually, I puffed out the breath I'd been holding unconsciously.

"Justin. We talked about this. You made a decision. As between us, it was a one-way door."

"Is it really?" I was pleading without words.

"There's a kid involved now. For the sake of Simon and Ron, I think it has to be, Justin."

But she didn't know. If she knew, maybe she'd change her mind.

"I think there's something I have to tell you."

"Justin, do you really?" Casey had acres of patience, but I could tell, by her copious use of my name, I was coming close to the end. It was time to cash in all my chips.

"I really do because it might be in the news." That wasn't the reason, but it sounded true.

"What are you talking about?"

"Lori Pope is investigating some priests for molesting kids from Saint Ignatius."

This time, her frown was from lack of comprehension.

"Did you know them, the priests? Are you going to represent them?"

"Monsignor Cobb and Father Morales. Yes, I knew them. They led trips to Guatemala."

"Oh, you mentioned going down there two different times. Do you have a conflict? Did you witness anything? You can't be a witness and defend them, you know."

"I...I'm not defending them. I would never—"

"Are you asking me to represent you? Sometimes the witnesses do have advocates by their side. Kind of a Gloria Allred type of situation." My anxiety must have been infectious because Casey normally didn't work that hard to fill in spaces in conversation. It was like she was trying to erect a wall of words to protect herself from what was coming. I couldn't protect others any longer.

"No, I think I may have to tell them what happened to me. I'm going to need you to help me as a victim advocate."

"Are you saying that...something...happened to you?" She squirmed, confirming my worst fears. I was repugnant to her now that she knew the absolute worst thing about me.

"No one would have believed me back then, so I didn't say anything. Sister Angela said it's what they needed to keep their vows." It sounded so stupid coming from my mouth. Only a silly child would have bought that line of bull.

"Justin, oh my God." Casey wrapped me in a hug. It took everything I had in me not to push her away. "I'm so sorry."

"I never wanted children. I didn't know how I could protect them. I didn't think a woman like you could ever love someone like me," I said, truths tumbling from my lips. "I don't want to have this hanging over me any longer. I know that Lori Pope isn't the best person in the world, but I think I'm going to help her."

"She asked *you* specifically? When?"

"In the summer, before the Cooley trial."

The shadow that passed over Casey's face disappeared quickly.

"I'm sorry. Whatever you need, I'll be there. Okay?" Casey smoothed a hand over my hair and patted my back.

"Can you promise me one thing?" I asked, though I had no right to the request.

"Anything."

"Don't marry Ron. Please. Not until this is over." Casey considered for a long moment, then nodded her agreement.

"If that's what you need to bring these people to justice, Ron can wait."

With Casey Cort by my side, I knew I could work with Lori Pope, take on the diocese, and get justice long denied.

ABOUT THE AUTHOR

Aime Austin is the author of the Casey Cort and Nicole Long Series of legal thrillers. She is also the host of the podcast, *A Time to Thrill*. When she's not writing crime fiction or interviewing brilliant creators for her podcast, she's in a yoga pose, knitting, or reading. Aime splits her time between Los Angeles and Budapest. Before turning to writing, Aime practiced family and criminal law in Cleveland, Ohio.

Made in United States
Orlando, FL
17 June 2022

18909544R00209